EVERYTHING WORTH COUNTING

MIHAELA BALAN LARSEN

BE YOU
VERY WELL

BE YOU
VERY WELL

ebook ISBN: 978-84-09-78098-3

Paperback ISBN: 978-84-09-78100-3

First published October 2025

This is a work of fiction. Any resemblance to real people or events is coincidental.

mihabalan.com

To my parents MIHAI and ELENA,
If you only knew how much you are missed.

PART I

1

ZIMNICEA

"For all of us, there is a word we say with tenderness and respect and that is our connection with life—Mother. Mother has always been, is, and will be the sublime symbol of our fecundity on this earth." Ion Neagu's voice traveled through the wall between the kitchen and my room.

"Here are three songs dedicated to mothers," a female voice followed. "First song—'When You Truly Are A Mother.'"

I could hardly differentiate the distorted melody from the background static and buzzing sound of the speaker that seemed as if it wanted to escape the radio.

When I opened my eyes, my head was under the blanket and my hands were clutching my knees. I must've sweated all night because my pajamas were wet and cold.

With the blanket wrapped around me, I got out of bed. The sun's rays were shining through the window, up which frost was still crawling in the shape of tree branches. That day, the sky was magnificent, a blue so profound it resembled the famous stained walls of the Voroneț Monastery.

I entered the kitchen where my father was seated at the corner table with my mother on the chair to his left. The limited space afforded us only the three chairs by the table, one for each. His face was buried in the wide-open newspaper *Scînteia*, while my mother sat quietly listening to the radio. You could see the steam rising from the coffee cups in front of them and smell its acrid flavor.

Right after the last song ended, Ion Neagu began reading the news from Bucharest. The plan for improving the economy was going well, productivity being over three percent better than in any Western country. In Dolj county, the citizens performed the traditional dances *hora* and *călușș* in front of the cultural house in celebration of six hundred new lambs being born since the beginning of the year. Meanwhile, the presidential couple, Nicolae and Tovarășa Elena Ceaușescu, were visiting Nigeria at the end of their African tour.

The coming of spring left Romanians in a conundrum. Every morning, we stood in front of our closets, wondering whether it was the right time to give the winter coat a rest and put on a lighter jacket. I planned to pick the short woolen coat I had worn all winter but leave the scarf.

By eight twenty-five, George, my friend, neighbor, and classmate, rang the doorbell. He had come to walk with me to school. My mother answered.

"Good morning, Ms. Eva."

"George, aren't you going to be cold? Did your mother see you walking out of the apartment with this light jacket on?"

"Eva, let the boy be," my father protested from the kitchen.

George's mother had not seen him leave that day, nor did she pay much attention to him on any other day. Neither did his two big brothers, Ion and Lucian. They were probably both still sleeping after coming home late, as they did most nights, sometimes even escorted by the local police. I put my shoes on quickly, before my mother could yell at George for holding the door open and letting the heat out.

"What about a hat? Aren't you taking one?" she asked.

"Mama, it's spring already, it's March!" I pleaded. "Nobody in my class wears a hat now."

"Do you want to be in bed sick again?" She pulled the woolen hat over my head. "Today it's the fourth. It's the mayor's inauguration day. We need to be present. All of us. So come home early," she called after us before I closed the door.

"Are you coming to the inauguration?" I asked George as we walked down the stairs.

"Only if my mother is going, and she probably won't."

Outside, the air was still so cold that we could see our breath. We picked up two small sticks from the ground and pretended to smoke. As soon as we crossed the intersection to Victoria Street, I took off my hat and hid it in my bag. With finesse, I spat on my fingers and ran them through my hair.

"Last night I heard my father talk about Matilda's mother," I said to George.

"What about her?" His eyes opened wide, and he stopped to look at me.

"Something about her mother wanting to go to her parents' village. My father said she might want to stay there." I took a puff from my stick.

"Do you think she might take Matilda or her brothers with her?" he asked.

"I don't think so, but let's get to school—I don't want to be late." I pushed him by the shoulders. "Why don't you ask her in your letters? Just don't mention that I told you—my parents don't know I was listening."

"I will. It's just she never answers me."

"Maybe she loves you and doesn't want to say it," I said, watching his cheeks flush. We continued smoking and fantasizing about their romance all the way to school.

Later that day, my parents and I walked hand in hand to City Hall, where the inauguration of the new mayor was to take place. My father wore an open dark brown coat with a suit and tie beneath, and my mother a green woolen coat that ended just a little below the knees, leaving the rest of her legs visible to show her new stockings and the shoes with a small heel. Her coat, designed and sewn entirely by herself, was copied from the fashion icons of the fifties in Bucharest. It had padded shoulders and tied at the waist with a belt.

We, like many others, arrived ahead of time. Before entering the building, we came across the current mayor, Filip, and his soon-to-be successor, Luca Savici, who were having a chat by the entrance.

"*Săru-mâna, Doamna Eva*,"[1] both party leaders greeted us, nodding first toward my mother then my father.

"Good evening," my mother answered with a small nod.

"With respect, gentlemen," my father said, shaking their hands.

---

1. *Săru-mâna, Doamna Eva* – Kiss your hands, Madame Eva (A form of saluting women at that time)

"Do you have a lighter, Cornele?" the mayor asked my father, holding a cigarette in his hand.

"Of course," my father answered, pulling one from his pocket.

"Cornele, one can hardly find you at work these days," Mayor Filip remarked. "My wife tells me that last time she went to your store, the *alimentară*, you were nowhere to be seen."

"I was probably just unloading the trucks in the back or checking the stock. It's been busy these days."

"You are the one responsible," the mayor replied. "You should always stay in the front. Let the others do the work in the back. How else will I ever get good meat for my table?" He took a drag from his cigarette. "Look here, your new mayor"—and here he gestured toward Mr. Savici, who looked uncomfortable—"thinks he's caught God by the toe with his new position."

"What are you talking about, Filipe?" Mr. Savici asked.

"What am I talking about? I'll tell you! Today, you'll become one of the many puppets our beloved Chairman Codrin holds by the strings all over the city."

"I am nobody's puppet. I lead by my own rules." Mr. Savici lifted his chin and puffed out his chest.

"Ha!" Filip answered. "At least you have humor. Codrin is the devil, *dracu-gol*, Savice! Mark my words, the day will come when you find yourself so tangled in his strings, you'll suffocate."

My eyes drifted from one man to the other, and I smiled to myself at the thought that tomorrow morning I could tell George that not only had I met both mayors, but I'd also heard their deepest secrets. My father knew better than to engage in their heated conversation and instead bid them goodbye.

We ascended the three steps to the building, bypassed the guard at the entrance, and proceeded down the hallway toward the auditorium. Inside, people were already gathered in groups.

"Why don't you go and talk to Matilda?" my father suggested.

"But I don't really feel like it, and if I talk to her, George will get upset."

"Then, go count the chairs. Tell me later how many there are so we will know how many people were invited."

"I guess I can do that."

I walked between the rows of chairs facing the stage and began counting, pointing at each chair as I passed. Up on the stage, a long table sat in the center, flanked by five chairs. The wall at the back of the stage was decorated with burgundy curtains, similar to the ones hanging in every window of the building. Two tall Romanian flags were placed on each side of the stage, and in the middle of it all was a photograph of the Carpathian Mountains with a quote from the Communist Party saying: "Long live the Romanian Communist Party led by its secretary-general Nicolae Ceaușescu." Dominating the room was a portrait of Nicolae Ceaușescu, whose eyes seemed to follow every movement as though perpetually scrutinizing those below.

"Sixty-seven chairs in the room and five more on the stage," I said out loud, looking at Ceaușescu, wishing he could see me count.

Outside, the conversation was interrupted by the sound of a car approaching. Out of a black Dacia 1300 exited the man in question, Codrin Constantin, chairman of the Romanian Communist Party. He was a bulky man with a visible belly in front. His white hair was long enough to be combed from one side to another. A white bushy mustache rested above his lips. He walked at a fast pace to the entrance as if he were already in a hurry to leave. After a short glance at the old and new mayor, he made a sign with his hand, signaling that everyone should take their seats inside. The meeting was ready to start.

Inside the town hall, people were chatting loudly, and as they began taking their seats, my father asked, "Have you seen the Dinus tonight?"

"No, they're probably not coming." My mother clasped her hand over her mouth. "Costel! We forgot the wine and meat we promised for tonight."

"*La dracu!*"[2] he answered, smacking his forehead. "How could I forget! I even prepared it in a nice package for them and left it in the refrigerator."

"What do we do? Shall I go home and get it? I don't really understand what they're saying anyway," my mother offered.

"Can't we go after the meeting? We can stop quickly at home and pick it up?"

"No, we'll be late, and you know how they are! We're meant to go along with the other families."

"Alright, I'll go."

"Are you sure?"

"Yes, yes, I walk faster anyway. I'll be back before they finish."

My mother sat down on the chair next to mine. I looked back as my dad waved us goodbye, winking at me with a smile.

"Stand up!" yelled one of the officers standing in the corner of the room.

We all rose to our feet and watched the Party leaders

---

2. *La dracu!* – To Hell! (Damn it!)

enter. After a moment, the officer directed, "You may all sit down."

The incumbent mayor of Zimnicea, Filip, commenced expressing his regrets for stepping down, only to be interrupted by Codrin Constantinescu, who was impatient to start his speech.

"Zimnicea stands as a model city. While we may not compare to the country's larger cities, we're certainly on the right trajectory, wouldn't you agree?" Everyone nodded. "Because the government never sleeps, it is always thinking: how can we improve? How can we overtake our production goals and not just hit the targets? The solution is right here in front of your eyes as I present to you, citizens, your new mayor of Zimnicea." And he pointed straight at Luca Savici.

A round of applause followed.

Mr. Savici got up in front of everyone, put his glasses on, and looked around the room, as if to take note of how many people were clapping. When the room was completely silent and calm, he cleared his throat and, with a paper in his hand, began to speak.

"Today, under the wise and unwavering guidance of our beloved Party and the glorious leadership of Codrin Constantinescu,"—he gestured at the man—"I'll continue to build, to build…" He stopped, interrupted by the sudden sound of the water pitchers on the table in front of him shaking.

2

ERUPTION

As glass fell to the ground, the two big flags at the back trembled. People looked to their neighbors and a few got up from their chairs when a colossal shock wave powered through the room. Over the course of fifty-six seconds, it felt as though a gigantic underground beast was trying to surface, lifting the building on its back. For a fraction of a second, the vertical movements seemed to stop, only for the beast to rage even more, the swift rocking now horizontal, gaining more strength. The beast hollered, a cry that cracked the sky in two, leaving behind an echoing roar made of shouts from both inside and beyond the walls of the room.

A ringing filled my ears, and I squinted my eyes in pain. As though no longer friends and family, everyone pushed to get out of the building. My mother lifted me up in her arms and tried to make her way through the crowd. Resting my head on her shoulder, I saw a pregnant woman pass out on the floor, security guards pushing past her. Was she still breathing? I wish I knew. Wedged in between others, we managed to exit the building, only to be hailed by a gray cloud of dust shadowing the city and obscuring the sky. We tucked our faces inside our clothes to breathe. Around us, people ran in all directions, and the sound of sirens dominated the air.

The ground had stopped shaking but the chaos was just beginning.

When my mother put me down, I coughed, choking on the thick air.

"Breathe, Alex, breathe!" my mother cried.

My first thoughts were of my dad and George, but when I turned and looked toward our neighborhood I trembled. In its destructive wake, the beast had claimed some of the city's oldest buildings, which had been standing tall before its sudden appearance.

At that moment, my mother screamed as if she had just woken up from a nightmare. She grabbed my hand and started walking fast, pulling me behind her.

"*Doamne fereşte*,[1] Cornel!" she yelled.

Between the crowds of people gathering in the streets, we ran, we pushed, and we screamed his name.

"Cornel! Cornel!"

Of the tall blocks that lined the roundabout on Victoria Street, only some of the first floors remained; the rest of the buildings were razed to the ground. It was hard to take in the sight of the ruins, knowing that bodies and possessions were trapped inside. As we came to the corner of our road, connecting with Victoria Street, we turned left and looked ahead. Two of the buildings in our block were halfway destroyed, some parts on fire, ours included.

I could hear my mother's breathing getting heavier and

---

1. *Doamne fereşte* – God forbid

deeper as her cries got louder. Number four on the street Gheorghe Frenț was nothing but a pile of rubble jumbled together with our life's memories and our loved ones. Neighbors came running to look for their families, blocking the arriving fire trucks and ambulances.

Their headlights illuminated people digging bodies out from the ruins. Some were severely hurt, some were crying for help from underneath, while others were already covered with white sheets and being carried away by two people. We walked hand in hand between the mass of people and screamed my father's name, but in vain. We went and asked the ambulance if they had registered anyone by the name of Cornel Toma, but they didn't recognize the name.

After what felt like an eternity, we spotted George's mother being held by one of her sons as she was fighting the urge to throw herself at the motionless bodies of her other two sons, found in the ruins: George and Lucian. I drifted from my mother's hand and ran toward them and to the small body being lifted onto a stretcher. His angelic face was scratched and full of dirt, just as it was at the end of a summer's day after we had roamed around the neighborhood. Blood from cuts around his head covered his face as he lay there, motionless. My legs gave up on me, and I fell to my knees crying, for the pain that stabbed my heart was too strong. As my mother came to help me up, the men transporting the bodies covered George's face, lifted him, and took him away.

For the next several hours, everything was a blur. Strong headlights burned my eyes, machines patrolled from every direction as people worked with persistence. The cold had infiltrated our bones, making our mouths shiver. After a while, I found myself sitting alone on a block of cement with a blanket borrowed from the ambulance, waiting for my mother. One after another, I counted bodies wrapped in white sheets being carried to the ambulances in front of me: "…five, six, seven…" Suddenly, I recognized my mother's voice. That's when I knew.

I followed her cries until I found her draped over a shape covered in a white sheet. They had found my father's body.

I couldn't believe it. It was him lying there, so still. Only it didn't look like him at all. He didn't look at me with his big, kind, proud eyes; he didn't smile as he always did when he saw me. His glasses? Where were they? But beneath the stains of blood from his skull, it was him. His eyes were closed, his suit shredded to pieces, he lay motionless, just like George.

3

LEAVING ZIMNICEA

The next day, we woke up feeling drowsy and exhausted. We had slept on a few blankets on the floor of a cold and moldy room in the Dinu family's basement, surrounded by old furniture, boxes of clothes, and tools. Fortunately for them, the only casualty in their house during the earthquake was a black-and-white TV that had shattered to the ground. My mother was already awake, staring at the ceiling.

"What are we going to do, Mama?" I asked.

"Survive for now, Alex, survive," she replied.

The true meaning of survival, something I'd never really considered before, now seemed the most difficult task of all. How could I survive with so much pain inside? We lay there in silence until we heard a knock on the door. Elena Dinu slowly opened the basement door.

"I've prepared some tea and bread in the kitchen," she said with a soothing voice and closed the door after her.

We picked up our dirty and torn clothes where we had left them on the floor the day before, got dressed, and went to the kitchen. The Dinu family had two boys, ages five and six, who, not understanding the gravity of the situation, continued their morning routine of chasing each other around the house.

While we sipped our tea at the table, Elena mentioned that the radio had reported substantial damage in Bucharest, with hundreds dead and thousands injured. "March 4, 1977 will forever be remembered as one of the greatest tragedies the Romanian population had to suffer," she quoted. Approximately thirty percent of the city was in ruins, and the Ceaușescus would cut their Africa trip short and return to Romania.

We left their home shortly after breakfast, heading back toward our neighborhood. The walk felt long and painful. I could feel the burning sensation from the blisters on my swollen feet. The many times I slowed down, my mother kept her pace ahead of me, reaching back her hand for me to grab.

When we finally reached our street, she slowed down. On the side of the street, a Dacia, its headlights still on, lay smashed in half under a block of concrete. A radio was playing in the background from somewhere in between the ruins. I found a small black-and-white photograph of a boy I didn't recognize on the pavement. Two men were shoveling debris from the pavement into a wheelbarrow and carting it to the back of a truck. Others were digging through the ruins for belongings that could be salvaged.

"There's Ms. Catrina," I said, pointing to an old woman sitting on some rubble.

She was an eighty-six-year-old woman who had lived most of her life in our block. Almost every day, we would see her sitting on the four steps up to our building, chewing roasted sunflower seeds and talking to every inhabitant who walked in and out. She wasn't universally liked, but if you needed information or advice about neighborhood matters, she was the one to ask. Before my mother and I had a chance to go to her, someone yelled my mother's name from the other side of the street.

"Eva! Eva, come here!" two women, acquaintances of my mother, called out, greeting us with hugs.

"How are you feeling? Where did the two of you sleep last night?" the tallest one with wavy blonde hair asked.

"We slept at Dinu's. They picked us up very late last night," my mother answered.

"Tonight, you can sleep at our place," the other woman said. "We'll make space for you two."

"Have you heard any news?" my mother asked.

"Eva, I am so sorry. It's unreal to think about Cornel. It feels like only yesterday we were all at the table, cheering and dancing at Luminița's birthday."

As the women continued talking, they directed us toward a long table put together from several plastic tables. On it were hot pots of tea and coffee, along with wine, jams, biscuits, some slices of salami, and black bread. I took a seat on one of the empty white plastic chairs, poured myself a cup of tea, and grabbed a biscuit. Looking through the crowd of people gathered around the table, I locked eyes with a familiar face.

It was Matilda, the girl from the third floor—George's big crush.

We headed toward each other and met in the middle. Her face looked pale and tired, her auburn hair disheveled compared with how she used to keep it before. They had lost their apartment too, but the four of them had survived.

"Silly George," she said, beginning to sob. "With his damn love letters that would always get me in so much trouble with my father. But I kept them—I kept them all hidden," she cried. "Except that now, I don't even have those."

"I guess then it's no secret he was crazy in love with you. He only talked about you day and night. Anytime he had the chance," I said.

"The worst part is, I sort of really liked him too," she said, wiping tears from her eyes.

Her father called her name, and she ran back to him. I hoped that if George's soul had not yet left their home and he was still around us that day, he would see how devastated Matilda was to have lost him.

Thinking of him, a knot tightened in my stomach, but I tried to push the thought away. I found a seat by the table and just as I was about to take a bite of a piece of dry salami to settle my stomach, I heard the chatter getting louder and louder. What started as a small gathering among the neighbors was now a large crowd with people from other parts of the city joining in. Heated conversations flowed from one person to the other, their faces lined with exhaustion, and some people started to argue.

"How do you know about this?" one of them asked.

"Why should we accept this? We should revolt if necessary! These are our homes! They can't do this!" a man shouted to the crowd.

"They have bulldozers and trucks. The train station is packed with men!" another shouted.

I saw my mother weaving her way through the crowd, walking quickly toward me.

"Alex, we need to go," she said firmly, grasping my arm.

"What? Where?" I asked, trying to follow her fast step from behind.

"We need to leave now!"

"But why? Where are we going to go?"

"To the train station, just follow me and walk fast."

Running through familiar backstreets, we breathed a sigh of relief when we arrived at the crowded station. It was teeming with men who appeared to have just disembarked from a train.

"What are they all doing in this city?" I wondered.

One of them held the door open for my mother and me. From the entry, we could see the train tracks at the other side of the large hallway. To our left was a bar, unmissable with its two plastic tables and chairs, ashtrays brimming with cigarette butts, and blue lights that had likely been there since Christmas. Next to it was an empty sandwich stand, which was closed at that hour. A large chart displayed information about upcoming arrivals and departures. At the ticket counter, a woman in uniform with thick glasses sat behind a window, speaking impatiently with travelers through the round cutout in the glass.

My mother joined the queue in front of the office, while I sat down on a bench. With the tickets in hand, my mother hurried toward me, but a man in a black leather jacket interrupted her when she passed.

"Where are you going, *doamnă?*" he asked and inhaled deeply from his cigarette.

"None of your business," my mother answered shortly.

"I can easily make it mine," he answered and spat bits of tobacco on the floor. "Where are you going now with the whole city in crisis?"

"My husband died last night, so I'm going to stay with my parents."

"And where exactly would that be?" he pressed, positioning himself in front of my mother as the train pulled into the station.

"Leave us alone. We've been through enough already." My mother sidestepped him.

As soon as the doors of the train opened, we climbed up the stairs and sat down on the first two orange fabric chairs next to a window. The conductor blew his whistle loudly three times:

"*Atenție, se închid ușile!*" He warned about the closing doors and jumped on the train.

Twenty-five minutes later, the train let us off at its first stop, Izvoarele.

4

IZVOARELE

Atop a hill stood a small Orthodox church built of burgundy bricks and named after Saint Gabriel. It was surrounded by a colorful garden, and next to it was a small convent where the priest of Izvoarele and three nuns resided.

To better understand Izvoarele's layout, you had to walk all the way uphill to where the church sat. From this vantage point, a myriad of fields ran toward the horizon, surrounded by forests of tall trees. Look closer and you could witness the rural life of the peasants as they navigated the unpaved streets toward the fields. From this height, the thatched roofs seemed close together, yet in reality they were separated by gardens and courtyards where animals and vegetables thrived. The main street of Izvoarele was hidden from view, overshadowed by another extended street called Cotroceni, which was situated on a higher plateau and dotted with several houses. My grandparents' house was number five.

This house was just as ordinary as any other. Each dwelling had a small path separating its property from the street. Along these patches, wooden benches sat here and there, often occupied by a couple of women in their long skirts, aprons around their waist, and a traditional kerchief tied around their heads. Surrounding my grandparents' garden was a wooden fence, not more than one meter tall, with a small gate in the middle. It was always open, so you could simply walk in, unless you were intimidated by the white fluffy dog, Volk, who patrolled and barked from his fenced-in area on the right side of the courtyard. Walking along the uneven cobblestone pavement, you would arrive at the three steps leading up to the front porch, which encircled the entire house. Follow the porch around the corner of the house and you would end up in the backyard.

Like any other house in the village, my grandparents had a summer kitchen with a stove, a big wooden table, and a couple of chairs outside, where we usually spent our time.

Two days after we arrived in Izvoarele, my mother and I were outside, enjoying the sun's warming rays on our skin. With the snow gone, the ground was dry at last, letting the sprouts of tulips peek out of the ground surrounding the porch. A snowdrop would've best described the season, but there weren't any visible. An unexpected call was heard all the way from the street—someone was yelling my mother's name. It was Izvoarele's mailman, Mr. Apostoliță.

"Good day, Ms. Eva, is that you? How are you doing?" he yelled all the way from the gate.

"Good day, Mr. Apostoliță. We are just around the house. Do you have something for me?" my mother asked, walking up to him.

"I was a bit confused." He smiled. "The address is for

number five, but I know who lives here, so I wondered who Eva Toma was. Now I understand. These two letters are addressed to you, then. Did you move back home with your parents?"

"Ah, no. I mean yes. For a while. My son Alex and I. Our block got demolished during the earthquake. We're among those left without a home."

"Yes, yes, I've heard. May God help you and those poor people. All those homes destroyed, and so many people died in the earthquake. We were luckier here—nothing happened. We were just a bit shaken. My wife and I just hid under the table that night when it happened. We must all pray to God to ease your suffering. Sign here that you received the letters—they check to see that you signed."

"How's your wife feeling? I meant to come over and talk to her," she said, wanting to change the subject. "My mother tells me that she's out of the hospital?"

"She's home now. Supposed to be in bed after the operation, but she has already started fussing around the house. After such a long time in the hospital, now she has too much energy. Come over one of these days with your mother. Bring Alex too. I always have nephews coming around, so he'll have someone to play with."

"We will come by. Thank you for the letters," my mother said, motioning to leave.

"Good day, Ms. Eva."

The first envelope contained the front page of a newspaper, folded carefully inside a handwritten letter from one of my mother's friends. My mother first unfolded the page ripped from the newspaper, showing a big black-and-white photograph of Tovarăşa Elena Ceauşescu walking next to the ruins of the demolished buildings of Zimnicea.

Behind her was Nicolae Ceaușescu, surrounded by members of the Communist Party and citizens. I didn't understand why the city was more destroyed than when we left. It looked like a ruined city. The second letter was from the morgue, informing us to plan the funeral for my father's body.

5

THE FUNERAL

There are certain events in life that will never fade from one's memory: an ornate cake with a candle to blow out on your birthday, your first crush, the first rejection, memories of summer holidays, your father teaching you how to play harmonica. This was one of them—my first funeral. My father's.

It was with frustration that my mother, having no money of her own, was obliged to accept help with the funeral arrangements from my paternal grandmother, Catrina. It came with a condition: the funeral was to take place in their home in Alexandria, the city my father came from, and he was to be buried in the Catholic cemetery, even though by marriage my father became Orthodox.

What felt like a hundred years later, the ceremony in church ended, and all of us followed the four men carrying the casket to the grave outside. The priest's loud rituals of prayer and song were overpowered by the hoarse voice of a woman, crying and begging for the dead to come back. It was my mother's. She had thrown herself on the ground next to the grave, as if she was about to crawl in. That's when the reality of never being able to see my father again finally hit me. With everyone's eyes on us, all I could do was lower my head and count the seconds until this would all be over.

Back at my grandmother Catrina's house, a gathering of family and friends spread around the living room, at the center of which was a table with food, snacks, cakes, wine in plastic bottles, and *țuică*, the hard Romanian liquor.

Among the noise of glasses clinking and toasts in my father's honor, there were the shouts of my cousins from underneath the tables and in between people. Loudest of all was my cousin Ionuț, the son of my mother's youngest sister, Alexandra, who had come all the way from Petroșani to attend the funeral. His mother, tired of him intruding on the adults talking in the kitchen, prodded him to go and play with me. After I refused a couple of times, I was certain I heard him swear at me, a Romanian expression only adults were allowed to use, and I wondered if I should tell on him to make him stop bugging me. But my grandmother Catrina, seeing me sitting alone, came next to me and put an arm around my shoulder, speaking so close I could almost taste the glasses of wine she had had for lunch.

"Alex, why don't you stay with us for a few days while your mother settles back in Zimnicea?"

Before I could reply, my mother sat down on the chair on my other side.

"He can't stay with you here in Alexandria," she said, sipping from a glass of wine. "He doesn't have clothes, and I need to enroll him in school."

"He can go to school here in Alexandria, just like Cornel. His grandfather and I can take care of him."

"There's a great school in Izvoarele, close to where we are staying."

"You're not thinking of sending him to that dreaded school in the village, are you?"

"What's wrong with it? I went there, and I turned out fine," my mother answered.

"Eva, be realistic!" Catrina said, facing my mother. "He's ten years old—we can offer him a better life."

I could see my mother's face turn red, but she remained silent.

"I'm sure Cornel would have approved of it," my grandmother continued in a softer voice.

"Perhaps. But for now, it's just me alone, and I'll make sure he has a good life," my mother said with a cold stare.

"You'll have to go to City Hall and request a new home. A thirty-four-year-old widow with a child…" She sighed. "What a tragedy!"

"I have no money to pay for a new home," my mother noted.

"Eva, we can help you."

"Oh Catrina… If only it was as easy as that," my mother answered.

My grandmother looked at her with indignation and let out a long sigh. At that moment, it occurred to me that I had only visited her during holidays and always together with my parents. Whether it was because of her nosy nature or the endless stories she told, which we were never sure were true or not, I never felt very comfortable around her.

The tension was finally broken when my other grandmother, Violeta, came to let us know that if we wanted to get back to Izvoarele that night, we should leave before my grandfather got too friendly with the wine. Before we left, my grandmother Catrina slid two ten lei banknotes into the pocket of my coat, together with a whisper.

"You're all I have left of him! You must come see us," she said, cupping my cheeks with her hands.

To hope for a silent ride home in the horse cart was wishful thinking. My Aunt Alexandra and Ionuț were coming back to Izvoarele with us to stay for the night. Ionuț was only eight years old, shorter than me, with messy brown hair. Most of his front teeth were unevenly shaped and had not fully grown into place just yet. He carried a great deal of energy with him and not once stopped kicking his legs throughout the whole journey.

6

A DAY IN LIFE

Like clockwork, Petrică, the rooster, woke us up at dawn with his wretched crowing. My grandfather, a man in his seventies, slowly got out of bed, pulled his woolen pants over his night tights, and donned a white cotton shirt on top of his white undershirt. He tightened everything around his waist with a wide black belt, grabbed his black sheepskin vest from a chair in the kitchen, and went outside. The morning air was chill and fresh, and the only sound in the whole village came from the chicken coop and the ducks clucking for food and water.

He splashed his face several times with cold water from a bucket and lit his Carpați cigarette. While he smoked his cigarette in peace, my grandmother Violeta joined him outside.

By 1977, when my mother and I lived there, my grandparents were left with a small garden where they grew vegetables, mainly potatoes, and fields with acres of corn and even more with grapevines. By the end of autumn, after everything was sold and taxes were paid, if there was any money left for the year, it was a great achievement for my grandfather, who knew nothing better than his work and loved nothing more than his lands.

Woken up by the sound of my grandfather loudly coughing, I grabbed a jacket from the chair next to the bed and went outside.

"Good morning," I said to the two of them, my breath condensing in the cold air.

My grandmother was by the outdoor kitchen, preparing my grandfather's lunch for later. She wrapped a piece of *mămăligă*, the Romanian polenta, in a cloth with a lump of sheep cheese and our bacon—*şuncă*. She smiled at me and asked how I had slept, while my grandfather continued smoking his cigarette, holding an old newspaper in his other hand.

"Do you know how to read, boy?" he asked, taking his eyes off the newspaper.

"Yes, I learned in school. I'm almost eleven years old," I answered irritably.

"Then you shouldn't see this," he said, placing the newspaper on the table. "Violeto, by the time you finish with that lunch, I could have fed and harnessed Valentina and Țugui twice!" he said to my grandmother.

"Then why don't you? Who is stopping you? Go harness your horses and then come get your lunch," she answered firmly.

He finished his cigarette, put the butt in a glass jar, and went to the stable, mumbling something only he could understand. I stood by the bench next to the table and looked at the front page of the newspaper. The main page showed a black-and-white photograph of our beloved Nicolae Ceaușescu, walking side by side with other members of the Party through the fields of corn and wheat.

Right next to the big picture was a note of yet another villager shot dead, having tried to revolt against the regime that stripped him of all his land and rights.

During the week, my grandmother Violeta worked from nine to three at the village's school library, where she had taught literature for the last thirty-three years. My mother spent most of her days traveling back and forth to Zimnicea by train, gathering new copies of documents and identity papers that were lost together with our home.

As for me, "the man of the house," as my grandfather put it, I was entrusted with clear tasks: to feed the birds, pigs, and dog, clean the pigsty, sweep the porch around the house, fetch two handfuls of potatoes from the basement, peel them and soak them in a bucket of water, and bring more water from the well in the valley to fill the plastic containers. Adjacent to the house, near the outdoor kitchen, was a compound split into three distinct sections. The first was the pigpen, housing two small pigs. This was followed by a chicken coop and finally a horse stable at the end, adjoining the street with a large double gate, which was wide enough for a horse cart to pass through.

I took a big plastic cup and filled it with a mix of middlings and oat bran, along with a bowl of maize, to keep Petrică from leaping at my head. I fed the pigs a modest amount of grain and plenty of water. Afterward, I turned my attention to Volk, our dog, by the gate, who seemed uninterested in my presence and contented himself with yesterday's leftovers and water.

Never had that porch been swept so well, nor those potatoes peeled with such precision. I felt a sense of pride in my work, momentarily distracting me from the events of the previous week and the yearning for our old home.

Flashes of George and me running around the school's

hallway came to my mind. I could taste the bread and scraped butter I often had for breakfast and smell the scent of meat that clung to my father's uniform when he came from work and hung it in the hallway. It was all so recent yet so far away. I felt like now I was living someone else's life and had no idea where it was leading.

My thoughts were interrupted by the noise of the front gate opening. Clad in her black attire, with her red hair tied in a ponytail and her gaze lowered, a slender figure walked along the porch toward the back of the house. It was my mother.

"Mama!"

"Alex, what are you doing?" she asked.

"I was just getting ready to bring some more water from the well. I already carried five buckets. How are things back in Zimnicea?"

"Chaotic. So messy and stressful, Alex." She sat down on the bench next to me. "Hundreds and hundreds of people are waiting outside the City Hall looking for answers and help."

"Have you seen anyone we know? Have you seen George's mother?"

"No, I haven't seen her, not yet. My feet are killing me." She took off her low-heeled shoes and flared her toes wide. "What have you been doing here alone all day?"

"Working around the house. Grandmother gave me a whole list of things to do."

"Maybe we should consider sending you to help your grandfather. He could also use some help in the fields."

Before a minute could pass, the front gate swung open again, and there was my grandmother. Tall and slender, with long white hair always put in a bun, light blue eyes, and a humble demeanor, she walked slowly onto the creaking porch, holding a cloth bag in her right hand and a letter in the left.

"Eva, we've received a letter from Ana in Spain," she said, showing it to her.

"From Ana, really?" my mother asked.

"Ana?" I asked.

"My sister! The one that lives in Barcelona."

"What does she say? Open it!" my mother said.

Other than the fact that she was the oldest sister and the stories about how she used to order around the other two sisters, my mother and Aunt Alexandra, I didn't know much about her. Losing interest, I got up from the table and went to the back of the yard, an abandoned lot behind the outdoor kitchen, filled with dry grass and all kinds of vegetation. I didn't recall seeing anyone go back here except for me. At the far-left end of this unkempt lot was a tall old walnut tree supporting what was once intended to be a treehouse. The deck, about two meters high, stood on four thick wooden posts. An unsafe-looking wooden railing encircled the space. I climbed up the short planks nailed to the trunk of the tree, carefully placing one foot on the floor to test it. The deck itself was a nest for old leaves, dirt, and bird poop.

For a split second, as I leaned against the corner of the railing, I felt a sense of calmness I had craved for the last few days. The view from up there spread widely from our neighbor's yard all the way to the empty fields ahead. It felt promising.

7

THE INVISIBILITY SPELL

I didn't know anything about refurbishing treehouses. Nevertheless, I started by ripping away the overgrown vegetation, cleaning the spiderwebs, old branches, and dry leaves, clearing out some abandoned bird nests, and sweeping the floor.

Once that was done, I snuck into my grandfather's shed, a tiny room filled with all kinds of tools that were hung from hooks on the wall and arranged in several rows by size. Next to the wall stood a table with a bench vise and several machines, the purposes of which I had no idea. I took the biggest hammer I could find and a handful of nails. Exactly how long had it been since I last touched a hammer? Two, three years ago, in second grade, maybe?

Suffice it to say, within half an hour, sixteen nails had been driven through the railing and into the posts and the tree.

"What a difference!" I said to myself. "My own kingdom."

Every day during this period, my mother would return

from Zimnicea, stressed out from the chaos at the City Hall. My grandmother listened to her with patience and support, but my grandfather always stormed inside the house, swearing at the Romanian bureaucracy. When this happened, I climbed up to my tree house. It was simple and small, with only a few hay bales borrowed from the horse's stable, arranged in the shape of a wide chair.

And it's not like it was easy to get there either, especially since I had created my own imaginary world. In my fantasy, there was fighting—not wars, but with dragons from the abandoned lot. Both red and blue dragons tried to keep me from climbing the steps on the trunk and getting into the treehouse. The red dragon would breathe long streams of fire from its nostrils, and the blue dragon would whip fiercely with his big tail. And what was my power? My invisibility spell! Protected by this spell, I could fight them with my stick. At least in those fights for survival, I always ended up triumphant.

"The sweet taste of victory!" I exclaimed once I climbed up.

It was on a mid-March afternoon, while my mother and grandmother were preparing dinner, that I decided to test the power of my invisibility spell with the dog. Volk, a mixed-breed and who had once been a street dog, was medium-sized with big, white fur. His coat left balls of hair all around the garden. On the left corner of his mouth, he had a big scar from his days on the streets, when teenagers had tried to kill him with a wire. My grandfather saw them and brought the dog home. Ever since then, Volk had been completely devoted to him. My grandparents were the only people who could pet or touch him. Volk's main fear was people.

I was intrigued by his unfriendly behavior toward me. I

brought him food several times, yet I had made no progress in getting closer to him. On that day in March, while he was sleeping peacefully on his side, I walked slowly and carefully along the porch, approaching his enclosure little by little. As often before, I cast my invisibility spell and reached out with my left hand until it touched the soft fur on his head, then petted him.

He turned and sank his teeth into my arm as if it were a piece of meat, shaking my hand up and down. At the sound of my screams, he stopped and realized what he had done. He let out a low growl and went into his cage. Within seconds, my mother and grandmother came to me and checked my arm, where blood was starting to flow. My grandmother brought out medicinal alcohol to disinfect the wound. The sting of the alcohol seemed to hurt more than the actual bite. My mother ran to the neighbor across the street, who had a horse carriage, and asked him to urgently take us to the nearest hospital in the village, Smârdioasa.

While we made our way to the hospital, a burning feeling came from my swollen arm. But even this didn't hurt as much as the reality that my invisibility spell only worked in my imaginary world. What is the use of imagination if we are victims of reality?

"I just wanted to play with him, that's all," I told my mother as she berated me for approaching Volk.

"Why can't you play with other things, make friends here in the village?" she asked, seemingly talking more to herself. "Trying to pet that dog while he was sleeping," she continued, shaking her head in disbelief. "Of course he was scared."

"I thought I was invisible. I thought I could pet him without him seeing me."

"Why would you be invisible? What are you talking about, Alex?"

"All I wanted was to be invisible. I feel invisible to everyone most of the time, anyway."

"Is that what you think, Alex? That you're invisible?"

"It's just how I feel," I answered. It was only once I said those words out loud that I realized that's exactly how I felt.

At the hospital in Smârdioasa, the assistant took me right in upon seeing my swollen arm. While she cleaned and patched me up, I received a shot in my belly and several in my left arm. When I finally left the clinic, it was close to midnight, and I was almost asleep. Our neighbor drove the horses hard as his family was waiting for him.

Surprisingly, when we opened the gate, Volk did not leave his cage but remained inside, his muzzle resting on his paws. My grandparents were waiting for us with their hearts heavy in their chests. The familiar scent of homemade fries, *mămăligă* with shredded cheese and *şuncă* slices on top, garlic sauce on the side, awakened my senses as we opened the kitchen door.

8

ON A SUNDAY

On a lazy Sunday in April, five villagers gathered around the large wooden table outside the kitchen. Three sat on a bench on one side, two on the other, each holding a small glass. In the middle of the table was a one-liter bottle of home-distilled *țuică*. For it was Sunday, the sacred day of the week. It was said that God rested on the seventh day, and so would the village. It wouldn't be a proper Sunday without villagers wearing their traditional outfits: white embroidered shirts with three buttons at the neck; black suede vests with traditional patterns and a pocket on each side; high-waisted trousers with the shirt tucked in and a wide belt; boots that reached almost to the knee; and black shepherd's hats. No matter how dangerous, political topics were not excluded from the table, nor were the loud folk songs from the radio in the background, masking their discussion.

Măi Vasile, Măi Văsile,
What land could bear a man like you?

The land with flowers can bear me,
For I have loved three sisters.
One on the hill and one downhill,
And the other one on the country lane.[1]

Perched in my treehouse, absorbed in Rebreanu's novel *Ion*, which I had borrowed from my grandmother, I noticed my mother coming.

"Alex? Alex, are you here?"

"Yes?" I leaned on the freshly nailed-down railing.

"Ah, there you are!" she exclaimed, walking all the way to the foot of the walnut tree.

She inspected the four steps anchored to the tree's trunk, grabbed a lower branch, and with youthful enthusiasm climbed her way up to the treehouse.

"Look at this!" She surveyed the place. "So, this is where you're always hiding."

"I cleaned it up myself."

"It's quite a difference! Ask your grandfather for a tree stump—you could use it as a table."

"I'll do that. How was church?"

"It was fine. We are the talk of the village. You know what they say—*gura lumii nici borta vântului n-o astupă.*[2] You know, your grandfather began building this treehouse back when my sisters and I were very young, but he never finished it. He said it terrifies him to look at it."

"Why is that?"

"Maybe because we used to hide here with my mother when he would come home from the village reeking of

---

1. "Măi Vasile, Măi Văsile" – An old folk song
2. *Gura lumii nici borta vântului n-o astupă* – Not even the hole of the wind can stop people's mouth

alcohol and itching for a fight. He'd force us out even in the dead of the night, and we would crawl here, all four of us, with only a blanket to cover us in the cold winters." She lowered her head.

As if complementing her black mourning clothes, her face was pale and looked aged over these last days. Even the vibrant red of her hair, so often admired, seemed faded. I felt so sorry for her.

"I can't picture Grandfather like that. He's always so peaceful and quiet."

"He changed a lot over time—he got old. He doesn't drink so much anymore either. How about we do something this Sunday?" She suddenly perked up.

"What can we do?"

She thought for a second.

"I'll show you something, just follow me."

We both climbed down from the tree and made our way outside the courtyard into the dusty rural streets. We could feel the stares and hear the talk of the neighbors sitting outside by the benches next to the street, looking in our direction. But we continued walking slowly toward the hillside, side by side, until we arrived at a crossroad where the road split in two. It felt like the end of the village, with the pointy roof of the church always guarding us from above. My mother chose the street to the right, a narrow gravel path that headed uphill and into the forest.

By the time we reached the forest, we were breathing heavily, fresh forest air filling our lungs. I couldn't see any animals nearby, but there were sounds of them moving around the trees, hidden behind the green foliage. Distant sounds of birds singing and talking to each other came from afar. The grass on the ground was moist and slippery, and occasionally you could spot a snowdrop peeking through the green blanket. I followed behind my mother, who was walking with her long black skirt raised in her hands, when she suddenly stopped.

"There it is! We're here!"

Following the yellow rays of sunlight that slipped between the trees, we found ourselves in a clearing. It was a field of grass with an old, thick tree here and there. I realized we must be in the meadow at the top of the hill. My mother ran toward the thickest tree, arranged her woolen cardigan on the ground, and we sat down, resting our backs against the trunk, letting the spring sun heat our faces.

In front of us, the meadow extended in waves downhill and then uphill again, and I imagined in the summer being able to run all the way from end to end and back. With her eyes closed, my mother leaned on me, drawn into her own thoughts. We stayed like that until the sun was about to set.

We arrived back home just in time for an early Sunday dinner with a few of our neighbors, some of whom were too drunk to walk. My grandmother had prepared a traditional Romanian pork stew, with shredded cheese on top, and *mămăligă* and pickled cucumbers on the side. It was during dinner, at the table and in front of everyone, that my grandfather, urged by his neighbor, a man whose children only worked in the fields, asked when I would start earning my living.

"The boy has never dug a centimeter of dirt in his life," the neighbor said.

"He's so thin and frail that if the wind blows any harder, we might not find him one day," added the other.

I looked from the neighbors to my mother, who remained silent as their voices grew louder, fueled by the alcohol. She had promised my grandmother Catrina that she would enroll me in the "wretched village school." Even besieged by the loss of the man in her life, I was still surprised that there was no reaction from her that night.

And thus, it was decided by my grandfather and the neighbors: the following week, I would begin working in the fields.

9

WORKING THE GARDEN

After a few days working side by side with my grandfather, I woke up feeling the strains of exhaustion and soreness in each bone of my body. Yawning, with my arms crossed in front of my chest, I leaned in the kitchen doorway in my pajamas. My grandmother was by the stove outside, boiling the freshly squeezed milk in the cauldron and preparing our lunch in a satchel. I took a bucket of cold water from the plastic water tank and splashed it all over my face. I was awake. The scent of freshly mowed grass and the green apples I had picked the other day filled the morning air.

Changed into my work clothes, I took the bucket of chicken feed and leftovers for the pigs and fed the impatient animals in the yard.

Afterward, I went to the stable, where my grandfather was preparing to harness the horses to the cart.

"Morning," I mumbled as I walked into the stable.

"What's with you?" he asked.

"What?"

"You look like you're holding the world's problems on your back."

"I'm just tired. Yesterday, you had me shoveling all day, for hours on end."

"Eeeeh, stop complaining. You've only been working with me for a couple of days. What are you going to do in the summer when it's time to harvest?"

Harvest in the summer? I sure hope not, I thought to myself.

"Take the hair out of Valentina's eyes after you place the bridle. You want her to see, don't you?" He interrupted me as I was preparing the horse. "Animals don't understand what you say to them. Everybody can guide a horse, but they must feel you to listen to you."

I placed the heavy tools—two differently sized rakes and a hoe—and other smaller ones in the cart. The usual lunch of polenta with a piece of cheese, onions, and salt went in a bucket.

By the time Valentina and Țugui pulled the old wooden cart into the street, the rest of the village was awake. My grandfather tapped the horses, and I jumped in the slow-moving horse cart.

On the outskirts of Izvoarele, aside from the fields of wheat, grape, and corn, my grandfather cultivated half a hectare of ground which he called a garden. Here, the main vegetables produced were potatoes, but onions, some tomato plants, radishes, and carrots also had their place.

"We're just easing up on the year," my grandfather said. "After the sun burns the earth, the work gets harder."

The sun was warming my back, and within hours it became harder and harder to lift the shovel from the ground.

"Rather than fast and sterile, better slow and fruitless!" he said, laughing.

The days felt long and lonesome in the fields, and when I looked out at the horizon the views would blur together. It felt as if the valley of fields grew larger each day. One day, when I turned to my right, I saw my grandfather shading himself under some bushes with small red berries and smoking a cigarette.

"Hey, Alex boy, take a break once in a while, you're going to kill yourself!" he shouted.

I dropped the shovel on the ground and went to sit down next to him under the bushes.

"You don't like to work here in the fields or what?" he asked.

"It's hard, *Tătaie*, and there is nothing to do."

"What do you mean nothing to do? I'll give you more to do then."

"No, I mean it's wilderness… empty. We do the same thing for hours."

"It's lonely," he continued after a drag of his cigarette. "Alex, one day maybe—I'm saying maybe—you'll be grateful for these quiet hours. The ground speaks to you, the birds speak to you. Who knows, maybe one day you'll be grateful for the harvests of this ground."

"In the fall, you mean?"

"Then too, if we are left with anything. But this ground could be yours someday if you put your mind to it. Your grandmother only gave me girls. What should I do with three girls? Two, actually! One left us."

"I'm not sure this is the path my parents planned for me."

"Look, Alex, you're a big boy now, you've matured—I'd like to think so, at least. What part of your so-called 'planned life,' as people from the city say, are you still living?"

The question left me speechless. Nothing that was happening in my life had been part of the plan a few weeks ago.

"Let's eat. Don't think so much," my grandfather said when he saw me lost in thought.

With his dry and rough hands, he broke off a piece of *mămăligă*, cut a piece of cheese, and handed them to me. We each took a piece of onion, dipped it in salt, and ate our lunch.

10

AT YUGOSLAV'S

The local tavern, found on a little offshoot of what they call the main street, was the heart of the village.

On Saturday afternoons, the tables outside the tavern would be crowded with men sharing a bottle or two of wine. The clientele was diverse, ranging from the mailman, Mr. Apostoliță, at one table, to Priest Tănăsescu on the other, with subjects covering everything from reforms and taxes to the need for God to wash away our sins. Each of them preached their own religion.

Without a tavern, a village is dead, frozen into autonomous and non-communicating entities. But other villagers who saw themselves as more refined would visit the barbershop at Yugoslav's for socializing. Yugoslav's had just as much alcohol, and the discussions were just as heated. My grandfather, Ilie, was a well-known man in Izvoarele and someone who lived his whole life driven by routine. For the last thirty-five years, he had spent his Saturday afternoons at Yugoslav's, having his beard shaved and his hair cut.

Yugoslav himself was a man of few words in his late fifties. When he spoke, his views were often contradictory, accepting and opposing anything from Party politics to religion. What made him appeal to most, caused others to have their reservations about him.

The first time my grandfather took me to Yugoslav's, I was impressed by the rural decor of his barbershop, which was nothing but a little extension in front of his house.

"Yugoslave, I see you're busy today," my grandfather shouted from the street, leaning on the fence.

"Don't worry, they all leave if they see you coming!" Yugoslav answered.

Another silver-haired neighbor was sitting peacefully in the barber chair, his head tilted backward and shaving soap all over his face, with Yugoslav working his beard with the razor. There were two other neighbors hanging around, one sitting on a step at the entrance of the house, and the other standing up, smoking a cigarette.

"Do you have a cigarette, Iorgovane?" My grandfather opened the gate and entered, waving for me to follow.

"There you go, Comrade Ilie." He flicked his white pack of cigarettes, with a green logo and the name printed on the side, until one cigarette came out.

"Did you start the sowing already? Gheorghe told me he saw you around your garden the other day," one of the neighbors asked my grandfather.

"Yeah, I did. Better late than never," he replied, then turned toward me, put his hand on my right shoulder, and added, "and now I even have help."

"I heard," said the neighbors, laughing. "How do you like Izvoarele, Alexandre?"

"I like it just fine, for now," I answered.

"How's your mother doing? Is she still going to Zimnicea, or what is she going to do?"

"She goes sometimes, but not as often," I answered.

"Can you cut my boy's hair, Yugoslave?" my grandfather asked.

"Definitely. How would you like it, Alex?" asked Yugoslav.

"I don't know," I said, shrugging my shoulders.

As soon as he finished with his customer, I was told to take my seat in the barber chair. When Yugoslav went into the kitchen of his house, I thought it was to bring a magazine or two so I could choose a hairstyle—that was the custom when my father took me to our barbershop in Zimnicea. But no! He returned with a metal bowl in his hand, placed it on top of my head, and started cutting around it, working the scissors from one side to the other. For the next step of the haircut, he simply removed the bowl and began trimming the top of my hair.

"So your hair doesn't come into your eyes like a horse," he explained.

During the haircut, I focused my attention on the cabinet in front of the chair, the sole piece of furniture in his barbershop. Considering that cabinets are often used as decorative furniture to stow items out of sight, this one was different. It was a wooden frame, with a glass sliding door displaying everything contained within. Inside, there were two fancy soaps wrapped in wax paper, a golden pair of scissors which I assumed he never used, a Russian doll, and three white towels perfectly folded. And what did I spot all the way in the back? Yes, two bottles of *țuică* and a few small glasses. Several cigarettes later, Yugoslav finished my haircut, and we headed home.

Without a doubt, 1977 must've been the worst and most embarrassing year of my life. I missed not sharing a bed with my mother and ached to be able to tell George about everything that was happening. I missed my father taking me to a barber who knew what a ten-year-old boy's haircut should look like. Instead, I walked behind my grandfather with my head down, pretending I was counting stones to avoid the looks of the villagers sitting outside their homes. I imagined by now they were probably thinking that I walked around with a bowl on my head.

My grandfather opened the gate, and I followed. I could hear the radio blasting Romanian music all the way from the street.

Taking care not to scare Volk again, I sat down on the porch steps, hoping that he would come to me while my grandfather went to the other side of the house. Little by little, the big dog came closer, until I felt the pressure of his snout on my knees. I rubbed him behind the ears and kissed his soft fur, finding warmth and a comforting sense of reality. Covered in hair and dog saliva, I got up and went into the backyard, where my grandmother was rolling dough on the table and my mother was kneading a cheese mixture for a pie.

Their conversation stopped as soon as I rounded the corner. My mother's expression changed from tense to a suppressed laugh, and my grandmother gave a disapproving look at my grandfather.

"What do you say to his new haircut?" my grandfather asked.

"I think he'll break hearts at his new school," my mother replied.

"Why do you insist so much on sending him to school? I desperately need people in the fields. Every kid in the village helps with their land, and I have to hire people," my grandfather said.

The four of us had dinner at the table outside—chicken soup with homemade noodles and *mămăligă*—as we listened to my grandfather's continuous pleading for an extra pair of hands in the fields, while my mother firmly stated that I would be enrolled in the village school, instead.

11

FIRST DAY AT THE NEW SCHOOL

Shortly after turning seven years old, I started school in Zimnicea. In the days leading up to the first day, my father had me memorize the oath of the Pioneer Organization for young communists, even though I wouldn't be required to know it until fourth grade:

"I, Alexandru Toma, as I join the ranks of the Young Pioneer Organization, pledge to love my homeland, excel in my studies, uphold diligence and discipline, and honor the red tricolor neckerchief."

Early that morning, dressed in my school's uniform, I walked hand in hand with my mother to a pompous square building with large windows, the "Anastasie Panu"—school. The uniform, long blue trousers, an orange blouse with epaulets, a red neckerchief in the colors of the Romanian flag placed in the breast pocket, and a blue cap, was obligatory for both girls and boys.

Once we entered the school's yard, my knees trembled seeing the crowd of students, teachers, parents, and grandparents congregating together. My mother held my hand until the last minute, when the director rang a loud bell and we were told to queue up, one line for each class. I looked back at my mother, who couldn't hold back her tears. She stood under one of the trees in the yard, with her gloves and purse in one hand, and waved at me with the other.

My first teacher, Ms. Păcuraru, was a round woman with curly blonde hair and light skin full of small moles. She often wore a skirt that ended just below the knees and a sweater, which made her look stylish for that period. If she rested her hand on your back when walking between the rows of benches, our cheeks would blush from pride. But when we were called to her table to receive a couple of whips over our hands, tears started flowing down our cheeks. It was a balance.

Years later, when my grandmother walked me to my first day in the village school, I felt nothing but fear and anxiety at the thought of what it would be like. We crossed the main street, turned a corner, and continued until we reached a small, low bridge constructed from wooden planks. It spanned a shallow stream littered with trash. I could see the school of Izvoarele all the way from the bridge. But just like in my fantasy world in the backyard, there were obstacles to cross. Here, the obstacles were real—two boys and a loud-mouthed girl approached most kids who wanted to pass.

"Who are those kids?" I asked my grandmother that first day.

"They're Gâscă's kids. He's a drunk, and their mother is as well."

"Are they also going to school?"

"I don't think so. The last time I saw the girl in school was last fall. She went for a few weeks and then dropped out again. I don't think the brothers ever attended. They're nothing but trouble. Stay away from them."

I was convinced I could feel their eyes following me until we were out of sight.

Izvoarele's school was nothing but a large house in the middle of an empty field. Inside was a hall that separated a couple of classrooms on each side. At the end of the hall was the director's office and the small library, where my grandmother worked.

I was introduced to my teacher, Ms. Ecaterina, a young woman with a long face, a prominent bone structure, brown eyes, and long hair tied in a tight bun.

As soon as I entered the classroom, eleven pairs of eyes locked onto me, examining me from head to toe, as if I was about to perform on stage, with as much judgment as curiosity. Inside the room, the air felt thick with hopelessness and neglect. There were hardly any seats left on the benches, except for one small spot next to a blond boy with an unkempt appearance and muddy black shoes. I sat down next to him, but he did not lift his head from his notebooks, nor did he say a word.

The few minutes of free time between classes felt short and chaotic. Kids were jumping on the benches, running in and out of the class, loudly shutting the door after them. Two classmates sitting behind us found entertainment in slapping and making fun of the blond kid beside me.

"Did your cow lick your hair, or did you forget to wash it?"

"You smell like sheep!"

His cheeks flushed, but his eyes didn't leave his book.

When my grandmother said she worked in a library, I imagined one of those enormous halls, where hundreds or thousands of books, indexed by genre and author, would fill shelves so tall she would need a ladder to reach them. But when I went to visit her that day, I entered a small triangular room, with an old sofa chair placed at the window, a few shelves with books, and a couple of stacks on the floor. Two kids, supervised by my grandmother, sat on the floor with a notebook and pen in their laps, doing their homework.

Back in the classroom, the blond boy was still in his seat, eating an apple.

"You don't like to go out during breaks?" I asked him, walking slowly toward the bench.

"Sometimes I do," he replied. His voice was timid and creaky, and for the first time he looked straight at me, and I could see his big brown eyes.

"I'm Alexandru, Alex, but I guess you know," I said, extending my right hand for a handshake.

"Yes, I know." He shook my hand. "I'm Păpădie."

"It's the first time I've met someone with this name. Are you from Izvoarele?"

"Around Izvoarele, close by."

"I'm from Zimnicea. My mother and I are only here temporarily."

"So I've heard."

Păpădie returned his attention to the school book. His right index finger hovered over the words, and his lips moved without sound as he read to himself at a snail's pace. I wondered why he was still struggling to read at our age, but later I noticed that he was not the only student in class with that problem.

After the bell rang, everyone assembled inside the classroom again. The two boys at the bench behind us entered last, slapping Păpădie on the back of his head on the way. I turned around and glared at them intensely. My blood raced through my veins as I fought to control my temper.

12

THE RECOVERY PLAN

A few days later when I arrived home from school, my mother and grandmother were sitting at the table outside, facing each other, both wrapping their woolen vests around them to shield them from the cold spring air. My mother had her head buried in a newspaper, holding it open and raised in front of her face. When she heard my steps on the porch, she hurriedly tried to put it away but wasn't quick enough, as I ran up and grabbed it. I opened the copy of *Flacăra roșie* in the middle and discovered an article that filled the two center pages.

The headline read, "Ceaușescu Unveils Bold Recovery Plan After Devastating Earthquake Strikes Bucharest—Bucharest, Romania, April 18, 1977."

On one side was a black-and-white photograph of a street with buildings torn in half but in the process of repair. In the background, there were cranes and large trucks loading rubble, Ladas and Dacias parked here and there, and people standing around glancing at the buildings as if they were historical monuments. I ignored my mother's request to return the paper, stepped away, and began to read the content of the article out loud:

"In the wake of a powerful earthquake that rocked Bucharest, Romanian citizens eagerly anticipated the unveiling of an extensive recovery plan. The resilient nation faced an unprecedented challenge, and on April 18, Comrade Nicolae Ceaușescu, the First Secretary of the Romanian Communist Party, addressed the nation, outlining a path toward rebuilding and offering assistance to those in dire need. Commencing his speech with a moment of silence to honor the lives lost, hospitalized individuals, and families left homeless, Ceaușescu conveyed condolences and gratitude."

"You can stop reading now," my mother said.

"Why? It's a newspaper article, and we're among those people who were left homeless. Can't I read what their plan is?"

My mother exchanged a silent glance with my grandmother, and I continued reading aloud.

"Acknowledging the unity and strength of the Romanian people during these challenging times, Ceaușescu commended their unwavering support for one another and their dedication to rebuilding their beloved city. 'Our people have successfully endured this crisis,' he proclaimed, 'and under the resolute leadership of our Party, we have rapidly restored normality to public life.'"

The government pledged financial support in the "Recovery Solidarity and Humanity Fund" opened by Nicolae Ceaușescu following the earthquake, to be used for rebuilding schools, improving hospital facilities, providing housing for the homeless, and assisting earthquake survivors left with disabilities.

"That's the part I wanted to get to," my mother

interrupted. "Homeless and jobless, but I don't believe for a second they'll do anything for us."

"Shhh," my grandmother hushed her, "don't speak like that, Eva! There's someone at the gate."

I closed the newspaper and placed it on the table, keeping an eye on the figure by the gate. He whistled loudly, waved his hand, and yelled, "Eva Toma? Come here!"

My mother's face lost all color at the sight of him, and she quickly walked to the gate. There, a tall, bony man in an impeccable suit, hat, and leather briefcase awaited her. I felt like I had seen him before, and his stern appearance piqued the curiosity of several neighbors who had gathered by their fences.

The dialogue between them was brief. He handed her an envelope and walked away, casting a menacing glance over his shoulder.

"What did he want?" my grandmother asked her.

"It seems I have to start working back in Zimnicea," she said, reading the letter from the envelope. "They've assigned me to Crișana's textile factory. I start on Monday at eight in the morning."

"How will that work? You'll have to get up at five to catch the train and arrive on time," my grandmother asked.

"But until I receive my salary, how will I even pay for the train rides? I spent everything we had on rides to Zimnicea to get our new documents." My mother sat down at the table, grasping her forehead.

"We could ask your father to help you. I also have a little saved up," my grandmother offered.

"I'll pay you back, though I can never repay you for everything you have done for us."

"Eva, be serious! You're my daughter. Alex is my grandson. This is your home just as much as it is mine. How many daughters do I have left? One is all the way in Spain and barely remembers us. One is in Petroșani with her family. You're all that remains here. We're going to be fine."

"I just don't see how," my mother said, starting to sob. "With no home and a low-paid job, how will Alex and I ever be fine?"

"Give it some time. A solution will come, you'll see," my grandmother said gently, caressing my mother's back.

13

THE FIGHT

My heart was pounding profoundly, and my pajamas were soaked with sweat from another nightmare.

This time, my father was sitting in his usual chair by the window in the kitchen, cross-legged, with his arms holding the newspaper that covered his face. He wore the same suit as in the other nightmares, as if it were his uniform—the suit he wore the last time I saw him, torn and dirty, but he didn't seem to mind.

I walked into the kitchen, and for a split moment I thought this was real life. I called him several times: "*Tata! Tata!*" At last, he lowered the newspaper from his face and looked at me, puzzled, with no recognition in his eyes. Suddenly, together with his chair, he began moving further away from me, as if the kitchen was opening into a dark void. Despite my efforts, my legs wouldn't move, no matter how hard I tried. My mother's hoarse voice, singing the same song she had sung since I could remember, finally woke me up.

Then a merchant arrived
Full of money, with great fanfare,
Buying children
Whom their mothers didn't love.
He came to our gate.
I came out and scolded him:
"You nor the emperor
Have money to buy my boy!
Go to the village, for it's big,
Leave, leave!" and he left.[1]

In the last few weeks, nightmares had occurred more often than dreams, to the point that I was frightened to go to sleep. It wasn't just my father who appeared in these nightmares but all the people I had known in my few years of life. I constantly wondered: *Will I ever see them again? What happened to them?*

Frustration from lack of sleep plunged me into numbness. I neither cared nor asked anymore whether we would ever move back to Zimnicea. I paid little attention in school and rarely did my homework. Whereas before I would try to eavesdrop on my mother and grandmother's conversations, now I was indifferent to their discussions. Every so often, I helped my grandfather without showing any enthusiasm. I spent my time alone in the treehouse whenever I had the chance.

That's why on a cloudy day in April, right before Easter, I found myself in a small, cluttered office, staring down at its red carpet full of muddy footprints. I was with two boys from my class, Paul and Lucrețiu, sitting on wooden chairs facing the man behind the desk in front of us. The desk was

---

1. "Cântec" by George Coșbuc

full of documents, papers, newspapers, magazines, pens, and bottles of ink. The stocky man with a puffy mustache and small square teeth screamed agitatedly at us. Every once in a while, he would get up from his chair to deliver a powerful slap across my cheek, leaving me nauseous and with a high-pitched ringing in my right ear. He was the school principal, famous in the small village of Izvoarele for his ability to maintain order and discipline in his district.

Paul and Lucrețiu were the kids who often slapped and made fun of Păpădie—until that day, when they snatched his apple and ran outside in the courtyard to a group of popular girls. An uncontrollable feeling of rage came over me as I tightened my fists and went after them.

"Give the apple back to Păpădie," I demanded.

The two boys looked at each other and started laughing out loud. One of them said, "If you want it, you must catch it first."

He threw the apple to the other, and I jumped on him, pushing him to the ground. As if that was not bad enough, I started punching him until his friend came to pull me away. That's when I turned toward him and punched him in the face as well.

The group of girls who had just been playing around with the two boys now pulled away in shock with their hands covering their mouths. The other kids gathered around to admire the spectacle until the principal arrived. He dragged us by our ears into his office, where we were then schooled, especially me for being the one who started the fight.

"Hooligans, that's what you are! How can you create such a spectacle and scene in the yard of my school? Fights are not permitted on school grounds, not in my school, *domnilor!*[2] Maybe there in the big city in Zimnicea, you can behave like this, but not here, not here! With all the trouble I went through to add you into a new class, right at the end of the school year, and this is how you repay me?" I felt the question was rhetorical.

A knock sounded at the door, and the principal, visibly annoyed, yelled, "Come in!"

It was my grandmother.

"There's your grandson, Ms. Violeta. What do you say to that?" he asked my grandmother, pointing at me.

"Maybe I could speak with you for a second, Mr. Baltag?" my grandmother asked.

When the principal went out to the hallway to talk to her, I could hear fragments of their conversation: "He has never behaved like this. He is a good kid. He's going through a lot right now."

Meanwhile, I was left with Paul and Lucrețiu. One hit the air precariously close to my face, showing his gap-toothed grin, and the other one told me how his big brothers would come to teach me a lesson. Their mockery, their threats, or the fact that the whole school would laugh at me, nothing mattered as much as the shame I felt when I thought of my mother and my grandmother's disappointment.

I ended up being expelled and was asked to gather my notebooks and go home. To avoid the looks of the other children, I kept my head low as I went to pick up my things from the classroom.

On the walk home, I debated several ways to explain the red marks and bruises that betrayed my face to my mother.

---

2. *Domnilor* – Gentleman

But as soon as she came home from work and saw me like that, she started crying. I had to tell her the truth.

"Alex, as if we don't have enough problems, you go and start fights?"

"I was just tired of seeing them attacking Păpădie."

"But he needs to stand up to them, not you. Who is this Păpădie anyway?"

"He sits next to me in class—or used to. He's from Smârdioasa and walks here every day just to come to school."

"I cannot imagine how the whole village is going to talk about this, and you know who'll get blamed for this? Your grandmother!"

"I know."

"I'll go to the school tomorrow and speak to the principal."

"But I don't want to go anymore!" I yelled in exasperation. "I don't like it there at all, especially now."

"If they take you back, you're going. I don't think you can imagine just how much a year missed from school will impact your student record. The only job in the city for someone like that will be as a cleaner," she threatened.

I left my mother in the kitchen and slunk into bed until my grandparents arrived home. By Friday, my grandmother had managed to soothe the principal's anger and convinced him to give me a second chance.

14

THE WRONG STREET

A whistle from outside, followed by Volk's barking, interrupted my morning. I opened the kitchen door and looked out onto the street. A blond boy with a round face full of freckles waved at me. It was Păpădie.

"Aren't you coming to school anymore?" he yelled.

"Just wait a minute," I replied.

I grabbed my two notebooks and, with a faint air of reluctance, went out to the gate. To show his gratitude, Păpădie offered to walk with me to school. It wouldn't be every day, as it added too much to his already long walk from Smârdioasa.

He rarely said anything, as if talking required a lot of effort from him, so we started our walk in silence.

Around us, the fields displayed yellow-gold tones, and here and there we saw a herd of cows or a flock of sheep. Shepherd dogs ran around them, and sometimes a boy would sleep by the gate to the field, hugging a whip, his hat atop his head, shielding him from the sun.

It occurred to me that the reason I felt so comfortable living in the village was that every single detail of a villager's life is based on routine. Routine is the basis for thriving for both animals and villagers, tightly intertwined like a well-made rope.

Every morning at the same hour, the cows knew when and where to go. Sometimes a boy and a dog guided them to the fields where they would grass; other times they went by themselves. Just before sunset, the village streets were blocked by herds of cows returning. Each cow knew exactly which home it belonged to and where to stop. The owners, afterward, followed their own routine of milking their cows. Every evening, villagers came to collect the many liters of fresh milk, which was then transformed into yogurt and cheese. It was their life cycle.

When we came to the small bridge over the garbage-filled stream, we saw the short figure of Principal Baltag in the distance. He was standing by the school entrance, talking to two teachers. As we approached, they turned their heads toward us with dismayed looks. We said good day to them all, but only the teachers returned the greeting. Principal Baltag kept his cold stare at us all the way to the class.

"Which of Moromete's sons left for Bucharest first?" Ms. Ecaterina asked, looking over the class. "Anyone? Have you read the book, or did you just say you did? Albert, what about you? Which of Moromete's sons first left for Bucharest, and why?"

"Aaaa, umm, I think it was Achim?" Albert answered, trembling.

"You think, or you know it was Achim?"

"It was Achim," he repeated louder.

"True, it was Achim," the teacher answered. "And why did he go to Bucharest? Who can tell me?"

"He went to sell milk and cheese to get money to send home to his father," answered Oana, one of the students two rows back from me.

"Exactly," the teacher said. "But did he actually send any money to his father?"

A knock on the door interrupted the class, to which the teacher responded, "Enter!"

A man in his fifties came in, dragging his son Vasile by the shoulder. Vasile was a student in our class, but he rarely attended school. His face was red and puffy, and his eyes were swollen from crying, with snot running down from his nose. His father spoke bluntly and said to the teacher, "Tovarăşă Ecaterina, please beat him, beat him like we do to horse thieves. This one only listens with fear!"

Vasile lowered his face and started crying again. The feeling of shame from standing in front of the class burned more than the quick palms of his teacher slapping him.

Going home that day, after I crossed the bridge, I decided to take a different street, for a change of scenery. After a minute, I noticed plastic bottles and a chair missing one of its legs littering the side of the street. Most of the houses along here were small, made of dried mud bricks, with colored fabric sheets instead of doors. Rusted metal parts, once belonging to cars, littered the open, unfenced gardens. The sound of kids crying in the background gave me chills, and the few people outside at that hour were staring at me. They wore colorful clothes, long skirts, and blouses adorned with golden ribbons. It seemed as if my curiosity had led me to unforeseen discoveries, and I realized then that this was the *cătuni* neighborhood, as our neighbor Constantin called it.

Halfway down the street, a carriage hitched to a skinny-looking horse stood in front of a courtyard with a wire fence. When I passed the carriage, I turned my head slightly so as not to stare. That's when I saw a girl roughly my age, wearing a floral-patterned pink skirt and a red T-shirt, her tangled black hair covering half her face. She looked back at me, and our eyes locked. I recognized her and she recognized me. It was the girl from the bridge!

These few seconds of distraction provided the perfect opportunity for her mother, who was chasing her, to catch and pull her by the hair. I quickly turned away and continued walking as fast as I could, eager to escape her angry screams.

15

CONTENTMENT

"Alex, come here," my mother yelled all the way from the backyard.

"I'd rather not," I answered, sitting on the high kitchen doorstep.

"Don't be a little chicken."

"I'm not a little chicken. Don't call me that."

"Can you be so sure? Are you scared to come out back?"

"No, I'm simply busy right now, and a boy cannot be a little chicken. I don't look like one."

"But you act like one." She laughed. "Well, fine, if Muhammad won't go to the mountain, the mountain must come to Muhammad."

With her red hair swinging from side to side, she jumped playfully around like a little kid, hiding both her hands behind her back.

"Left, or right?" she asked.

"For what? What is it, Mama?"

"Just pick one."

"All right, left!"

"You won!"

When she opened her hand, a plump, ripe red tomato was revealed.

"My first tomato!"

"It's not the only one. There are a lot more back there—you've taken good care of them," she said.

"Can we taste it?"

"Yes, let's share it. Let me bring some smoked meats and cheese to go with it," my mother said.

She came back with a plate of *şuncă*, *pastramă*, cheese, a few slices of onion, and the tomato from the garden. She placed it on the kitchen table outside. With my hand, I took a piece of *şuncă* from the plate, dipped a slice of onion in the salt, and bit loudly from it. *The most refined food a man can taste!* I thought. I took a moment to peruse my surroundings. In front of me was my mother, working attentively on an embroidery for one of her colleagues at work, once in a while pausing to take a piece of tomato and cheese from the plate. The dark circles under her eyes and a recent loss of weight made her look bony and tired.

My grandparents' garden was now shaded by the large acacia tree that proudly bore its white flowers like clusters of snowdrops, giving us privacy from neighbors passing by on the street. On a patch of grass around the porch, a few tulips bloomed. Next to them, like a sentinel, a large bush of red peonies stood tall, spreading a strong fragrance which I could often smell all the way from the street.

Life in Izvoarele flowed differently—it was slower, gentler. Even with its cracked blue wooden shutters on the two windows in front and the bare yellow bulb in the kitchen hanging from the discolored ceiling, my grandparents' house was like a portal into a world of comfort and peace. After two months, I now treasured waking to the sound of animals asking for food in the early dawn, the constant background noise from the loud radio kept outside by the kitchen door, the bucket showers, and even the occasional cleaning of the stinking pigsty. In the evenings, the whole village smelled of hay and polenta. Some nights, when I couldn't sleep, I went outside and sat on the rotten porch, breathing the cold May air, and looked up. From a sky full of stars, two of them shone brighter to me, like diffused lights breaking through the darkness.

Between the four of us, there was harmony and care for one another. I thought about how my grandmother would start baking something fresh for us as soon as she set foot in the house. Then she would yell so I could hear it all the way from the treehouse: "I prepared a pie for you! It's still hot. Come and eat before it gets cold."

And then there was my grandfather, a man of few words, especially now that I had started school and couldn't help him as much. I was surprised when I saw him digging out a seat from an old swing that my mother and her sisters had used as kids. He replaced the missing ropes with new ones he traded for with a neighbor and hung them from a branch of the walnut tree by my treehouse.

"Ms. Eva! Ms. Eva, are you home?" Mr. Apostoliță yelled from the street, interrupting my thoughts.

"Yes, I'm coming!" she said, gently putting her embroidery on the table and walking to the gate.

"I think you have a letter again, Ms. Eva."

"Where do I sign?"

"Here." The mailman pointed with a finger. "So, how do you like living in Izvoarele? I heard your boy is now enrolled in school."

"Yes, he is. He cannot miss his studies," she said, handing back his pen.

"He's lucky. Baltag is a very good man. He improved the school a lot. Did you see that now they even have a football court?"

"Yes, Alex told me they play there after school sometimes."

"Are you going to stay here?"

"I'm not sure just yet."

"I heard that you're taking the train every morning. I was afraid I might not find you home at this time of day. You must've received the check from City Hall from the relief fund?"

"No, I didn't," my mother answered. "Instead, I got placed at Crișana's. That's why I take the train. Today is my day off."

"I see, so that's why."

"Don't listen to the talk of the village, Mr. Apostoliță. You know what they say, 'the word of mouth is free.'"

"True, true. Well, in that case, I'll be going. I have many more deliveries to make."

"Have a good day!"

"Goodbye, Ms. Eva." He waved.

The letter was from my Aunt Ana in Barcelona, and my mother opened it quickly, reading a few words out loud here and there from which I understood that she should call her immediately. My aunt's name often came up in conversation between my mother and grandmother, thanks to the letters she was sending, but I never gave much thought to it—until now, when I saw my mother sitting at the table with the letter in one hand, looking disturbed.

Naturally, the simplest solution for a call was to use the

village's only phone at the mayor's office. With a pack of Carpați cigarettes and Alvorada coffee beans, he would allow the call, albeit with the expectation that it might be overheard. Instead, my mother opted to wait until the next day to use a payphone near the factory she worked at.

16

IN THE TRASH

In those times, the most thrilling word on people's lips, a word so intoxicating that as soon as Romanians heard it, their minds instantly projected them into a life full of luxury and freedom, was "Occident" or, as some might know it, "The West."

For many, the dream to live in the Occident was just that, a dream lingering in the back of their minds. For others, it became their purpose, so intense that they would risk their lives to achieve it. With an open port to the Danube River, which served as a national border with Bulgaria, Zimnicea was highly popular with the latter group. Daily, newspapers reported on people getting caught trying to swim across the river. They were labeled by the border guards as *frontieriști*, but mostly they were simple, brave men who risked their lives for their dream. Among these stories, there were also whispers of hope, tales of those who succeeded, shared mostly in hushed conversations among the villagers.

"What are those?" I asked my mother, who pulled several documents from her bag.

As she carefully arranged them on the small table in our room, she answered. "Papers."

"For what?" I sat on the side of our soft sprung bed.

"For a passport," she said and sat down next to me. She took my hand in hers and looked me in the eyes. "Tomorrow morning, I'll take the train to Bucharest. I managed to get an appointment at the embassy, and I want to apply for a passport."

"What for?"

"I've been talking to Ana. If I come to Barcelona, she'll help me to get a job. This could be our way to a better life."

My heart started beating fast, and I just stood there looking at her.

"When I'm settled, the first thing I'll do is bring you. I won't leave you here alone, I promise."

"You're going alone?"

"I don't want to, but I have no other choice. They'll never approve a passport for both of us. They need to think I'll come back."

My mind blanked while she continued talking. All I heard were fragments about Red Cross visas and family reunification.

I didn't wait for her to finish before I got up and stormed out of the house and straight to my treehouse, where I cried uncontrollably, hugging myself and holding my legs close to my chest. I skipped dinner and only went in when it got too cold outside. The next morning, pretending to still be asleep, I listened as my mother dressed silently. I felt her hand softly caressing my head and her lips on my cheek. I turned my head to the other side and told her, "Go away!" in a rough voice.

She remained still for a few seconds, then went out of the room. My heart trembled as I listened to her quietly making her way out of the house, out the gate, and into the dawn. I envisioned myself left alone at my grandparents', having been deserted by both my father and now my mother, who would move to Spain and eventually forget about my existence.

That notorious day, as I was walking home from school, I again saw the girl from the gypsy neighborhood standing at the bridge, this time accompanied by her two brothers. When they noticed me, they gestured to the students ahead to cross the bridge quickly.

"Look who's here—the city boy!" the girl said, approaching me, one brother following her and another blocking my way back.

"Get out of my face," I said, lifting my head up to meet the eyes of her brothers.

"No, we won't," the older one answered. "What are you going to do?" He smiled at me, his mouth open, revealing his two missing front teeth.

"He thinks he's something special, coming from the big city," the girl said to her brothers. "That's probably how he got accepted to our school."

I rolled my eyes at the thought of my having received special treatment at the school and tried to make my way past by putting my right arm ahead and trying to squeeze in between. But they hardly let me pass, stubbornly blocking the way. When I finally made it through, the girl pushed me from behind, sending me over the edge of the bridge.

I fell on my hands and knees onto the garbage that was littering the stream. It caused great amusement for the three of them and the other students witnessing the show. I tried to pick my notebooks up from among the trash and climbed up again.

"What is your problem?" I yelled back at them. "My books and clothes are ruined. It's not funny!" But my anger only made them laugh more.

"It's not, right? You know what else wasn't funny?" the girl said, stopping her laugh. "You came onto my street and stared into our garden until my mother caught me and pulled me by the hair. That wasn't very funny for me either."

"That was not my fault. I just looked in your direction for a second. She would've done it anyway."

"Not if she hadn't caught me, she wouldn't."

"Why were you on our street anyway?" asked one of the brothers. "What were you doing there?"

"I didn't know it was your street. Do you own it?" I asked.

"Yes, and if we catch you walking there again, I'll cut your legs with a scythe. Go back to your grandmother's house, or better yet, go back to your own city."

Defeated, dirty, and stinking of trash, I turned around and walked away from the bridge, their laughs and insults in the background.

When I finally found myself out of their sight, I couldn't stop my legs from trembling and felt tears flowing down my cheeks. The first thing I did when I arrived home was to get a few buckets of water and scrub myself with soap, hoping the scent of garbage would go away. I remained in my treehouse until the evening when my mother arrived home and came up to find me. She hadn't qualified for a passport, and her disappointment made my day a little better.

17

VERONICA

"Good day, Mr. Viorel. Hot today, isn't it?" I greeted our neighbor, who was leaning on his wooden fence, looking out into the street.

"Good day, boy! Oh, it's scorching," he answered, moving the straw in his mouth from one side to the other and staring curiously at my bags placed on the ground.

The two bags I carried were big and heavy, and each contained several bottles of freshly squeezed cow's milk and big chunks of cheese.

"How much do you want this time?" my grandmother's friend Lucica had asked earlier when I walked in. She had been stirring rice into a pot of milk she was boiling on the stove. Occasionally, she slurped a mouthful from the spoon, to see if it needed more sugar.

"You can stuff a whole cow in each, if you have them. I can carry it!" I answered, my stomach growling at the scent of sweet rice pudding.

The road from Lucica, who lived a few streets downhill, seemed unbearably long and steep when carrying the bags, forcing me to make several stops to rest my aching arms and fingers.

In front of our gate was Ramona, another neighbor who was "at it again," shouting and talking endlessly in the street, obviously angry about someone and wanting the whole village to know. Viorel yelled at her to keep quiet, only to be shut down by his wife and daughter, as always.

"Let her be," said Aurora, his wife. "The street is free. Everyone can do as they please without anyone else interfering. You should only care about your yard or your own house. Leave her alone to chatter if she wants. If she's stupid, you don't have to be stupid too."

"Each in their own nest," added Florica, his daughter.

Deep inside, Viorel knew that he had just as much right to speak up if someone bothered him and the peacefulness of the neighborhood. However, he knew better than to start an argument with his wife and daughter. So, he concluded then and there that, yes, the village street is free for everyone.

Laughing to myself, I picked up my two heavy bags and walked through the gate quickly, thinking that I could blame the delay on the milk not being ready when I came to pick it up. But I stopped short. Turning the corner of the house, I saw someone I instantly recognized standing face to face with my mother by the kitchen table: the girl from the bridge. At first, I feared she might be there to tell my mother a lie about what happened, but as they both turned toward me, I noticed the girl's red eyes and flushed cheeks.

"Come here, Alex, don't just stand there," my mother urged.

The girl remained quiet and avoided my gaze, seemingly fixated on the floral patterns of the tablecloth.

"Mama, what's going on?"

"I heard from a little bird what happened at the bridge the other day," my mother began, nodding toward the girl, "and I thought a chat with Veronica—her name, by the way—would be good." After a brief pause, when none of us said anything, she continued, "We had a great talk, and I think we understand each other."

Veronica didn't look up from the table.

"How old are you, Veronica?" my mother asked.

"I'll be nine in November," she replied.

"See? You're almost the same age. My Alex will be eleven in September," my mother said, smiling and looking at each of us. "Aren't you in school, Veronica?"

"Mmm, no, not really." She hesitated. "I mostly take care of our home. I used to go."

"You didn't like it?"

"I don't know. Some things I liked, but I got punished a lot, and I was too tired from working at home. My mother also..."

"What's with your mother?" my mother interrupted.

"She wasn't very happy when I wasn't home to take care of her and cook for my brothers."

"I see," my mother said. "Are you two hungry? Veronica, are you eating with us? We have bean stew with *mămăligă*."

"If you have enough," Veronica answered.

"Alex, why don't you show her your treehouse, and I'll prepare the table."

Ashamed and angry, I dropped the bags on the ground in front of my mother and gestured at Veronica to follow me.

Why did she need to get involved in my affairs? It was so embarrassing, knowing that my mother, of all people, found the girl who had pushed me off the bridge. And what was I supposed to do with Veronica now?

As soon as I opened the gate to the backyard and Veronica saw the treehouse, she ran up to the walnut tree, climbed the makeshift stairs, and within a few seconds she was already at the railing, looking down at me. Then she turned and looked away, her face lit up at the view of green fields meeting the light blue sky, like in a painting.

18

COSTEL CARP

Weeks went by without any more mentions of Ana or Barcelona. It seemed as if my mother had made peace with our life with my grandparents, at least on the surface. But gradually, her behavior started to change.

At home, she sat on the kitchen doorstep looking up at the sky and rarely talked. Her irritation with everyone around her became noticeable. Even my grandfather felt uneasy telling jokes at the dinner table, so as not to upset her even more.

Every week she came home with a page ripped from a magazine with a model of a pantsuit or a dress, and fabric she bought on credit from a store in Zimnicea. My grandmother argued with her to stop going into debt over dresses and summer suits, telling her to put money *la saltea*, for darker days. But it was all in vain. She wasn't listening, insisting that this could make her more money than her job.

On a Saturday morning, before my grandparents

returned from clearing the paths between the rows of grapevine, I went to the backyard to pick the cherries that were hanging low on the trees, so that my grandmother could bake a pie. Climbing up the tree and resting a plastic bucket on the branch next to me, I plucked the cherries with one hand and stuffed myself with the other until my stomach started to complain and my face was stained cherry red.

There was a name I kept hearing between whispers. The previous night after dinner, we all sat at the outdoor table—my grandparents, my mother, and two of our neighbors, Constantin and Gabriel. The sweet early summer scent in the air mixed with the fiery smell of *țuică* in their glasses, when Constantin thought he heard thunder in the distance.

"May there be thunder and lightning all month," said my grandfather.

"So the clouds will be weeping all summer," added Gabriel.

"So our corn stores will be full for winter," said Constantin in his stutter.

With one ear on the villagers' talk and the other to my mother, I overheard her say to my grandmother that she had been asking around for news of Costel Carp and his mother, but had not heard anything.

Spitting out another cherry stone, I sat in the tree and thought of the day he and my father took me fishing for the first time.

For the last twenty years, there hadn't been a Thursday without my father and Costel going fishing. The first time they took me with them was just after I turned six. As we embarked on Costel's blue boat, he told me he would take us to a special place, a "surprise." Both Costel and my father taught me how to bait the fishing hook and cast the line. We were at the end of a channel, on the outskirts of the Danube, where the only fish we could catch were "black eyes," as Costel liked to call bass. Thinking back, the place must've been carefully chosen beforehand. Without paying attention to the cork bobbing in the water, mesmerized by the vegetation surrounding the canal, I suddenly felt the bite of a fish. It seemed as if the fish wanted to unbalance me and pull me into the water.

"Ha!" I sobered up from the surprise and pulled back.

My father reached around from behind and helped hold the rod.

"Reel it in again, but this time slower," he advised.

The fish surfaced as if to take a breath of fresh air, then continued fighting even more forcefully. After a long struggle, my father helped me land the fish and put it in a metal bucket filled with water so it would last until we arrived home.

We never wanted to leave that place, but with the sundown, the presence of the local "guards"—the water mosquitoes—convinced us it was time to return home. By the time we left the canal, we were enveloped in a cloud of them. As you slapped your leg to kill one, two more attacked from behind. That day, the three of us brought home a bucket full of fish for Friday's dinner. We were dirty and reeked of fish, our bodies covered in mosquito bites. I remember it as one of the best days of my life.

Climbing down the cherry tree, I could hear the rhythmic sound of my grandmother's old sewing machine echoing through the garden. It came all the way from the other side of the house. I knew how my mother would be sitting, arching her back to see precisely where the machine's needle penetrated the material.

Back in Zimnicea, there were times when I grew tired of the smell of oil from her sewing machine, the scraps of textile, thread of all colors strewn around the apartment, and the steady *ch-ch-ch* of the needle puncturing the fabric.

I left the bucket of cherries on the kitchen table and went to see her. In one corner of the room was an old oak closet, and by the wall was a large wooden chest used to keep my grandmother's marriage dowry: hand-embroidered tablecloths, linen bedding, and woven woolen shawls, each showcasing fine craftsmanship and domestic skill. Several carpets adorned the floor and walls, giving the room a traditional feel.

"Aaah, Alex, you scared me!" she gasped, looking at me over her shoulder.

"Didn't mean to."

"Aren't you with your grandfather today?"

"No, he said that he, Leon, and Grandmother are enough. Maybe tomorrow I can go and help them. Shall we do something?"

"I'm a bit busy, Alex. Why don't you go ask Veronica if she wants to go out and play or come over?"

"Mama, I can't go to her house. Her street is weird and dangerous. Why don't we go to the fields? We haven't been in a couple of weeks. They're probably full of flowers by now."

"I'm a bit tired after working all week. It's also very hot outside…"

"Oh," I said. "I guess I'll go get the milk before Grandmother arrives home." I turned to leave.

"Wait, Alex!" she yelled and paused for a second. "Let's

go!" She left the material on the sideboard of the sewing machine and stood up.

"We're going to the fields?" I asked.

"No, even better. Have you been to the pond?"

"I heard the kids from school talk about it," I said.

"Then come."

19

THE VILLAGE POND

It was already lunchtime when my mother and I walked side by side to the pond. At that hour, the village streets were quiet, not a single person in sight. The house of Izvoarele's mayor, Mr. Valentin Cocioată, perched proudly on a corner leading to a stretch of wide-open fields. The fence around his garden was tall enough to maintain some privacy but low enough for curious villagers to peek over.

The house itself, painted with a mixture of white and green, with the colors seemingly coordinated with the white flowers and green bushes in his yard, looked spacious, and compared with other properties, clean and well-maintained. To the locals, it was the village's patrimony.

"It's not nice to look in people's gardens, Alex," my mother said.

"I was just having a peek," I answered, catching up to her.

When we reached the tall grass on a nearby field, we

could hear the giggling noises of a boy and a girl, hiding in between the green grass, thinking no one could hear them.

Both my mother and I recognized the couple: Maria, Constantin's daughter, and Grigore, a young fellow from a Hungarian family in a nearby village.

The whole village knew their sad love story. Constantin had made it clear that he would never approve of his daughter marrying a boy of Grigore's status, and even worse, from a different village. He was betting on the fact that the boy would never dare to ask for her hand in marriage, knowing his feelings toward him.

"By the time Kabucs's boy, Grigore, gets the *inima-n dinți*[1] to ask for Maria's hand, she will have reached retirement," Constantin would say.

My mother and I locked eyes for a second and, pretending not to hear them, quickly cut through the fields. Further ahead, there was a thick cluster of willow branches overshadowing the pond behind them. Like a beautiful girl with long hair, the willow allowed the ends of its green leafy branches to dip in the water.

The landscape was lush green and abundant with vegetation and wildflowers. Echoes of loud laughter from the pond reverberated throughout the valley.

"Do you hear that?" I asked my mother.

"Yes, it's just a group of girls."

I peeked through the willow branches and saw three girls in the pond, splashing water at each other.

"Who are they?"

"I have no idea, but it's not like we're not allowed to go there too. There is room for us on the other side, over there." She pointed to a grassy area away from the girls.

---

1. *Inima-n dinți* – To take his heart in his teeth (Courage)

As soon as they saw us, the girls stopped their playful antics and looked at each other.

"Good day, girls!"

"Good day, miss," they replied.

"What a warm day for a bath, right?" my mother asked.

"It's cold at first when you dip your feet in, but we've been here a while and don't feel cold anymore. Right, Elisa?" The smallest girl turned to the one next to her.

"Yeah, I'm not cold, although my skin got all wrinkly, like Ioana's shirt." They all laughed.

"I think I'll get out now," Elisa decided.

Their shoes and dry clothes lay on their side of the grass.

As the girls walked out of the water, my mother took off her sandals, gathered her skirt, and dipped her feet into the water. I, on the other hand, remained on the grass, captivated by the last girl emerging from the pond.

Her white slip, crafted with lace, was wet and stuck to her body. I could see the shape of her curves and what I imagined were her nipples.

"Alex, aren't you coming in the water?" my mother interrupted.

"Just a minute," I responded abruptly, without taking my eyes off the girl with the blonde hair and pale skin.

I don't know if I stared for a minute or an hour, but at my mother's insistence, I finally got up and went into the pond. My mind barely noticed the cold water. It was as if I had walked straight into a fire, so convinced was I that I was in love.

They must be sisters, I thought. Their handmade shirts, woven from four layers of cotton, had intricate embroidery with red bows at the neck and sleeves. Typical of *boieri* families, the higher-ranking landowners in the villages.

Politely, the girls bid my mother farewell, and I stole a final glance at the girl as she walked away with her sisters.

"Could it be that my Alex is in love?" my mother teased.

"What makes you think that?"

"You were staring so intently that I don't think you noticed you went into the water with all your clothes on." She laughed.

"I did, didn't I?" I said, looking at myself. "How long have I been in the water like this?"

"For as long as it took for that poor girl to put her clothes on and leave," my mother replied, still laughing.

As if by magic, the sun cast its warm rays toward us, and we settled in the sun to dry off. We listened to the chorus of hundreds of birds singing in the background. After a nap, we made our way home.

"Come, come, Alex, Eva!" my grandmother called out from across the street when we entered the yard. "Viorel's cow is giving birth. Come here and help us!"

My mother and I entered Viorel's garden, from where we often picked chamomile flowers for tea. The cow's moans of pain echoed from the shed. We found her lying on her side, surrounded by several of Viorel's children and his wife, all attempting to soothe her. Eventually, the village veterinarian arrived, looped a rope around the calf's legs, and together we pulled out the newborn—first the legs, then the entire body. Seeing the cow, which provided us with milk, so proud and content with her calf was gratifying. The mother and newborn's survival sparked a celebration in the village.

My grandfather, always keen on festive occasions, brought his accordion and a few bottles of *țuică*. Viorel's wife and daughters prepared food for everyone, and the evening was filled with dancing and laughter. The thought of the girl with the golden hair lingered in my mind, not leaving for even a moment. That night, I went to bed smiling, hopeful that she might appear in my dreams, giving me the courage to speak to her.

20

IONUȚ ARRIVES

On the morning of June 23, I was en route to the Izvoarele train station, a narrow building nestled among tall wild grass on both sides. Simultaneously, my eight-year-old cousin Ionuț was on a train headed to Izvoarele, traveling alone. He sat by the window in an orange plastic chair, clutching his luggage with one hand and resting the other on the armrest, his eyes fixed on the rapidly changing landscape, which only intensified his nausea. When a wave hit him, he reached for the plastic bag in his trouser pocket, but looking away from the window made him reconsider, and he put it back.

Earlier that morning, he had arrived at the train station in his hometown Petroșani, accompanied by his mother, Alexandra. She had bought him the ticket to Izvoarele, walked him to his seat on the train, and made sure he was settled. She left him with firm instructions.

"Ionuț, look away from the window if you feel sick, or use the bag," she advised, patting the front pocket of his trousers and straightening his shirt collar.

"Don't talk to strangers or respond to vendors. Stay in your seat until the conductor announces, 'Next stop, Izvoarele,'" she instructed, emphasizing her words with a wag of her finger.

Back in Izvoarele, my mother and grandmother had given me directions to the train station before they left for work, as if I hadn't been there before.

"Now, when you two boys get home, remember your chores. Show him how to feed the animals, and you both should start cleaning the horse's stable," she instructed me before walking out the gate.

"*Mămaie*, we'll manage," I said and leaned back in my chair.

"You should also help your grandfather. There's so much work that he even had to hire two extra hands. Imagine the embarrassment with two healthy boys at home."

After they both left, I followed suit.

Quickening my pace as I heard the distant rumble of the train, I stepped onto the open cement platform beside the track just as it pulled in. The sight of the locomotive, with its noisy engine and smoke billowing from beneath, struck me as something out of a gothic tale.

The doors opened and a short figure, clad in loose linen shirt and pants, with the legs rolled up as if bought with room to grow, jumped down the steps of the train, looked toward me, then ran straight to the bushes. After the long trip, Ionuț's stomach had evidently made up its mind.

"Remember the baby chickens and ducklings we had during your last visit? They're all grown now. Two didn't make it, and *Tătaie* gave some away to the tax collector," I was telling him as we walked the dusty streets of Izvoarele. "*Mămaie* insists on taking the ducks to the stream for a swim and a bit of exercise. I've already taken them a few times."

"We're going with the ducks?" he asked.

"Yes, first thing in the morning, before helping *Tătaie* in the fields. We'll leave them and collect them on our way back."

"I can't wait to ride in the horse carriage with *Tătaie*," Ionuț said.

I smiled.

"I have something to show you when we get home," I said.

"What is it?"

"It's a surprise."

"Please tell me, I'm terrible with surprises."

"Alright, alright. We have our own tree house in the backyard, and *Tătaie* fixed up the old swing next to it. So we have our very own swing too."

"Really? A tree house!"

"Yes, a tree house."

"What else have you been up to? My mom said you went to school in Izvoarele. How was it?"

"It was okay," I lied. "Different from Zimnicea. Most weeks we do more manual labor than studying. Fine by me," I continued. "I even made a new friend. His name is Păpădie. You'll meet him soon. He drops by now and then, now that school's out. And you, how was school for you? Any bad grades?"

"My math teacher, the *cap sec*,[1] just wouldn't let me pass. I was so frustrated with her *în pisicii măsii*[2] that I barely managed to keep my mouth shut and not yell at her. It

1. *Cap sec* – Dry head (Stubborn)
2. *În pisicii măsii* – In my mother's cats! (Damn it!)

wasn't until June that she finally gave me a good conduct grade, so I didn't have to repeat the year. You can imagine when my father heard that I only passed the year at her mercy, how *i-a sărit muștarul.*[3] He didn't stop lecturing me about it for days. I was so happy when my mother said that I could come to Izvoarele for a month."

"I can imagine." I laughed, picturing the scene.

---

3. *I-a sărit muștarul* – His mustard jumped (He snapped)

21

THE LADYBUG

After living with my grandparents for the last couple of months, I considered myself somewhat of an expert on their home. Yet, in the short time my cousin spent with us, I realized how much of a novice I actually was. The times spent in idleness, what we called *frecând menta*, were different for each of us. I would often climb to my treehouse and lose myself in a book. Ionuț, a much more active and energetic soul, liked to explore each corner of our grandparents' place instead.

One day, overcome by Ionuț's persistence, we went into our grandparents' bedroom. The room had a small window where very little sun entered. This helped keep the air cool, especially compared with the other rooms of the house, where we could barely sleep at night during summer. Their bed was flawlessly made, with not a single wrinkle to be seen, as if they had never used it. One of their closets had a door ajar from where we could see the traditional clothes they used for holidays and celebrations. Next to the closet was a table with small drawers on each side and a round mirror on top of it.

Ionuț gasped when he saw the music box placed on the side of the table. In the corner, shining in the rays of sunlight that came through the small window, my grandfather's accordion sat flawlessly polished on a chair. I smiled at the thought of how many people that instrument had made laugh and dance over the years, including my father.

"What a beautiful smell." Ionuț held the soap nestled among the folded bed sheets to his nose.

Turning away from him, my breath caught when I recognized a black-and-white photograph stuck in the frame of the round mirror. It was my father and me, standing in front of our building before my first day of school. Meanwhile, Ionuț's attention was on flipping through our grandmother's dowry. I took the photograph, looked at it closely, then slipped it into my pocket.

"We should go," I blurted out. "There's nothing interesting here."

We stepped back outside near the basement entrance, in front of the weathered doors lying angled against the ground.

"Shall we go inside?" Ionuț suggested, nodding toward the basement.

"We're not supposed to, especially when they're not home."

"They don't have to know," Ionuț countered.

"What if we get caught?" I said after a pause. "And what would we even find down there?"

"What wouldn't we find?"

Our eyes settled on the large doors, hinged on each side, locked with a chunky padlock speckled with rust. I knew from experience how heavy they were. Once opened, nine steep, short steps descended into the room below, where the entrance was the sole source of light.

With the sky getting darker and threatening rain, we remembered the chores we were supposed to be doing, and for the time being abandoned our mission. We quickly put the animals in their coop, then sat on the porch under the shelter, watching the sky turn a menacing black. Lightning danced playfully through the thickening clouds.

Soon, my grandmother appeared in the garden, clearly agitated.

"The rain is coming! Did you cover my baby chickens?" she asked.

"Yes, *Mămaie*. They're safe, and we secured the coop so the chickens and ducks can't escape," I assured her.

"Good, good. Is your mother home, Alex?"

"Not yet."

"Oh, God help us!" she exclaimed, arms outstretched to the sky. "I pray to Saint Ilie, the patron of rain, for the miracle we need in this heat. We need it for our plants, vegetables, and fruits to survive the winter." As if on cue, heavy raindrops began to fall.

"*În pisicii măsii*," Ionuț blurted out, "look how black the sky is!"

"Shhh... careful *Mămaie* does not hear you say that!"

My grandfather arrived in a hurry and yelled from the street, asking if Eva was home yet. When we yelled back she wasn't, he turned the cart and urged the horses toward the train station, thunder accompanying him on the way. I didn't breathe easy until a few minutes later, when I saw the cart with my grandfather and mother roll in, both soaked to the bone. In the moment, Ionuț and I dashed into the rain to assist in unhitching the horses, reveling in the mud with our bare feet. That night, we slept with the windows open to the sound of summer rain.

By the time I woke up, the rain had stopped. The morning looked dark and cold. I could sense the bitter smell of coffee brewing, so I knew my grandparents were up. I left my mother in bed and went to the kitchen. The door to the outside was open, and there I could see my grandmother placing the bread dough in the oven. My grandfather sat in his chair by the entrance, as if waiting for the right moment to go outside. In the back of the kitchen, next to the carpeted wall, was a small bed occupied by Ionuț. He sat leaning against the wall, counting the drops of rain dripping from the roof into the plastic bucket outside on the porch. I snuggled under the blankets beside him as Grandmother handed us each a cup of warm milk with a spoon of honey.

"*Tătaie*, how do you see when you go down in the basement?" Ionuț suddenly asked.

"What do you mean, how do I see? I turn on the light, that's how I see. How else? What's it to you anyway?"

"I was just wondering, that's all."

After a few moments, my grandfather said, "I built that basement all by myself—I only had your grandmother to help. Months and months we dug for that basement."

"So, when you turn on the light, there is a lightbulb down there, you say?" I interrupted him.

"Yes, so you can see the shelves in the back."

"I see," I said.

"Don't worry, you two are way too short to reach the pull cord. Don't even think about it." He laughed.

It didn't take long for the sun to make its appearance, and we all went outside to start our day. In between the wet leaves of grass and flowers, Ionuț and I found a ladybug. Tradition said that whoever finds one must sing her song and let her fly away so she can bring luck to your home. I scooped her up and kept her in my closed palms, then Ionuț and I sang out loudly:

Ladybug, bug,
Fly off the leaf,
Wherever you will fly,
There will be my home.

Ladybug-bug,
And wherever you fly,
There I will get married…

Then I opened my palms, and we watched her fly away, my grandparents joyfully laughing from the table. My mother remained in bed for most of that day.

22

INTO THE BASEMENT

A few days later, when Ionuț was searching for matches, he accidentally found the key to the basement hidden under the white doily on the first shelf of the kitchen cabinet. Without a second thought, we moved to unlock the padlock. A few turns right and left, *click*, it opened! We removed the heavy chain from around the handles and together started to lift one of the doors to the side. Descending the stairs, I was struck by a strong smell of moisture, dust, and naphthalene growing more pungent with each step.

I passed by the sacks of vegetables and fruits, cans of pickled vegetables, jars of fruit compote, all stacked on shelves. Pieces of smoked meat were hanging from the rafters, displayed like in a butchery. Following the line of dried garlic hung on the wall, I advanced further into the basement. With each step, the air grew heavier and thicker.

"What's going on in there? Do you see something?" Ionuț asked from outside, looking down through the open door.

"I think I see the cord for the light bulb. It's next to the pillar here in front."

"Turn it on, turn it on!"

"It's too high, like grandpa said."

"Is there nothing you can stand on?"

"I'm looking… Aha! There's a bucket!"

"Good!"

"No, it's still too high. I can't reach it," I said, balancing on the bucket.

"Should I bring a chair?"

"Why don't you come down here, and I can lift you up?"

"*În pisicii măsii*," Ionuț swore as he made his way down the stairs, "the damn lightbulb."

Light as a feather, I lifted Ionuț by his legs, and he pulled the cord.

"There! *Tătaie* thought he was smart."

For the first time, we could see all the way to the back of the basement. There was nothing more than a handful of wine barrels, one next to the other. Each barrel had a small tap at the bottom, with a plastic measuring cup and a glass underneath.

"Alex, have you ever tasted his wine?"

"Once in a while, when he leaves the table and there's some left in the glass," I said, and we both laughed.

"I do the same when my mother has her neighbors over," Ionuț said. "As soon as they walk to the door to leave, I clean all the glasses."

"Shall we try some?"

We approached the first barrel on the right, which turned out to be dry white wine. After a cautious sip, we both made faces—it was not to our liking. The second barrel offered red wine, but its aroma reminded me of my dad's old leather boots, not a favorite either. By the time we had tried a cup from each barrel, giggling and wrinkling our noses, we realized we hadn't found any that we liked.

"That's why he comes down here so often—he's got all this wine, just look at it!" Ionuț slurred.

"What are those down there?" I said, pointing at something in the back.

"What?"

"Those glass jugs behind the stairs."

"I don't know, but I do see some spiders on the walls," Ionuț said, looking around.

"Let's check the jars."

Laughing uncontrollably, we stumbled into a few glass bottles placed by the wall, causing a racket as we headed for the large jars, containing cherry liquor, *vișinată*, and *afinată*, the blueberry liquor.

"That's where he's hiding the good stuff," Ionuț said.

"I don't think we should drink any more. We can just taste the fruits at the bottom instead," I suggested.

"Good idea."

Next to the jars, we found a small strainer on a plate, which we used to fish some of the fruits out.

"We'll just take a few so *Tătaie* doesn't notice," I whispered.

The cherries had an invigorating taste after soaking in alcohol for a long time, and it was hard to stop eating them. However, after all the tasting, laughing, and singing we had done in the basement, we both started feeling a little ill and decided that it was time to get some fresh air. So, holding each other's arms for support, we climbed up the stairs, two at a time. Out in the fresh air, the red glow of the sun warmed us—a welcome relief.

As I was struggling to lift the heavy door to close the

basement, I looked over to Ionuț, who remained still, staring down the stairs.

"You mind giving me a hand with the door, Ionuț?" I asked.

No answer.

"Ionuț?"

That's when he started throwing up all the way down the stairs of the basement. The sight of it made me nauseous as well. We sat down on the ground for a few minutes, trying to recover, holding our heads in our hands.

"What are we going to do now?" I asked.

"I don't know, I feel horrible. I can barely see. Why is everything spinning?" Ionuț groaned. "*În pisicii măsii!*"

"We have to clean that up, Ionuț. Can you imagine if *Tătaie* or my mother sees it? They'll be home soon." The thought sent a wave of panic through me.

Ionuț sat there, holding his head in misery while I fetched a bucket and filled it with water. Armed with cloths from the kitchen, I began the daunting task of cleaning the stairs.

"You have to help me, Ionuț. It's your mess."

"I know, I know… but I feel awful," he moaned.

"Me too, but we have to clean this up. You start from the bottom, and I'll start here at the top."

Slowly, Ionuț got up and staggered down the stairs.

"Try to hold your breath, so you don't throw up more," I suggested.

Together, we cleaned the stairs as best we could. Afterward, we carefully closed the basement door, returned the key to its original place, cleaned the bucket, and disposed of the soiled cloths. Exhausted and still feeling the effects of our indulgence, we trudged up to the treehouse for a well-deserved nap.

As we laid our heads down on the hay, the world continued to spin wildly in our vision, like images on a carousel, refusing to settle. The gentle sway of the treehouse in the breeze did little to ease our churning stomachs, and we both hoped sleep would come quickly and bring some relief.

Sleep did come but we woke up to a burning sensation on our behinds. Startled awake, we were met with the sight of my grandfather looming over us, his face a mask of fury. The horse whip, so thin and quick, felt like it was throwing fire with every lash.

"*Minți crețe*[1] that you are!" he bellowed. "Going into my basement and making a mess of my year's work, all my wine and liquor!" The whip cracked again and again.

"Of all the places you could've run around, you chose my basement! Not once did you offer to help in the fields, yet you found time to wreak havoc down there!"

He then turned to Ionuț, pointing the whip at him.

"And who came up with this idea? Was it you, Ionuț?"

"No," Ionuț stammered through tears.

"Then who? You, Alex?" He turned to me. "I was just telling your mother how mature you've become. But I was wrong, I was very wrong."

I stood there, unable to muster the strength to respond or defend myself, silently enduring the punishment. Below the tree, my mother showed up, telling my grandfather that this was enough, that he ought to come back down. He climbed down, mumbling angrily to himself.

"This time we really *dat cu mucii în fasole*,"[2] I whispered to Ionuț.

---

1. *Minți crețe* – Curly minds (Stupid idiots)
2. *Dat cu mucii în fasole* – Smashed the boogers in the beans (Screwed up)

"*În pisicii măsii!* I never want to drink again," Ionuț replied, his voice shaky.

"I don't feel sick anymore, though," I admitted.

"Me neither, but my butt hurts," Ionuț said, and despite the pain and the tears, we found ourselves laughing together.

23

SAINT ILIE

It was only recently that Grandfather Ilie turned seventy-one years old, and while he claimed that he felt "in the prime of his life," his appearance told a different story. His white hair, once light brown, was now thinned and unruly, covering his forehead. The wrinkles around his eyes and forehead, his rough hands full of calluses, and his bony face around his pronounced nose spoke of decades of laughter, hardship, losses, and sorrows in his life.

A fire had trapped his parents and two of his brothers in their house, ending his childhood at the age of fourteen. He and another brother, Gigi, who survived the fire, were left alone. Only a couple of years later, Gigi succumbed to pneumonia.

He never attended school nor had any inclination for it. All he knew was how to work the land. In his early years, he worked at a governor's farm in a village called Creţeşti, in another part of the country. He saved up everything he earned, returned to Izvoarele, and bought his own land. It was easier to buy in those times—all they needed was money. Since he had spent all his savings on the land, he found shelter under the blue sky until good-hearted neighbors offered him a roof over his head.

That's how he met my grandmother. She was one of the daughters of the families that helped him with shelter in those times. At night, she would sneak out to the stable where he slept and read stories to him. He was captivated by her brightness, her childlike way of retelling the stories she had read in her books, her humble attitude toward life, and the fact that she never saw him as just a poor land worker. They fell in love, and a year later they got married. Together, they bought another piece of land on which to build a house.

They worked the land in the morning and built their house for the rest of the day. As soon as the house was ready to be inhabited, their first child, Ana, came into the world, followed by Eva and Alexandra. To the end of his days, *Tătaie* Ilie would consider Ana's departure from her homeland, her roots, as both a betrayal and his own personal failure.

On July 20, we celebrated Saint Ilie, the protector of crops, bringer of rain and thunder. Gathered outside were my grandparents, my mother, Ionuț, and me. The day was so warm that finding an appetite for lunch was hard. Ionuț sat next to our grandfather, biting his nails, while I settled in the shadow at the kitchen doorstep, opened the newspaper *Flacăra Iașului*, and began to read aloud. An article claimed that in Huși, a city in the eastern part of Romania, the agricultural production cooperative had already finished harvesting the wheat.

"Just as in 1965, no other area in the country has reached the same yield as Huși," I quoted.

"What a lie! How do they know their performance is leading if here, in Teleorman county, we haven't even started harvesting?" my grandfather asked.

As I was about to continue with the article, a whistle came from the gate, and Păpădie waved from the street.

"The gate is open!" I yelled, closing the newspaper.

"Good day to you all," Păpădie said, making his way around the porch.

"Good day? Is that how you salute women in your family? Good day?" scolded my grandfather.

"Kiss your hands, Ms. Eva, *Săru-mâna*, Ms. Violeta," Păpădie said to each of them.

"You must always salute the oldest one first. At least, that's how it was in my time," my grandfather said.

"Maybe he didn't know I was the oldest, Ilie. Maybe he thought I was the youngest," my grandmother answered.

"Ha! If you were the youngest, why do you only have those three shovels left in your mouth, huh?"

"It's from your strong farts at night. All my teeth fell out," my grandmother retorted, and we all laughed together.

On the radio, a new song was starting, and my grandmother shushed us with a sign. The five of us remained silent, listening to George Enescu's rhapsody dedicated to his country.

A few days later, with much sadness, we bid Ionuț and his silly antics farewell as we put him on the train back to his hometown. He wore the same clothes as he had when he first arrived, including an empty bag thoughtfully placed in his pants pocket, in case of emergencies.

24

DOES THE COB LOOK LIKE A DOLL?

My grandfather began the corn harvest at the beginning of August. Every morning, we woke up at dawn and prepared for the day. Together with Vasile and Gheorghe, two teenage boys my grandfather had hired from a nearby village, we drove to the fields in the horse carriage, feeling lethargic.

Looking over the fields, the rows of corn seemed endless, the heat and sun almost unbearable. I picked up a wicker basket and a sickle and headed straight to the first row on the left side of the field. With one hand, I held the stalk in the middle, pulled it toward me, and cut it from the bottom with the sickle. I then ripped the corn cob from the stalk and placed it in the basket. When I lifted my head, I could see the two boys working quickly and steadily on the other side of the field.

Within a few minutes, my basket was full. I bent down and hoisted it onto my shoulder, holding it with both arms and feeling the coarse weave against my face. As I walked back toward my grandparents, sweat dripped from my forehead into my eyes and ran down to my mouth. It burned my eyes, itched my nose, and wetted my lips, tasting salty and dusty. When my grandfather saw me approaching, he helped me lower the basket and empty it. Afterward, I returned to my row.

Hold the stalk, cut it, rip the cob, and toss it into the basket. After a few trips with the full basket, my palms burned more than the sun's scorching rays on my back and neck. I could feel every blister forming in my palm and every small cut from the sickle's tip when it accidentally grazed my arms and legs. Surrounded by an infinite number of stalks and startled mice, I was alone. My mind began to drift, and my thoughts became my only companions.

I thought about my mother, how stressed and worried she had become over the last couple of months. I tried to imagine what it must be like to work in the factory for eight hours a day and then commute another hour. I wished she weren't so distant and would talk to us. I wished I could do something when I heard her crying in the dark, thinking no one would hear her. I wondered if we were destined to stay here in Izvoarele, as I couldn't see how we could afford a place of our own, unless... Unless she remarried. No, that could not happen. I decided that I ought to speak to her soon. But how would I even start?

The image of my father kept appearing in my mind, but I forced it away. I refused to think about him. It would only make me cry and slow me down. I thought about George, how he would've loved to work the fields with us. He probably would have made a wig out of the long, silky threads growing on the ears of corn, and we would laugh until our bellies hurt, just as we used to. Why do they call corn cobs 'dolls' here, anyway? Maybe it's because they do look like a doll, with their blonde hair.

I thought about my friends from the village, Păpădie and now also Veronica, and how different and difficult their lives were, yet they still found reasons to laugh and dream of better days ahead. Păpădie walked several kilometers a day to go to school without his father's approval, and Veronica, coming from a very troubled family, wore shredded and dirty clothes. Nonetheless, she was insistent on us teaching her how to read whenever she came around.

I had lost count of the number of baskets I carried back and forth. Returning with another full one, I saw my grandfather sitting in a low chair, a piece of straw in one side of his mouth, wearing his old, ruffled hat, his back hunched as he picked the "dolls" from the ground and sorted them into their pile. Every once in a while, he looked out at us, his expression one of satisfaction and contentment. Next to him stood my grandmother, with a kerchief on her head, legs covered by a long summer skirt, and her tan arms showing beneath the short sleeves of her shirt.

"Alex, aren't you hungry or thirsty?" she asked as she saw me approaching.

"Both," I answered.

"We'll have lunch then," my grandfather decided. "Vasile, Gheorghe! Come, boys, eat and drink something," he yelled into the field.

My grandmother brought a large tablecloth from the carriage and placed it on the grass in the shadow under a big tree. She then laid another smaller cloth in the middle and set a big round wooden plate with *mămăligă*, salt, and onion on top of it. She then cut pieces of *şuncă*, *jumări*, and cheese and added them to the plate.

With our stomachs full, we stretched out on the grass, each of us with one hand behind our head and the other on our belly. Gheorghe took out his hand-carved flute from his sachet and leaned against the trunk of the tree. He played *hăiduceasca* for us until a neighbor rode by to talk to my grandfather about the miners' protest in the village of Lupeni. It had now lasted for more than three days and forced Ceaușescu to interrupt his seaside vacation to make an appearance.

Days went by, and the barn at home was finally stacked full of corn. Now, it was time to scrape the kernels from the cobs and fill them into sacks.

25

THE TRAIN RIDE

I wasn't sure what I despised most: the flies from our neighbor's dung heaps or today's early morning bath with soapy water from a bucket. During summer, it was a refreshing necessity, but now in September, the cold impact made my heart skip a beat, feeling as if at any moment I was going into cardiac arrest.

But I had no choice. My mother had gotten it into her head that we were to travel by train to Constanța, a city about three hundred and fifty kilometers away, for the day. Despite my insistence, she wouldn't tell me the reason. The only clue I got was that we were to visit an old friend, and it would be the "surprise of the year" for me. At that time, I had no idea of the many more unforeseen surprises that awaited us that year.

By five in the morning, we were already out of the gate. My mother's red hair, freshly dyed and styled in waves, had been set in curlers overnight. She wore a plaid hourglass-shaped dress that fell just below the knees, with a knitted cardigan on top. I was dressed in my plain black trousers, a white shirt with a red tie, and an old brown woolen vest that an older cousin had left behind—my least favorite item in my limited wardrobe.

We boarded the morning's first train to Bucharest. Our seat numbers, 567 and 568, were in train cabin number 56, on the fifth wagon. The cabin contained eight seats in total, four on each side, facing each other. I rushed inside and got the seat by the window, and my mother sat next to me. Under the window was a yellow-painted tin table. The brush marks, and the painter's poor skills, were clearly visible. Beneath the table was a gray, miserable, and sticky basket, with husks of seeds stuck to it. The curtains hanging on the window seemed to tell the same story of heavy use.

Twenty-five minutes later, the train slowed down, and the conductor stepped out to open the doors. "First stop, Zimnicea!" he announced.

For five minutes, I remained glued to the window, scanning the station for a familiar face in what once was my hometown. I envisioned running off the train, all the way to Strada Gheorghe Frentz, Nr. 4, our old street, where memories of my father and my best friend still lingered.

"Did we remember to bring some apples or something to eat?" My mother broke the silence.

"Yes, we have apples," I replied, still fixated on the window.

"When we arrive in Bucharest, we'll buy something to eat. You must be starving," she continued.

"Mother?"

"Yes?"

"Why haven't you ever taken me to our street in Zimnicea?"

After a brief pause, she answered, "I don't think you'd want to see how it looks now."

"What do you mean?"

"I mean that, for your own sake, it's better to keep our old street in your memory the way it used to be, not how it is now."

"Is it that bad?"

"They started rebuilding it, but the funds from Bucharest ran out two months ago. It's left unfinished, dirty… unrecognizable."

Outside, the conductor's whistle sounded loudly three times, and I could hear him climb up the steps of the wagon and close the door behind him. The train slowly started to move again. Four hours and twenty-five minutes of inhaling the thick air in the cabin, and we arrived in Bucharest. As the wagon door opened, the crisp autumn breeze was a refreshing shock. We disembarked the train one by one, jumping down from the high steps. It felt like an assembly line as everyone moved side by side. My mother held my right hand tightly and clutched her purse to her chest while we descended the uneven stairs toward a tunnel connecting to the other platforms and the main station. A heavy scent of urine dominated the tunnels. We ascended the seventh exit to the left, arriving at Bucharest's main central station, the North Railway Station.

True to every other Romanian train station, the floor was decorated with petite mustard-colored tiles, with a thick layer of dirt and cigarette butts. Amidst the noise of chatting and shouting travelers moving around without clear direction, a loud woman's voice resonated from the speakers. Some passengers juggled luggage in one hand and a ticket in the other, searching for their train and wagon number. The elderly occupied most of the seats by the wall. Occasionally, an elbow would jostle me, leaving behind just a hurried *scuze* as the person rushed ahead.

Together with the other passengers, my mother and I stood in the long queue at the information desk. I glanced at a mother embracing her son, a teenage boy dressed in an army uniform. She cupped his face in her hands, tears in her eyes, gazing at him as if the sun had just risen between the clouds.

"Do you have everything with you, Lecule?" she asked him repeatedly.

"Yes, Mother, I have everything I need. But I must get to my platform before the train leaves," he replied.

"Don't worry, the train won't leave without you," she reassured him.

"No, I'm sure the train would graciously wait just for me before it departs. Without me, it might not even make the trip at all," the boy answered.

"Promise you'll write to me more often this time," the mother implored.

"I promise I will."

"And eat some of the food I packed for you. You're skin and bones," she insisted.

"I will," he promised.

He kissed his mother on the cheek, hoisted his rucksack, and descended the stairs to the platforms. The mother remained motionless for a few moments, as if holding on to the hope that he would return and never leave. Finally, she turned, her head bowed, and slowly made her way out of the station.

It was now our turn.

"Good day, when is the next train to Constanța?" my mother asked at the ticket office.

"The next train to Constanța arrives on Platform Two in fifteen minutes and leaves in twenty," the woman behind the counter replied.

"From Platform Two?"

"That's what I said," the woman repeated.

"Thank you," my mother said.

We moved from waiting in one queue to another, this time at one of the shops in the station, where my mother bought two packs of Eugenia biscuits for the road. By the time she finished paying, the announcement came over the loudspeakers:

"Attention all passengers! Train 23471 from Timișoara to Constanța arrives at Platform Two in four minutes. Attention!" The woman's voice echoed through the large building.

"That's our train, Alex, we must go," my mother said, holding my hand and leading me toward the platform.

Three and a half hours later, we disembarked at the Constanța train station and descended the steps to the exit. The tobacco smoke I had inhaled during the second train ride, mixed with the fumes from the heavy traffic outside, left me feeling nauseous and tired.

Several yellow taxis sat idling in front of the station. My mother walked ahead and opened the rear door of the first taxi in line, gesturing for me to get in first.

"Where to, *doamna*?" the driver asked.

"Navy headquarters," my mother answered.

26

THE VISIT

"And with whom are you meeting?" asked the secretary at the open desk inside the office.

"The deputy secretary," answered my mother.

"You may be seated, and I'll inform you when he's ready to receive you," she said, pointing toward the three empty chairs by the wall.

My mother and I sat quietly, taking in our surroundings. The office hallway looked grand and luxurious. The ceiling of the building was so high that I almost twisted my neck looking up at the grand chandelier. The floor was solid marble, inlaid with golden details, and modern carpets lined the center, so pristine it seemed as if nobody had ever walked on them. Everywhere you looked, there were paintings of marine ships from old times, portraits of admirals, and photographs of important people shaking hands.

A couple of minutes later, the receptionist gestured for us to follow her. She led us to the end of the hallway, stopping in front of a tall white door, which she opened for us. Inside, at the desk, dressed in a navy-blue military uniform, sat my dad's old friend, Costel Carp. He rose from his chair when he saw us, and I ran toward him.

"Look at you, Alex, you've grown up so fast!" he exclaimed, lifting me up. "You'll soon be taller than me, but I hope not heavier too."

"Why didn't you come to see us anymore? We missed you!" I said, staying in his arms as if I was still a small boy.

Costel and my mother greeted each other with a close hug. Looking at him, I almost couldn't recognize him in his uniform. He appeared more robust, his shoulders broader, and he seemed to have gained some weight. His black hair, slick and combed back, complemented his clean-shaven face, now without a trace of his usual mustache. The office looked the size of half my grandparents' house, with three large windows at the end giving a view of the sea.

"Come, sit down. You two must be tired after such a long trip," Costel said, gesturing toward the two chairs in front of the desk.

"How long has it been?" my mother asked him.

"Almost three years, but it feels like an eternity," he answered. "I never forgot our many years together, the Friday dinners, and so much fun we had—the three of us, four since Alexei came," he said, glancing at me. "Cornel…" He paused, as if holding back tears. "He was the brother I never had. How I loved that man."

"You and I both," my mother replied.

"I thought I felt the ground beneath me shake when I heard the news," Costel continued. "I tried to come to Zimnicea, but I couldn't leave my work at that time. It's been busy here since the earthquake. I cried every night for weeks. When I went to pick up my mother a few months ago, I couldn't believe my eyes when I saw what was left of our neighborhood."

"Yes, I know. I'm glad you managed to bring her here," my mother said.

"Yeah, well, my mother is a difficult woman, as you know. She feeds me more than necessary, tries to run my life, but what can I do? I can't live without her. How about you? I heard you two moved to Izvoarele?"

At this question, my mother erupted into tears.

"It's hard, Costel, it's very hard. I cry myself to sleep almost every night because I don't know how to live, how to survive. How can I offer a future to this little boy here?" she said, glancing toward me. "And I miss Cornel so much, you have no idea."

Costel walked over to her side, bent down, and hugged her tightly as she continued to cry.

"I have nobody to talk to," she continued, her voice choked with emotion. "My parents have their own problems with the land and the restrictions. At work, I'm limited in whom I can confide. They keep an eye on us all day. Sometimes I feel like I'm being followed from the moment I set foot in Zimnicea until I take my train home. I don't know, maybe I've become paranoid. But I'm glad for you, that you got out of that city and got a job here," she said to Costel.

"You know it wasn't necessarily my choice. I had to do it. They cornered me," he replied, returning to his desk chair. "And I can't complain… It's better now. I've paid my dues in the last two years. I've done many things I'm not proud of lately, but once you get in, you can't get out. I really had no choice."

"I understand," my mother said, trying to compose herself.

"You mentioned on the phone you wanted to discuss some papers?"

"Yes, not quite papers, but something very delicate. Alex, maybe you could go to the window and look at the ships?" she said to me. Turning to Costel, she added, "Costel, you're my only savior, and I hope I can count on you."

"For what exactly?" he asked.

Quietly, I walked to the window, feeling a mix of worry and confusion. On my way, I playfully poked Costel's shoulder like in old times, and he responded with a similar playful gesture. There wasn't much to see outside, just a few gigantic ships docked in the port. Two cranes were busy loading goods from trucks onto one of the vessels. Beyond the ships, the restless sea stretched to the horizon.

Even with their whispering, fragments of their conversation reached me from across the office.

"So, let me get this clear," I heard Costel say to my mother. "You want to board a ship to Spain? There are no ships to Spain from here… In this idea of yours, would you at least consider going alone for a few months? It's very risky traveling with a child."

"I know, I thought about it, but I can't leave him behind, Costel. I've already lost my husband. I can't bear the thought of leaving my son here," she said, pausing for a few moments. I looked away from the window and saw her eyes on me before she continued, "Please do this for me, Costel. For the memory of all those times we shared, for Cornel. I need to make sure I can offer my boy a better future."

"Look, Eva, you know I would do anything for you and Cornel. But what you're asking is very dangerous, for both of us. I could lose my position, my house, everything. Think about your parents, their land, and who knows what else," Costel said.

I turned around. *Why would something happen to my grandparents?*

"I know, I know," she murmured, her eyes fixed on the carpet.

Costel remained silent for a few moments. He then pulled out a pack of cigarettes from his coat pocket, extracted one, and lit it with a match. Taking a few deep drags, he leaned back in his chair. I felt so confused and let down by my mother, and I couldn't wait for us to leave so I could tell her that I would not go anywhere. The thought of leaving my grandparents, my friends, and Izvoarele gave me a lump in my throat.

After he finished his cigarette, Costel finally said, "There's only one way to do this, and here's the plan."

27

THE PEASANTRY IS WAKING UP!

From the moment we left the office until we were back in Izvoarele, we were never alone—cab drivers, people drifting throughout the train station, and other travelers with us in the cabin. Several times, I couldn't contain myself and asked my mother if what I had overheard was true. She shushed me instantly.

When we returned to Izvoarele, it was so late that the streets were pitch black. The only lights were faint flickerings from a few neighbors' windows. Not a single creature was in sight, and even the dogs had ceased their barking. My mother led me by the hand, but I still struggled to keep up with her.

We walked in silence to my grandparents' house until my mother could no longer contain herself. She began to explain her intentions and the plan she had devised with Costel, or at least a part of it. She knew me well enough to understand that, in my exhausted state, I wouldn't overreact.

When I woke up the next morning, my mother had

already left for work. Lying in bed, I replayed the events of the previous day in my head: the encounter with Costel and my mother's plan. I couldn't believe that life was about to change so drastically for us again. Had she truly lost her mind? What had gotten into her? I wished I could talk to her, to try and convince her that it wasn't a good idea. If only I could speak with my grandmother about this, maybe she could persuade her to reconsider. But I remembered the one thing she had strictly forbidden me to do: to tell anyone about the plan or act differently in any way. For the time being, life was to go on exactly as before.

And so, I tried. I got dressed and went to school, with the new school year just beginning. As I walked my usual route, I noticed the streets of Izvoarele becoming increasingly crowded. The landless, along with both the poor and wealthy peasants from Izvoarele and nearby villages, were gathering in what seemed like a burgeoning riot. Their heavy steps and loud voices echoed through the streets.

"The peasantry is waking up!" they shouted. "We want our land back!"

I wasn't surprised. Riots had become a common occurrence in the village lately, a result of the rural systematization program that aimed to relocate more peasants to the cities for factory work, seizing their land and harvests. However, this time, my concern was deeper, especially for my grandfather. A few days earlier, several peasants, instead of selling their grape and corn harvests to the Cooperative Agricultural Production association, had hidden them in the village outskirts. The authorities discovered this and confiscated everything. Two mornings ago, when the peasants went to retrieve their sacks, they were met with the military lying in wait among the bushes, and they were arrested on the spot.

The rioters veered off onto a street to the left, presumably heading toward the Party office, where later that day, the fate of the imprisoned peasants was to be decided. The riot cast a shadow of fear and worry over everyone at school, as most students had fathers or other family members involved. Păpădie had been absent for several days. By the second break, rumors had spread that a hundred and fifty soldiers had been dispatched from Alexandria to quell the riot, authorized to end it at any cost.

School ended early, and I walked home in silence with my grandmother. For a moment, my mother's reasons for wanting to leave started to resonate with me. Orchestrating an escape seemed reckless and risky, but was staying here equally dangerous?

Later that day, we gathered around the dinner table—my mother, grandmother, and I. Quietly, we dipped our spoons into the vegetable soup, which had turned cold by the time we finished our bowls.

My grandfather walked in, followed by his neighbor, Constantin.

"Close the door, Constantine!" he instructed. He took a seat on the bed by the wall, removed his straw hat, and held his head in his hands. His forehead was marred by a large bump, and one of his eyes was bruised.

"Have a seat, Constantine!" my grandmother said, rising to offer him her chair.

"*Țuică*?" my grandfather asked.

"Only a little bit, if you have to spare," Constantin replied humbly as he took the offered seat.

My grandmother fetched a bottle of *țuică* from the

basement and served each of the men a glass. Meanwhile, my mother and I began clearing the table.

"*Noroc!*" My grandfather raised his glass.

"*Noroc!*" Constantin responded in kind.

The men emptied their glasses, and my grandfather promptly refilled them. With his left hand covering his eyes, now brimming with tears, he said, "For all the sorrows and suffering of our people."

My grandmother, my mother, and I retreated to my grandparents' bedroom and sat on their soft, springy bed. Just when it seemed the day couldn't get any worse, my mother took my grandmother's hand into hers and told her the plan.

"I was afraid that this day would come sooner or later," my grandmother said. She took my hand into hers, and we all held hands together. "I hope you know how risky this is for you and Alexandru."

"Mother, I wish it wasn't like this. If Cornel lived, it wouldn't be," said my mother, starting to cry. "But without him…"

"I know," my grandmother interrupted. "We are always going to be here, waiting for you. Although there is little chance of coming back if you leave like that."

After the riot in September, villagers had to swallow their tears and continue harvesting. Little by little, the villagers' lives became more secluded, each to their own. The once joyful streets of Izvoarele were now quiet and empty. If a neighbor popped their head up above their fence, peasant hat on and a straw in one side of the mouth, it was only to duck back into their yard seconds later. It felt like everyone was waiting for something. But what?

When my mother informed my grandfather, behind closed doors, about her plan to escape the country in the upcoming weeks, he took the news badly. He stood there on his chair by the kitchen window, while my mother, seated on the kitchen bed, explained to him all the reasons why she wanted to raise her child in another country. As soon as she finished talking, he took a liter bottle of *țuică* and went into the horse stable, where he also spent the night.

During our last days in Izvoarele, he barely spoke a single word to either of us. His eyes became small and red from crying, and his hands shook from drinking; he looked at us as if we were the rose's thorns stabbing his heart. He was about to lose yet another daughter to the hopes of a better future in another country. And yet he couldn't find any tangible arguments to convince her that she should stay.

28

THE ESCAPE

On October 27, in the early hours, two lone figures walked hand in hand along the unpaved road of the village. Uncertain of the future, they surrendered their destiny to the hands of fate. A thick mist enveloped the village, reducing visibility to just a few meters ahead. The morning was astonishingly peaceful and quiet.

My mother's now-old woolen coat let the wind blow through to her thin stockings. In one hand, she juggled both a suitcase and her handbag, and in the other firmly held mine. I was wearing the same coat I had arrived in from Zimnicea, now short on me and worn out. A sweater my grandmother knitted for me, two shirts, and school-uniform pants comprised my entire wardrobe. Despite my mother's tenderness and affection in the preceding days, showering me with promises, I couldn't stop sobbing all the way to the train station and throughout the entire journey.

After several grueling hours and two train rides, we arrived in Constanța. My eyes were swollen and red from crying, my head throbbing with pain that intensified with each step, feeling like a heavy weight pressing down on my neck. The gloomy, rainy weather outside perfectly mirrored my emotions.

Outside the train station, Costel leaned against his car, dressed in his navy uniform. He threw his cigarette on the ground and came forward to pick me up, but I was not having it that day. He gently set me back down and instead took my mother's luggage and stored it in the trunk of his car.

With the two of them talking in front, I sat quietly in the backseat, looking out the window.

The tall, gray, gloomy buildings of the city passed by in a blur as we drove through Constanța.

The image of my grandfather's teary eyes as we walked out of his gate that morning was etched in my memory. It ripped my heart apart to see his pain, the way he remained there on the kitchen's threshold, with his hat in his hands. If he had wanted to blurt out his pain and disappointment to us, he didn't. He remained quiet and sad.

At that moment, I couldn't imagine happiness in my life again. I turned ahead to look at my mother, who was chatting with Costel, and wondered how she could act so blasé as if nothing of importance was happening.

"Look at the fountains, Alex," Costel said, catching my reflection in his rearview mirror. "We're going to drive by them in just a few minutes."

The fountains were in the middle of a lush space between the large streets, with flowers and trees surrounding them, an arranged analogy of a small park. What Costel had intended as a beautiful distraction, the vibrant scenery with the fountain at its center, only served to draw me deeper into memories of the fields in Izvoarele, where I had spent days running around, and the pond where I had hoped to see the girl with golden hair again.

I thought of Păpădie and Veronica's reaction when they would stop by my grandparents' house and learn that I didn't live there anymore. I hadn't seen Păpădie to thank him for being my friend in a new school where others avoided me, and I couldn't say goodbye to Veronica, the girl who once pushed me down from the bridge and into the trash. I had left like that, out of the blue, without a word.

Costel parked the car in front of one of the most majestic buildings I've ever seen—the Casino of Constanța. Its impressive structure, with elegant curves and grand windows, looked out over the sea. The three of us walked inside the building and into the restaurant, where Costel chose one of the tables by the window, overlooking the port.

"It's here already. The ship docked at its mooring this morning," he said to us, as we sat down at a table.

"Where?" my mother asked, turning to look out the window.

"All the way to the right. Do you see that dark blue ship, almost black in this light, several stories tall?" Costel pointed out.

There she was! Standing proudly in all her robustness. She looked enormous and grotesque to me. As rich as the plate of steamed salmon with vegetables looked, suddenly I couldn't stomach any more. After a quick toast, Costel settled the bill, and we headed back to the car. The final moments were drawing near, and a storm of emotions churned in the pit of my stomach.

Costel drove us through the gated fence surrounding the port, flashing his badge at the security officer, and then parked the car a few meters away from the ship. Rain had begun to fall, and stormy gusts of wind caused the boat to rock in the waves. The atmosphere was tense with the impatience of passengers eager to board. They emerged from the port building in large groups, their tickets and papers checked as they exited. Under raised umbrellas, they hurried toward the side of the ship, followed by baggage handlers pushing their loads of suitcases on squeaky metal carts.

Costel began explaining the layout of the ship—three decks accessible to passengers, with the uppermost one barely visible through the fog and rain. There, passengers with first-class tickets resided, while the second deck was designated for economy class. The first deck contained restaurants, bars, and entertainment rooms. Below all these, in the hull of the boat, was where the staff were, and this was where we would be staying.

"I managed to arrange kitchen staff papers for your mother to get on board and into the maintenance corridors. The ship's purser is a friend of mine, and he's aware of your situation. He promised to keep you both safe and well-fed during the journey," Costel said, glancing at me through the rearview mirror. "Alex, I need you to be brave and enter the boat through the passengers' entrance."

"Aren't you coming with me?" I asked, my confusion evident.

"I can't. I'll be escorting your mother inside, but I can't justify a child accompanying a staff member. The idea is that you can easily blend in with the passengers. All the people who are walking to the ship have already had their tickets and papers checked when leaving the station, so they shouldn't be checked again when boarding."

"What?" I exclaimed and turned to my mother. "Mama?"

"Alex, please!" she implored. "I'm sorry, but there's no

turning back now, and you must do this quickly before all the passengers board."

I leaned back in my seat, overwhelmed by the enormity of what the day had become. After a brief silence, Costel continued.

"Once on board, right at the entrance, there's a staircase leading to each level. Walk calmly up to the first deck. As you enter, you'll see a long hallway. Walk down that hallway, all the way to the back, until you reach a door with a round glass window. That's a storage room with supplies and materials. Inside, there's a staircase that connects to the staff deck downstairs, where your mother will be waiting for you. I know this boat like the back of my hand. There are a few cabinets in that room. Hide in one until you hear the boat's horn and feel it start to move. Then, take the stairs down."

"I promise I'll be there waiting for you," my mother reassured me.

"I'm sorry I don't have more time to say a proper goodbye, Alex. Maybe one day we'll see each other again. Right now, there's no time to waste. You need to go!"

I exited the car, slamming the door as hard as I could. I fought the urge to run away, all the way back to Izvoarele. But an old lady, struggling to hold a small bag in one hand and bracing her umbrella against the wind with the other, seemed like the perfect opportunity to sneak aboard.

I moved to her side, offering my arm for support, and took the umbrella from her hand. She seemed grateful for the assistance, possibly mistaking me for a cabin boy. Leaning on my arm, we proceeded together up the gangway toward the boat. What looked like the perfect picture of a grandson helping his grandmother inside the boat was, in fact, the trembling body of an eleven-year-old boy, scared and cold.

Once on the third floor, I slowly let go of her arm, turned around, and went downstairs to the first floor, as instructed.

The long hallway was bustling with passengers, all eager and anxious as they entered and exited their rooms, ready to start their journey. With my head down, I slipped between them until I found the storage room, where I hid myself between a rack of uniforms in a cabinet.

Squatting down, knees clenched to my chest, I sobbed uncontrollably. At the sound of the footsteps coming from the hallway, I wiped my face and swallowed my tears, praying that nobody would hear my heart pounding in my chest and discover me.

"Twenty-one, twenty-two, twenty-three," I counted the beats to myself.

I tried to think of what my mother and Costel were doing at that moment. Were they walking the same stairs I did? What if Costel's plan didn't work? What would happen to me?

PART II

29

THE ARRIVAL

If someone had asked us how long we'd been on the ship, our answer would likely have been vague: "Three days, a month, maybe a year?" By then, we had grown accustomed to the boat's constant motion, left and right, up and down, as if we were on a swing.

My mother was leaning on the deck's railing, the sun's rays reflecting off the clear blue water making her squint her eyes. The city ahead of us appeared to sit on a hill, as if gazing back at us. A patchwork of uneven houses and buildings, each in different colors and styles, framed against the clear blue sky.

"Come and see it, Alex!" My mother waved at me.

Lazily, I stood up from where I had been sitting on the deck and went to the railing. As the scenery grew sharper, I felt the distant memory of my stomach's turmoil from the initial days at sea starting to come back. For most people on the boat, this place before us represented home. But for us?

Thirty minutes later, as the boat's horn bellowed, shaking the entire ship, my mother and I sat impatiently by her bunk bed, dressed and with our suitcases packed. We were now well acquainted with the back door from the kitchen, leading to the narrow stairs ascending to the maintenance room on the first floor. By the time we made it up there, the hallway was already filled with the hectic noise of passengers preparing to disembark. Bellboys were scrambling to assist with luggage, rushing and shouting.

Hand in hand, my mother and I placed ourselves in the queue that was slowly advancing across the wooden gangplank bridging the ship and port. Impatiently, I lifted myself up on my toes to see why we were moving so slowly. Ahead of us was an open booth with two police officers stopping each passenger to check their documents and occasionally rifle through their bags. I gave my mother a worried look, and in return she raised a finger to her mouth, signaling to keep quiet. I could feel her body tremble through her hand.

Step by step, our turn was slowly approaching. As a last resort, I looked behind me for the familiar face of the old lady I had boarded with, but didn't see her. My mother's grip tightened so much that my hand hurt.

The couple ahead of us, an elderly man and a younger

woman, picked up their suitcase from the ground, greeted the officers, and went ahead. It was our turn.

"*I documenti, per favore*," said one of the officers, holding out a hand.

My mother put our suitcase down and started looking through her bag. At last, she found our Romanian identifications and handed them over without saying a word. The officer read her name out loud—"E-V-A T-O-M-A"—and ran his index finger over the document, staring at the unfamiliar language from our identification.

"*Passaporto?*" He looked sternly at my mother.

I froze. I had no idea what her plan was from here on out.

"Eva Toma?" said a voice from behind the officer. A woman not much taller than my mother, with unusually short dark hair and wearing a skirt suit, spoke privately with the two officers and then, with a smile, addressed us in Romanian.

"Let's get out of here. Follow me, please," she said, already striding ahead.

My mother placed a hand over her chest as if trying to keep her heart from jumping out. Without apprehension, we followed her closely, maintaining a normal pace through the bustling harbor. Amidst the din of disembarking passengers and the clanking of cranes transferring goods between ships, my ears tuned into a new, distinct melody—words spoken in their own rhythmic cadence. It was Italian, a language both foreign and faintly recognizable.

We passed the main station of Civitavecchia and arrived at an outdoor parking lot, stopping in front of a brown Italian car. Its design captivated me: four round headlights, a large and a small one on each side, a logo at the center, and a flawlessly shaped bumper beneath. The wheels had round silver hubcaps, like I had only seen in magazines.

"Wow," I uttered, touching the paint with the tip of my fingers.

"Do you like it?" the woman asked with a hint of pride.

"Yes, very much," I replied.

"I named her Giulia," she said, once we were all in the car. "She's an Alfa Romeo Giulia. My name is Ionela, as I suppose Costel told you."

"Ionela, you have no idea how terrified I was when the officer asked for our passports. Costel told me you would handle it, but I didn't know when or how," my mother said.

"Just like home, friends and connections go a long way here."

"I cannot thank you enough," my mother responded.

"Well, I owe one to Costel. He helped me years ago, and I understand how difficult this must have been for you. I was once in a similar situation."

"When did you leave the country?" my mother asked.

"A few years ago, and it was thanks to Costel that I managed to get out. Afterward, I was lucky enough to meet my husband and get married."

"Congratulations!" my mother said. "What do you do now?"

"I work at the Consolato Generale di Romania a Roma," Ionela replied, her pronunciation impeccably Italian.

Both my mother and I exchanged confused glances.

"It's the Romanian Consulate in Rome," she clarified in Romanian. "I'm taking you to a city called Latina—Lazio in Italian—which is about seventy kilometers from here."

"What are we going to do there?" my mother asked.

"In Lazio, there's one of the largest camps, known as

Lagarul Rosi Longhi. I'm dropping you two there," Ionela explained.

"I thought you could help us get on a bus to Spain, where my sister lives," my mother said. "Costel told me you could help us with the necessary papers."

"The only thing I can do is get you into this camp, and I've arranged an interview with the commission team that can get you papers as political refugees," Ionela responded.

"We're asking for political asylum?" my mother questioned.

"Yes, to avoid being sent back to Romania, you'll need political asylum. Then we can look into getting you both to Barcelona."

"What is political asylum?" I asked.

"It's a set of documents that lets you stay in other countries," Ionela answered.

My mother sat back quietly, her eyebrows furrowed and a look of worry on her face as we took the highway to Lazio. After some time, Ionela broke the silence.

"Look, I know you're both tired and scared right now. I've been in your situation," she said, glancing at my mother through the rearview mirror. "The camp has other Romanians, so you won't be alone."

"How many people live there?" my mother asked.

"I honestly have no idea. Maybe fifty at a time? I really don't know. Why?"

"It's just that, when I spoke with Costel, I was expecting a different path for our journey to Spain. I wouldn't have come if I had known my son and I would end up in a camp. Can't we just take a bus from here? How far is it?"

"I told Costel that there's no easy way out of this. You need to get approved for political asylum before anything else can happen," Ionela explained.

"When will we meet with the commission team?"

"Tomorrow," Ionela replied. Seeing the look on my mother's face, she added, "Don't worry. I'm driving to the camp tomorrow, so we can prepare for the interview together. I'll be with you every step of the way and translate for you."

"This truly comes as a shock to me," my mother said, her voice catching as if she was about to cry. "I'm also very tired." She put an arm around me.

"I know, I understand. But you need to trust me. I'll do everything within my power and beyond. Costel is very dear to me, and I've given him my word."

Each time Ionela turned her head to check her mirrors, her long earrings swung like tiny chandeliers. With her back straight and seat moved forward close to the steering wheel, she kept her focus on the Italian traffic, once in a while yelling at the other cars as if they could hear her.

After more than an hour of driving with minimal conversation, the road became increasingly narrow and steep. The region looked deserted, with few buildings or houses visible except for one tall, robust structure that stood prominently beside the street in the middle of this emptiness. We approached hesitantly, slowing down until we reached the blue entry gates. A man in a blue jumpsuit pushed the gates aside to let us in.

Ionela parked the car near the building's entrance, stepped out, and opened the trunk to retrieve our suitcase. By the time my mother and I climbed out of the backseat, several people from the camp had gathered around, and two camp officials—a man and a woman—came to greet us.

A tall, skinny man dressed in pleated pants and a plaid brown V-neck sweater was introduced as the camp administrator, Mr. Giovanni. Following him was Ms.

Georgia, the camp secretary, a short, bulky woman with curly blonde hair. She carried a folder and a camera and motioned us inside to have our pictures taken. Ionela translated questions back and forth between the five of us. Clutching my mother's hand, I looked around. Seeing the people who lived there, gathered in groups and staring curiously at us, did little to alleviate my apprehension.

The camp building was as imposing on the inside as it was from the outside. A long hallway stretched from the entrance to the exit at the opposite end. The ground floor boasted colorful marble floors, polished to a shine, complemented by tall white walls and high ceilings. A chandelier hung in the center, casting warm light over the space. White doors lined the walls, leading to various offices. On the right side of the hallway, a set of stairs ascended to the first floor. From where we stood, I could see a landing midway up.

With Mr. Giovanni and Ionela ahead, my mother and I went up the stairs. We were shown two rooms where language classes were held and a smaller one called *Biblioteca*, a narrow room packed with books, so messily arranged and stacked all along the floor that it made my head spin. From the windows on the first floor, I could see a long alley split in two by shrubs in the middle and benches on each side. At the end of the alley was a modest-looking building with people constantly coming and going.

"What's that building?" I asked Ionela, pointing toward it.

Having anticipated my question, Mr. Giovanni quickly responded before Ionela could reply.

"Those are the camp's dormitories, bathrooms, cantinas, and recreation rooms."

"Are we not sleeping in this building?" I asked.

"No, of course not," Mr. Giovanni replied, laughing to himself. He paused before continuing, "We can't have people sleeping on marble floors. You are fortunate to secure two spots here. As long as I'm in charge, this camp will remain one of the safest and cleanest options available. Now, let's see the other side of the camp—I don't have all day." He waved Ionela to follow him.

His confidence made me reconsider my initial apprehensions about the camp experience. In fact, a smile crept onto my face at the thought of making new friends my age, running around in "the park," attending classes, and spending time reading in the library. His words painted a picture of a life that, while different from what we had known, held the promise of new beginnings and adventures.

But those wishful thoughts were quickly overshadowed by the stark reality of the second camp building. As we entered, a pungent mix of dampness, urine, and overcooked food assaulted our senses. Here, the first building's luxurious, colored marble floors were replaced by stark, concrete gray quartz, reminiscent of the school bathrooms back in Romania. The dormitory area consisted of five rooms, two for women and three for men, each containing several single beds. There were two large bathrooms from where the building's dominant odors emanated.

"Remember the water schedule." Ionela translated Mr. Giovanni's directive. "It's from seven to nine in the morning and seven to nine in the evening. Meals follow the same schedule."

"The same hours?" my mother queried.

"It seems so, yes," Ionela confirmed.

Further on, the last room served as a combined kitchen and dining area, known as the cantina. At the back of this room, a door led to a smaller space with a few chairs and tables and a small round TV in the center—the community room.

While Ionela ventured into the women's dormitories to secure an empty bed and sheets, I made my way to the men's dormitory. Mr. Giovanni had suggested a bed by the grated window, next to another Romanian boy about my age. The room was large and airy, resembling a hospital ward with its rows of beds and metal drawers serving as nightstands.

Underneath each bed, locked trolleys and bags were stored. Ionela left in a hurry, leaving us just in time for our first meal in the camp's cantina: pasta and bread, with a warm cup of bland tea.

* * *

A couple of hours later, on that particular windy night of November 2, in another corner of the world, a joyful figure stumbled drunkenly across the doorstep of Bar La Esperanza and into the narrow streets of the Gràcia neighborhood. At this time of night, the streets were packed with people who, since October 23, had been celebrating the return from exile of the honorable Josep Tarradellas and his appointment to President of Generalitat de Catalunya. The man's tailored French suit and his scruffy attempt at a handlebar mustache made his appearance resemble a noir detective, but his soft piano hands and taste in exquisite wines revealed his true nature. He was a noble Frenchman.

Stepping into the street, he retrieved a pipe from his right inner pocket, packed the bowl, and signaled one of the men around for a light. With the pipe lit, he took a long-anticipated drag. Ignoring the shouting from drunken men around him, he walked slowly toward a side street, where his motorcycle, easily recognized in the Gràcia neighborhood for its never-used sidecar, was parked. He put the key in the ignition and kicked it to life. On the short trip toward his home, the beam from the round headlight paved the way through the streets. At an intersection, the Frenchman took a right turn into the only street ascending a hill. The street was called Carrer de Verdi, and it went up all the way to Sant Gervasi, lined by houses of all kinds of colors placed next to one another as if in a continuous row.

The Frenchman parked his motorbike in front of a white two-story house. Enthusiastically, he tried to insert his key in the lock, but with no luck, until at last the door was opened from the inside by an elderly woman, wearing a headband and dressed in a large white nightgown with a detailed fringe.

"Aha! The key still works," he said while advancing inside.

"Yes, when I open the door." The woman closed the door quickly, clearly irritated to be woken up at this hour.

He advanced from the entrance to the living room and took off his blazer, leaving bits of tobacco ash all over the neatly cleaned floor.

"What do we have for dinner?"

"Dinner? I thought the monsieur decided to eat out tonight."

"I did. I ate lots. I don't really remember what," he said, stroking his mustache as if trying to remember.

"Is the monsieur still hungry, then?" she asked.

"Chère Agueda, you know I can't ever feel fully satisfied unless it's from your cooking," he said, smiling at her, opening his arms, and giving her a hug.

"Oh, Monsieur Laurent, you always know just the right

words to say to a woman who just wants to go to bed," she answered.

"We'll have time to sleep, Agueda. Shall we eat?"

"*Oui!*" she answered.

"Do you care to join me then?"

"*Avec plaisir*," she answered, and down to the kitchen she went while Monsieur Laurent poured himself a glass of '61 Bartolo Mascarello.

30

THE COMMISSARIAT

The first thing I saw when I opened my eyes was a blond boy resting his head on his pillow, gazing directly at me with a pair of the most curious green eyes I'd ever seen.

But yes, I remember him, I thought. We had made quick introductions the previous night. His name was Silviu. He had arrived here with his father, having fled from Romania as well. From the start, he made it clear not to expect a friendship just because we came from the same country. "People here, they come and go. It's not worth it," he said.

He also pointed out that since he had been there for several months, he had already claimed all the drawers of the nightstand for himself. Any personal belongings of mine would have to be stored in a box under the bed. He warned me not to expect to see him around the camp much, as he only came here to sleep or occasionally eat when the food was tolerable. Despite his height and assertive tone, I was surprised to learn he was only three years older than me.

Overall, he seemed like a guy who had endured a lot. And I wanted to be his friend.

"You snored!" he commented that morning as he got dressed.

"Oh, I was pretty tired," I replied, my voice hoarse.

Judging by the orderly behavior of the other refugees from the camp, I understood that the cantina followed the same routine every day, three times a day. You stayed in line, picked up a tray, forks, and a knife, then went to the serving area where one of the three kitchen staff served you your meal. There were no options or questions—you took what was given. Amidst the bustle of adults and kids moving around the room, I found a secluded table where my mother and I could eat in relative peace, away from the noise and agitation.

Shortly after breakfast, a shiny brown car with a soft purring engine pulled up in the parking lot of the main building. Ionela, looking weary and stressed, hurried out of the car. She quickly approached us, where we sat waiting in the hallway.

"I'm so sorry I'm late—Italian traffic," she said, sitting down next to my mother.

"It's alright," my mother responded, moving around on the chair, unable to sit still.

"I saw the black car parked outside. Are they here already?"

"Yes, they're waiting for us. What do we tell them?" my mother asked, biting one of her nails.

"The truth—why you're here and what you want," Ionela replied.

"I can't feel my heart," my mother said.

"Take a deep breath and relax. I speak fluent Italian. I'll do the talking and ask you for any details I need.

Remember,"—Ionela paused, looking directly into my mother's eyes—"they've dealt with thousands of people like you, and most of them got their asylum approved."

"Am I not going in as well?" I asked.

"I don't think so. If they need to speak to you, I'll call you," Ionela said.

Just then, Ms. Georgia opened the office door.

"Signora Eva? Signora Ionela? They are ready for you now."

Left alone in the hallway, I was engulfed by a sense of aimlessness. Minutes ticked by, and my growing anxiety compelled me to do something, anything. I couldn't bear just sitting idly, watching people bustle about purposefully, while I seemed to be the only one without a clear role or direction.

I got up. Twenty-five steps to the entry and twenty-six back. I estimated about fifty-six marble squares in the entire entrance and counted seven vintage-looking wooden chairs lined against the wall. The air carried a scent of carbon paper, tobacco, and the whiff of cologne from a man I ended up following upstairs, stopping right in front of the door of the *biblioteca*.

I gently pushed it open and peered inside. Even though the room had four tall shelves, most books were either haphazardly placed on them or scattered across the floor. It was as if someone had dug through them, searching for something, and left them wherever they landed. Compared with my grandmother's library, this one seemed neglected yet well stocked.

What was most puzzling was the fact that in the middle of the chaos, a man was seated at the round brown table, engrossed in a book, as if nothing around him mattered. When I stepped into the room, he briefly lifted his eyes to study me from head to toe, then returned to his reading. I pretended to browse through the books, casting occasional glances his way, trying not to be too obvious. Something about him reminded me of a character from a book I had read recently, though I couldn't pinpoint which one. He was short and skinny, with sharply defined eyebrows and a distinctly pugnacious face. His attire was notable for someone living in a refugee camp—a ruddy-tinted tweed suit, a red shirt, and a white handkerchief with red edges, intricately embroidered, protruding from his breast pocket.

"*Bună ziua*,"[1] I said, hoping for a response in my native language.

But the only response I got was a brief look before he again turned to his book. Feeling a bit awkward, I withdrew to the window overlooking the back of the camp, or "the park" as Mr. Giovanni had called it.

I watched three young children playing hopscotch, and nearby a group of three women sat on a bench. People moved in and out of the camp's buildings, each absorbed in their own thoughts. My attention, however, was drawn to a bench at the far end of the park, where a woman sat alone, her posture slumped, her back hunched, and her arms hanging listlessly at her sides. Her long black hair, purple sweater, and white vest were distinguishable even from a distance. The fact that she didn't seem to make any movements for the few minutes I stood observing her sparked a worried curiosity.

"Alexandru?" Mr. Giovanni entered the room, calling my name.

"*Da?*" I answered.

He began to speak, but I couldn't understand him.

1. *Bună ziua* – Good day (A form of saluting)

Realizing my confusion, he gestured toward the stairs, and I followed him downstairs.

In the large hallway, my mother and Ionela were talking with a woman from the commissariat team. As I descended the stairs, Ionela quickly ushered me under her arm and introduced me to two men in suits holding leather briefcases.

Shortly thereafter, the group left for their car and departed, leaving my mother, Ionela, the camp secretary, and me in the hallway.

"How did it go? When can we leave?" I asked my mother.

"You're ready to leave already?" Ionela said. "I'm afraid it will take some time."

"How long? How long will we stay here?" my mother asked.

"Not so long, I'm sure. Unfortunately, I have to go back now, or I'll be late for my job. I'll come visit you on Sunday," Ionela said.

Seeing my mother's defeated look, she continued, "Have some faith, Eva. Things will get better."

"So now what?" my mother asked.

"Now, we wait," Ionela responded.

31

HUNGER

It must've been close to midnight in the middle of November when someone hit the light switch of our dormitories with a loud smack that woke us all up. *Boom!* Once the lights were on, a shouting in a foreign language followed, sounding like a loud army drill. This continued until we climbed out of the beds, scared and confused. Two police officers with large rifles hanging over their shoulders were standing guard by the door to each dormitory.

"*Vai fuori di qui, vai fuori di qui!*" one of them was yelling while the other one pulled a few of the slower men out of bed.

I didn't understand a word of what was being said, but Silviu was ahead of me, so I followed his lead. Each of us—men, boys, girls, and women—walked outside, in a line, with our heads down. Like me, most of them were barefoot, the cold creeping into my body like a fungus in a tree. One of the officers used the butt of his rifle to hurry us along, since a few of the smaller kids started to cry, slowing our movement as others bumped into each other on our way out.

"*Muoviti velocemente!*"[1] the other officer yelled, surveying each of us.

Once outside, my first instinct was to search for my mother among the crowd. I screamed and yelled her name —the thought that she might've disappeared scared me more than anything else. But then I saw her, standing on top of a bench, searching for me throughout the crowd.

"Mama, what's happening?" I pushed through and ran to her.

"Give me your hand, give me your hand!" she yelled, her right hand catching mine as she pulled me up onto the bench and hugged me tightly. "I don't know, Alexei. I think they were searching for someone inside, but I don't know."

Feeling the warmth of my mother's body, I closed my eyes for a few seconds. The sound of crying in the background, the panic and the terror brought me back to the night of the earthquake. This seemed all too familiar to me. Images of demolished buildings, a cloud of dust that made everything turn black, the sound of ambulances, and traces of blood came back to me as if I were still there. But as I opened my eyes and looked around, I realized that this was a different nightmare with a different story—this was someone else's nightmare.

Within a few minutes, two officers came out from the dormitories, escorting a man in handcuffs as others followed behind. The man was short in stature, bald, his face red and swollen, his shirt halfway unbuttoned, as if he was just getting dressed. He walked proudly, keeping his head high and looking ahead, unaffected by the many pairs of eyes

1. *Muoviti velocemente* – Move fast

staring at him. As he calmly made his way toward the police car, our eyes met briefly. His expression, so dreadfully fearless, sent a shiver down my spine.

My eyes must have betrayed my fear, for he threw a quick smirk toward me before his head was pushed down and into the police car.

I wondered how much misery he had endured in his life to find heading to prison, surrounded by violence, punishment, and loneliness, to be something so ordinary.

Other than the fact that his name was Frank Balaz and that he was a Hungarian refugee who had been living in Latina camp for the last three years, nobody seemed to know anything about him. Except, of course, for Silviu, who whispered to us as we got back into our beds.

"Frank was a part of a team of burglars who were working in Lazio county. I guess they finally got him," he said, pulling the cover on top of him.

"Are you serious? A team of burglars? What were they stealing?" This seemed like something out of the movies to me.

"Stuff from rich Italians, who else?" Silviu said. "Imagine being so rich and living in a mansion like the main house of the camp, full of art and expensive stuff, drinking champagne and old cognac, traveling to other countries."

"He would break in and steal their things?"

"Yeah, that's what I've heard. There are a lot of people here doing all sorts of things. People must survive somehow."

"Like what?"

"Shhhh," one of the younger men from two beds on the left shouted at us.

"*Vaffanculo*," Silviu answered, hiding his head under the covers.

"*În pisicii măsii*," I whispered, and we both laughed.

The following morning, I woke up thinking of Frank Balaz and looked suspiciously at anyone I passed. Who knew what other secrets were hiding beneath the worried looks of other refugees? Like Silviu said, "people had to survive somehow." We found the cantina quieter and emptier than usual. People eating at the tables all glanced around at each other, as if waiting for something bad to happen. Any outsider walking into that room would see the scared look in our eyes and the ineffable fear we shared.

The man I had seen in the library passed by us, and I gave him a slight nod. He nodded back. We forced ourselves to swallow our usual piece of bread and two hard-boiled eggs.

Two women of large stature walked into the cantina side by side, wearing nightgowns, as if they couldn't be bothered showering or changing anymore.

To make matters worse, my mother was having a hard time catching Ana on the phone since every time she called, she wasn't home. It had been two whole weeks since we had heard anything from Ionela, not a letter nor a phone call. There were times when the thought crossed our minds that she might have forgotten us in the camp, more than ever as the days went by. But then we thought it could be that we were just hungry. The mind plays tricks on you when you are hungry—hungry for real, essential food other than tea, bread, porridge, and vegetable soup, with meat only on rare occasions.

We ached for something or someone familiar in our lives.

My mother carried a book, papers, and a pen with her

at all times, determined to learn Italian. She was probably the only one who showed up every day to the classes offered by the camp and the last one to leave. She possessed a peculiar ability to get herself involved in everything that was going on, as if she wasn't fully aware of where we were or that we would eventually leave.

She did not miss a chance to learn a song or a dance, even when they were in Polish, Hungarian, Serbian, or Albanian. Often, I would see her with other people's young children in her arms, and Ms. Georgia got used to asking for her help around the camp.

On Saturdays, we sat together with another group of people, all of us crowded on a couple of chairs, squinting at a small black-and-white TV placed on a dining table, usually showing an old Italian movie. Needless to say, my mother and I were not far enough along in classes to understand what was said, but she seemed entirely absorbed by the pictures, their fashion, and the sound of the language.

Unlike my mother, I found great relief in going to the *biblioteca*, where I would endlessly search the books, hoping to find one in Romanian, and occasionally meet the man in the tweed suit reading a book. From time to time, I kept an eye out the window at the bench where the same woman sat for hours, looking desolate. The man did not speak much, but like a true gentleman, one day he introduced himself.

"Nowak," he said, extending his hand for a shake.

"Alexandru," I answered and shook his hand firmly.

"Poland," he then said.

"Romania," I replied, and he resumed his reading while I kept wondering, *Who does he remind me of?*

Outside the main building, to the right side of "the park" and away from the sun, was a pomegranate tree, clinging to the tall bushes that surrounded the area like a fence. Its leaves, now hanging without a rustle, were dark green, yet bore no fruit. By the root of the tree, on a small handmade wooden chair, often sat a short man of darker complexion wearing a strange, pointy, round straw hat. He used a pocketknife, thick rope, several wooden sticks, sandpaper, and colored pens to carve what seemed to be children's toys. Many days, I would sit on the ground next to him, watching him work his hands, shaping and polishing the wood with sandpaper, linking the pieces of wood together into different shapes, and adding facial features with the colored pens, giving them life.

So deep was his focus on his work that he often hardly noticed me around. I didn't mind, as his whole world was fascinating to me. As I watched him work with his rusty, aged hands, his eyes drifted toward me from time to time. I imagined how a whole world of wooden dolls was being created, each in a different shape and size, then spread from one house to another, like the human universe.

"God of the Dolls" was my nickname for him. I wanted to tell him but couldn't find the way.

Until one day, with my heart in my chest, I wrote the following questions for him on a piece of paper:

"*Come ti chiami?*"

"Nam," he answered. "*E tu?*"

"Alexandru. Alex."

"*Di dove sei?*"

"Romania. *E tu?*"

"Vietnam," he answered, then turned back and continued with his carving while I continued watching him in silence.

32

LETTER

November 19, 1977
Latina, Italy

Dragă Mămaie si Tătaie,

It's me, Alex.

It's raining outside, and I am writing to you from a school desk in the classroom, where I am supposed to be learning Italian. My teacher… She's not really a typical teacher. She is one of the refugees who offered to tutor us here. She has no degree or teaching experience, not at all like a Romanian teacher from school.

The scent of old books from the library makes me think of you—it's like your own scent. I can't stop feeling bad about the way we left. I am wondering… Is Tătaie still upset with my mother? Is it snowing in the village? I wish I knew how you are doing.

Mama and I are well enough here in Italy for

now. Don't worry about us! I used to count the days since the last time I saw you and Tătaie, but it only made me miss you more. I guess not everything is worth counting.

I don't know if you will receive this letter, but I will try to find a way to mail it to you.

With love,
Your grandson,
Alex.

On the third Sunday of November, it was pouring with rain and had been for several days. Light was rarely making an appearance anymore, and the sun had become a forgotten friend. It was gone, hiding behind the clouds. The gray clouds moved freely from west to east, as if on a mission to share their sadness with the world. They shifted their tones from lighter to darker, from happy to sad, as rain accompanied them. I found myself standing on top of one of the many empty desks in the classroom on the first floor, staring out through the large windows to the colorful roofs of the houses nearby.

Once in a while, voices shouting from the room downstairs stirred me. Several groups of men were watching sports on the TV there. Silence and solitude, the biggest fears of humankind, were like a grilled steak and a glass of fine wine in a refugee camp, an elusive luxury. Yet, I was intuitive enough to see where people were less inclined to go: the classrooms. Why would anyone want to visit classrooms that reminded them they were not home anymore and had to adapt to yet another language, when they could sit with others who shared the same agony?

"Stop staring blankly, for you are looking into hell's ass." My grandmother's voice suddenly popped into my head.

That's what she would say if she ever saw me sitting around looking aimlessly. I remember Veronica telling me one day that there was a poor old woman who spent her days sitting on her porch staring into the distance. The village rumor was that she had the power of casting spells and talking with the devil. She was so frightening that even the gypsies feared her. But she was alone, living in poverty, more frightened of people than they were of her. In the evening, she locked the door, banging it with her knee several times and counting out loud each time "One! Two! Three!" until the rusty latch managed to secure itself.

Between the empty, wet tree branches and colorful rooftop houses, my eyes were drawn to something moving through the small streets. It looked like the roof of a car. But unlike any other car, this one seemed familiar to me—it was Giulia, Ionela's car.

By the time her car had its headlights at the gates, I was already downstairs, yelling to my mother, "Ionela is here! Ionela is here!"

"She is?" my mother asked. We went quickly outside, not minding the drops of cold rain because we were so glad to see a familiar face. She gave me a bag with five oranges, two bananas, and two lollipops.

"You won't be able to share them with all the kids here, so maybe don't take them out of the bag," my mother whispered as we sat down at one of the empty tables in the back of the community room.

Throughout Ionela's visit, my mother poured her heart out, sharing all that had been troubling her. She had kept a lot of things to herself, for I had never heard her complain about the camp's safety, the dreadful cold, the conditions, the food, nor about waiting for answers and the uncertainty of our future. As much as it hurt to hear my mother in pain, the sweet and crisp scent of oranges and bananas hidden underneath my coat whisked my thoughts away. They took me back to our home during Christmas when the city was covered in snow.

"But why don't you go and visit the city of Latina while you're here? Nobody is forcing you to stay inside the camp every moment of the day," Ionela suggested.

"We've been around a bit, but now with the rain and all, there's not much to do but stay inside. How do we get to the city center from here?"

"There's a bus that goes to the center, just a hundred meters away. Once you are there, have some pasta—live the Italian life while you are here."

"I don't have money to spend on a restaurant, Ionela," my mother said, rather annoyed at her suggestion.

Ionela quickly took out a few lira bills and handed them to my mother, who, after much insistence, finally accepted them.

"Ionela, I need to ask you, have you heard anything about our case, any news?"

"No, I'm sorry, nothing yet. There isn't much to do but wait at this point—things like these take time."

"How much time?" my mother asked, taking Ionela's hands into hers. "I've risked everything to come here, and it's already been three weeks with no news. I can barely sleep at night, at the thought that I failed my boy and brought him here with no future."

"Eva, what can I do? Three weeks is nothing compared with how long others have already been waiting here. Just think that you are doing it to get to Barcelona, to your sister, and for Alex."

Right before Ionela left, I handed her the letter for my grandparents, which she promised to mail the next day.

Back in the cantina, I saw Nam talking with another man at the far end of the room. With my tongue touching the roof of my mouth, I forced a whistle through my teeth until he finally turned around and saw me. His face showed pleasant surprise when I reached my right hand inside my coat and took out an orange for him.

"Eva, Alex, here!" yelled the Polish woman, Elisabeth, waving for us to sit at her table.

Listening to the two of them talk about Elisabeth's husband's job at Fabiano's, a place in the city, my eyes drifted to the other side of the room, where the lady with the purple sweater was sitting alone at her table, poking at her food. She held her head down, as if she didn't have the power to keep it up anymore.

"That's Mila," Elisabeth said, seeing me stare at her. "She's from Serbia."

Rumor had it that she had been living in the camp for more than seven years, off and on. She arrived many years ago with her brother. At the time, he was twenty-seven and she was thirty-two. After a long wait, Canada approved their asylum papers.

They left for Canada, but within a year her brother got into some trouble and ended up shot dead in the middle of the day. Mila then decided to return to Serbia, where she found her parents' house in ruins. A nearby mining detonation had gone wrong, killed both her parents, and left her little sister in an orphanage, having lost both legs.

"Imagine!" Elisabeth said.

Apparently, she then suffered a stroke that hospitalized her for months, and subsequently she began talking less and less to people. She came back to this camp over a year ago, having no other place to go, and she was speaking only with camp and kitchen staff. Every now and then, the doctor who visited the camp would give her boxes of sleeping pills to help her get through the nights.

"I don't think she's in her full capacity," Elisabeth continued as the three of us turned our heads toward her. "Who could be?"

Later that night, I quickly ran to the library to hand an orange to Mr. Nowak, who thanked me in his native language, "*Dziękuję*."

Finally, after much internal debate, I mustered the courage to go to the bench where Mila always sat late at night, alone. Her reaction to my offering of the orange left me rather disappointed. She merely turned her head, glanced away, and then resumed sitting in silence, not even sighing.

I left another one underneath the messy sheets on Silviu's bed and went to sleep.

* * *

It was a rainy Sunday in Barcelona, gloomy and dark, the perfect opportunity to do those things around the house that there was never time for, Ms. Agueda decided. Her decision was not welcomed with much passion by her young helper, Gloria, who only wished she was up in her room where she could take off her shoes and rest, for her pregnancy was giving her back pain. Carrying a heavy ladder around the house, Ms. Agueda brushed the spider webs from the corners of the hallways.

Meanwhile, Gloria watered the plants and trees, removing dead leaves. Sensing that Gloria was becoming vexed with her for not allowing her to rest, Ms. Agueda did her best to keep the conversation going in a low tone, as it was only ten-thirty, and Monsieur Laurent was still asleep.

"You should be careful with Doctor Aleu. He's known to be a gabber around the neighborhood," she said. Seeing that Gloria had not yet responded, she continued, "But at least he's willing to help you along the way. What are Francesc's plans? I pray he doesn't leave you stranded, alone and pregnant, as often happens to young unmarried girls."

Ms. Agueda's questions stemmed not so much from interest but from an attempt to show compassion to the poor girl. Deep down, however, she disliked the fact that Gloria had become pregnant out of wedlock, tarnishing the reputation of Mr. Laurent's household in the neighborhood.

"He just needs to find the right time to break the news to his parents. Then we can move in with them. They have a big house with many rooms, up by Matarro," Gloria said.

"I guess that's just as good. It's not your own place, but at least it's something. What other options do you have, after all?"

"It'll be good for me to live by the seaside. I could take walks along the beach and have picnics in the summer," Gloria mused as she removed yet another dead leaf, putting it in a bucket.

"I think it's time we start sweeping up all this mess and throw the trash out before Mr. Laurent wakes up," Ms. Agueda said, descending the ladder's steps with a big duster full of spider webs.

She stepped out onto the terrace, letting the rain wet her duster, and took a deep breath to inhale the fresh scent of rain. Then she turned around and looked at Gloria. She was steadily sweeping the hallway with her head down and back arched, looking tired and miserable.

A feeling of compassion came to Ms. Agueda's heart as she remembered the day, many years ago, when she too was pregnant, the hardship of pregnancy, and making ends meet while taking care of a baby. All that struggle, only to lose him before a year had passed. She went inside, lifted the bucket of dead leaves for Gloria, and carried it out to the trash bin outside.

Gloria, surprised at her gesture, looked at her curiously. "You didn't have to do that, Ms. Agueda, I can carry a bucket. I'm young, remember?"

"I know, but you're also pregnant and shouldn't put in so much effort."

"I'm only three months pregnant. What will you do when I'm nine months along?" Gloria asked, smiling at her.

"By then, I hope the help I was promised will have arrived, and we will manage."

"Have you heard anything else about her?"

"Just that she is delayed, but I hope it's not for too long. I need someone urgently," Ms. Agueda said.

The noise of a door opening and closing was heard from upstairs, and that put an end to their conversation.

"Monsieur Laurent is up—leave this for now. We need to prepare coffee and breakfast right away!" Her figure tensed as she rushed toward the kitchen, with Ms. Gloria following behind.

33

SAINT NICOLAE

"It was 1975. I remember it as clearly as if it were yesterday. The North Vietnamese Army took control of our cities and advanced into the south, reaching my hometown. We were so scared that we tried bolting our doors from the inside at night. But little by little, more and more rumors about people fleeing came to light. If you had money, it was easier, but my family didn't, so we could only leave by boat," said Nam, his words coming out so roughly and slowly as if they hurt. "My family," he continued, after a small pause. "I had seven brothers and twenty-one cousins. My mother and father died a long time ago."

"Have you ever been married?" I asked.

"Yes, yes, my wife, Linh," his face lit up as he looked toward the sky. "It was three years ago when we managed to escape—me, Linh, and our two boys, together with my brother's family. Our boat was small, with only fifty people in total. We went for many, many days. People fainted from starvation. Then we met another boat of five or six men. They seemed good at first. We thought we had found freedom. They gave us food and a blanket, and we were happy. But then they took all our belongings and money, and they kidnapped two small girls who were on the boat with their parents. The parents tried to fight them but got stabbed. They threw the rest of us back in the boat and pushed us out to sea. Are you sure you want to hear more? It's not easy to swallow," he said, seeing my terrified face.

"Yes, yes, of course. What happened next?" I asked.

"First, we arrived in Australia. There were thousands of immigrants like us. The queues took days. They gave us food and clothing but said there was not enough for everyone—mothers and kids had priority. What could we do? Go back to sea again? We decided my wife and our kids should stay, find a place, and settle. We, the men, had to go back to sea. We didn't know how to navigate or sail very well, and at a certain point, when we thought we were close to a small island, we encountered pirates. They checked for our belongings, but they had already been stolen—we had nothing, not even food. They got mad! My brother, stupid with a big mouth, decided to fight them, but they shot him. The bullet went straight to his forehead, here," he said, pointing a finger to the center of his own forehead. "He fell into the water. They shot another guy who was with us as well. The rest of us managed to sail as fast as the wind would take us and arrived in the Philippines after many hard days and nights. From there, some of us were resettled to Italy with the help of an Italian UN commissioner."

I stood speechless for a moment while Nam continued carving his wooden toys. His expression was soft and gentle, as if he had a mind that trusted the universe. He put down his carving knife, measured the block of wood with a ruler, took his pen, and made a mark on the wood. He then sanded the wood, causing sawdust to gently float in the air around him. It was our process: when a miniature was carved, Nam gave it to me, and I placed it in one of my lines. One for each color and design.

"Do you know anything about your family now? Do you keep in touch with them?" I asked when Nam stopped sanding.

"Yes, yes, every Sunday I go to the city and make a phone call. They are out of the camp, and my wife found a job. The kids aren't in school, but they are good, healthy."

"Why aren't you there with them then?"

"I'm waiting for my papers. Australia is not easy to get into. But it's close, I can feel it. You just arrived, but I've been here a long time," he said.

"How did you learn to make these?" I asked, pointing to his wood crafts.

"My grandfather taught me. I can't find the proper wood, so I use sticks from dry trees. I go to the city center and sell them. Sometimes I make a few liras, sometimes I give them for free. Life here is lonely and depressing if you don't have something to occupy you," he explained.

"True, although sometimes loneliness is good," I said.

"It might be good for you, but I don't think it's good for your mother," he said, as we both turned our heads and saw her walking to us.

I got up from underneath the tree where Nam was crafting and met her halfway.

"Did you speak with her?" I asked.

"Just now," my mother answered with a bit of an Italian accent that she had picked up recently. "Such luck—when I called her, she was just walking into her apartment," my mother said as we continued walking slowly around the park.

"And?"

"She was not happy about the situation. Apparently, she promised the woman I will work for that I would be there by now. You should've heard her screaming and shouting." My mother laughed. "She will talk to the authorities in Spain."

"Do you think she can do something?" I inquired.

"I don't know, but she always had a spiteful tongue when she was mad. She said she will go to the consulate in Barcelona and the immigration office. Who knows, this time her temper might be able to help us! How I miss her. We used to be very close when we were kids," she reflected.

"And Aunt Alexandra?" I asked.

"Her as well, but Ana and I were the unruly ones, and because of that we were always getting into trouble. When our parents would go to a wedding, we would drink my father's wine, and Ana would smoke her filthy cigarettes. Then, we would go to the local bar and dance until my father would come and drag us home, by the hair." My mother laughed again. "Or all the time she borrowed books from the library, she would lose them, and my mother had to pay them back from her own salary.

If there's one thing that would upset Grandmother, it's losing books. I remember every time I borrowed a book, she would check on me every day. I believe the experience with Ana scared her. In general, my parents, especially my father, punished her a lot, and me as well for being with her."

"How did she end up going to Spain?" I asked.

"She hated life in Izvoarele and always complained about having to help in the fields. When she went with us, she would climb up a tree and sleep all day. So, when she turned nineteen years old and had finished school, she went to Bucharest looking to work. But after a year, we received an unexpected letter saying she was going to marry a Spanish man she had met there and would move with him to Spain. There was a photograph of the two of them in the letter. He looked older, bald, and happy, with a rose adorning his lapel. Apparently, he owned a bar in Barcelona and was going to take her there. She knew that if she came to Izvoarele, my parents wouldn't let her go, so she never came back. We haven't seen her since."

That evening, after I had just finished cleaning the last drop of tomato sauce from my plate with a piece of crusted bread, I leaned back in the stiff wooden chair and tried to follow my mother's conversation. She was explaining one of our Christmas traditions, which involved butchering a pig and preserving it for the year ahead, to the four other people at our table, including a Polish couple—Elisabeth and her husband.

Perhaps it was this tale of Christmases back in Romania or my thoughts of my grandparents while Nam was talking about his family, but that night I dreamed of the day before Saint Nicolae came to us, George and me, and not with a whip as the bad kids usually get in the tale!

It was December 5. I woke up early, and it was still night outside. I flipped the switch for the light, but the electricity was off, as was the heat. I went to the window. The brisk wind whistled through the windowsill, the cold creeping in through the two layers of windows, even with a blanket stuffed between them. Just like I remembered, in my dream the radiators were iced over, and the warm brick I had near my feet had turned cold as well. I nestled deeper into the unspun woolen sweater I slept in and looked out the window.

Outside was magical. Big fluffy snowflakes were pouring from the sky, and the whole neighborhood was covered in snow. Everything was quiet, not a light or a movement in sight. As soon as a tinkle of sunlight made its appearance in the sky, I woke up my parents. My mother dressed me in a thick purple jumpsuit with two sweaters underneath, a woolen scarf, and a hat, and I ran upstairs to get George. We spent the first part of the day building snowmen and throwing snowballs with the other kids from the block, while my father polished and waxed the runners on our sleds. The snow crunched under the jagged soles of our boots. There was a popular hill back in Zimnicea, several blocks away, where most of us gathered to go down on our sleds. Together with Matilda from the third floor and two other boys from the next block, we climbed the hill and went racing down.

After work, my father came with us as well, pulling us on our sleds and throwing snowballs at us until it was dark outside, and the streetlights turned on.

When we returned to the apartment, our frozen toes and noses hurt. Our stomachs growled at the scent of warm, cooked food.

"Look at you three, all covered in snow! How can you stay out in this cold all day?" my mother exclaimed. "And you, Cornel, you let them crawl like that! Shake all that snow off outside, not in my hallway," she said to us with a smile at the corner of her mouth.

After dinner, my father told both me and George to make sure we polished our boots so Saint Nicolae would come to us tonight.

"Saint Nicolae rarely comes to my place, *domnule* Cornel," George said, leaning back in the chair with a hand on his full belly.

"Well then, why don't you ask your parents if you can sleep here tonight? And maybe he will find you here," my mother suggested.

The next morning, on December 6, we woke up to find

our boots full of small Rom chocolates and bananas for both of us. George's big green eyes were wide open at the unexpected sight, and my heart was so happy that Saint Nicolae had found us both at home.

When I woke up from my dream, I felt nothing but a deep ache, like a sharp knife was still stuck in my heart. I opened my eyes. The room was dark and filled with the sounds of people sleeping. Silviu was tossing in his bed next to mine. I sat up on the side of the bed and stayed there for a while, thinking of my father. With tears running down my cheeks, I climbed out of the warm bed and went to the window. I pulled the brown curtains aside and stared at the view outside. Two long rows of pavement were lined with occasional benches. In between them, dead flowers and dry bushes dotted the ground, and several trees with bare branches surrounded the area.

At the side of the main camp building, a tall pole with the Italian flag fluttered strongly in the wind. I looked up at the sky full of stars and prayed that my dad would watch over us. I wiped my tears away and went back to bed. At that time, I didn't have a single clue what faith had reserved for us.

34

EVERYONE WASHES AND BEHAVES!

Six days before Christmas, as the sun rode high over Camp Latina, five lone figures climbed out of a minibus and up the steps of the main camp building. Two of them were delegates from the International Red Cross, and two were administrators from the Red Crescent organization. Over their clothes, they wore white and red vests with their organizations' logos on the back. Both Mr. Giovanni and Ms. Georgia went to shake hands and welcome them to the camp. They presented themselves in an intense and nervous manner, with words flowing from them, leaving little room for the camp officials to speak.

At last, they entered our building where we were all waiting. They introduced themselves to us and gave a short description of the history of the Red Cross and Crescent, together with the mission and responsibilities of their organizations.

"The fundamental mission of the Red Cross and Red Crescent movement is to prevent and relieve human suffering in any circumstances, to protect life and health, to ensure respect for human dignity, without making any discrimination related to nationality, race, sex, religion, age, military, social, or political appearance, both in cases of armed conflict and disasters."

Each of us kept our ears open, privately hoping that they would have a solution, and we would soon be on our way. In return, they expressed admirable looks and comments about our orderly behavior in the camp.

To these outsiders, the camp may have looked deceivingly close to a budget hotel. We had meticulously followed the administrator's instructions over the past few days: "Everyone washes and behaves." We had tediously cleaned all the tall windows and every panel on the walls, scrubbed the floors, and dusted the aristocratic chairs and the enormous chandelier in the main building. Thanks to an anonymous donation to the camp, our janitor was able to replace all the broken shower heads in both the women's and the men's bathrooms.

Instead of two showers per bathroom that had to be shared between twenty to twenty-five men, now we had all seven of them working. Some pipes and faucets were also replaced. Not only that, but for the whole twenty-four hours leading up to the visit, both lighting and heating were working without restrictions, and every bed received a crisp, clean pair of sheets. Even the menu in the cantina had been upgraded, offering a wider selection, including peas, cheese, beef, fresh bread, milk, butter, and croissants.

For entertainment, our Italian language teacher prepared a popular Italian song called "Alla Fiera Dell'Est," sung by a choir of seven kids, much younger than me, accompanied by the sound of an acoustic guitar played by one of the Polish guys from the camp. The atmosphere turned almost jolly as we all listened to the story of how the father ended up buying a mouse and sang along.

Alla fiera dell'est,
per due soldi,
un topolino mio padre comprò.

And so we talked and laughed with each other, played games, ran around, sat by the big row of tables arranged in the cantina, and ate and drank. And was there, after all, anything to make a passerby aware of our longing for the loved ones left behind, in a strange country awaiting an unclear future? Were we as happy as we seemed to be there together, or mostly miserable inside?

By the end of the visit, before they bid their goodbyes, we were pleasantly surprised by the sudden presence of a large man climbing out of their van. He was dressed in a Santa Claus costume, with a round belly and white beard. He was carrying two large bags of clothes, toys, games, and books, which were shared erratically among us after their departure.

I sat down next to my mother at a table in the cantina, where she was talking with the Polish couple, when out of nowhere I saw Silviu and his father, Mihai, entering the room. *That's a rare sight*, I thought. I waved at him, and he came over as soon as he saw me and sat in the chair next to me. As conversation flowed, I discovered the reason why he was almost never to be seen around the camp. He worked as a dishwasher at Paco's, an Italian cafeteria in the city center, while his father worked on a construction site outside the city.

"I wash dishes, take out the trash, clean tables, anything they ask me to," he described.

"And you like it?"

"Yeah, it's fine. I learn Italian and I get paid two hundred lire per hour, can't ask for more than that. How was the visit? Anything left to eat?"

"Not sure, there were a lot of people, but can you believe it? The camp even bought peanut butter. Have you ever tried it? To be honest, I didn't like it at all."

"Another good part about my job is that I get food, and I mean real food, every day," Silviu said.

"You're lucky," I agreed.

"You could come with me one day! Maybe I can ask Paco if he has something for you to do?"

"Thanks, but I think my mother would go nuts at the idea of me working in the city. She will say that it's too dangerous. I think in her mind, I'm just a small boy," I said.

"Huh, as if this camp is not dangerous," he said to himself.

"What did you say?" I asked.

"Never mind. You know that tall, overweight woman with a long head and a sailor cap who works in the kitchen? She talks very loudly and with an accent?"

"Yes, everybody knows her."

"Her name is Madame Maria, and the rumor is that she was a nun at a Catholic school in Alsace, France. She might look tough, but she's a true angel. When you go with the tray to get your food, make sure to smile at her and ask her something in French."

"In French? I can barely manage Italian, never mind French."

"No, but say things like *comment ça va aujourd'hui*. I learned this from a guy from Algeria who used to stay here."

"Look what I found!" my mother interrupted us. "A few

golden treasures in the pile of dirt, you might say." She held up a few pieces of clothing.

It was great fun for my small audience, Silviu and my mother, to see me parade in T-shirts that probably belonged to someone much taller and more robust than me. I got a pair of woolen trousers to be worn with cotton tights underneath to keep warm and make them fit my waist, and some sweaters with V-necks—the type I only used to wear to school. But my favorite item was *A Christmas Carol* by Dickens, translated into Romanian and given to me by Mr. Nowak, who went through all the books that Santa had brought.

That evening, after I bid goodnight to my mother and Silviu, I retired to bed early, feeling overwhelmed and satiated. How long had it been since I last felt so full and satisfied? It must've been when we lived at my grandparents' and my grandmother cooked stuffed peppers with *mămăligă* and sour cream.

Tucked in my bed, I flicked through the pages of the book, stopping to read about the Ghost of Christmas Present. From time to time, my attention drifted to the sounds of a woman sobbing in the hallways and the two men in our dormitory whispering about something or someone. Suddenly, a loud scream resonated through the entire camp building, followed by several others of a lower tonality.

My first thought was, *My mother!* I rushed out of bed and ran barefoot towards the exit.

I crossed the park as fast as I could and arrived at the crowd gathered in a circle in front of the main building. A window on the third floor was open, and the white curtains were flowing in the wind. I found my mother staring at the ground, her eyes fixed in shock and her right hand covering her mouth. When I looked down at the cemented pavement, I realized why.

The first time I had heard the term 'suicide' was when my grandmother told me the story of one of her favorite writers, Virginia Woolf.

"She was mad," my grandmother said. "She wrote in her last letter that she was hearing voices and couldn't concentrate. Can you imagine her poor husband and everyone she had left behind? She had so much passion and talent, such a waste."

Still, I struggled to comprehend why someone would choose to end their life, just as I couldn't fathom why the Serbian woman, Mila, had done so. But maybe she was hearing voices as well? Maybe she was mad, after all?

My mother took my hand and dragged me out of there. Within minutes, the high-pitched sirens of an ambulance were heard from down the next street while the camp administrator and janitor pushed everyone aside to make way for them to come in.

We stood by the side of my bed, with ambulance noises and the sound of crying in the background. She hugged me tightly, and I leaned my head on her shoulder. I could feel her heart hammering in her chest as she started rocking me from side to side until at last I fell asleep. Then she gently laid my head on my pillow and covered me with the blankets.

35

CHRISTMAS LETTER

December 28, 1977
Latina, Italy

Dragă Mămaie și Tătaie,

Here at the camp, we are a big group, people from all over Europe, but I also have a friend all the way from Vietnam. For Christmas, we didn't have any Christmas trees, snow, or much heat in the radiators for that matter. But the women placed candles and plastic lights everywhere. We sang carols in different languages, and the atmosphere cheered up a bit. The evening before Christmas Day, we put all the tables together in the cantina and sang an Italian carol called "Tu Scendi dalle Stelle" that we learned in language class. Some of us danced (not me), the men shook hands with each other and exchanged cigarettes, and the women laughed and talked.

On Christmas Day, both men and women were

divided into teams, and we took turns playing football outside. We had dinner with all sorts of sausages, biscuits, and chocolates. Madame Maria, whom you don't know, works in the kitchen. She made tiramisu for everybody, and it went down very well. The only two camp employees present produced a camera, and we took a few group photos, all of us together. And if you worry that we might have had a rotten Christmas, I think I can speak for my mother as well to assure you that you are mistaken.

I hope this letter finds you both healthy and full, warm and rested like two bears that go into hibernation and come out at the first sign of spring.

I keep you both in my heart,

Alex

36

EVEN THE BLIZZARD DIED OF COLD

In the shapeless moments before fully returning to consciousness, I lay with my eyes closed and listened to the roommates around me. I weighed up the events of the last days in my mind.

"Not just yet," I said to myself. "I'm not ready yet."

But the sound of voices from inside the dormitory picked up in volume, transitioning from whispering to normal within a few minutes. Everyone started to get out of bed, confronting the cold temperatures inside the room. Like my father used to say, "Even the blizzard died of cold." This was a different type of cold, for it was also humid and persisted in its stubborn plan to freeze us all to death. I didn't have a choice, so the previous night I put on two pairs of pants, one T-shirt, one undershirt, a sweater, and two pairs of socks that I had from Romania. An orange hat, which I had found among the donated clothes, covered my head. My first attempt at getting out from underneath the bed sheets was a complete failure.

"I can't, I just can't. I'm hungry, though, and a warm cup of tea wouldn't hurt."

One brave step at a time. So, I took a deep breath and pulled the covers to the side. I swung my legs out of the bed and sat there, watching the traces of my breath visible in the air. Before a minute had passed, my mother came, knocked on the door, stuck her head inside the room, and signaled for me to come with her for breakfast. Reflecting on it, those days were the first days I saw my mother wearing anything other than her skirt and dress. Now she even wore a hat—a woolen hat. She hated wool because it made her skin itch.

The camp did not have a good start to the year, especially now in January, as the worst misfortune had befallen us. The pipes in the bathroom had burst open, flooding the whole men's bathroom and even reaching one of the women's dormitories at the end of the building. The flooding was so severe that several beds had been drenched, leaving people with no other choice but to sleep two in a bed or on a blanket in the hallway. Heat was not an option either, and there were times when we thought it was colder inside than outside. And to make matters worse, food was not abundant. Every day, we would see people carrying backpacks and leaving the camp for a better place. A great queue started early in the morning with refugees, especially the ones with kids, desperately asking to be transferred or to hurry their cases.

To my sadness, among the people who left the camp were Silviu and his father, leaving me with an old Hungarian man who had taken Silviu's bed. I didn't know his name and wasn't interested in finding out either. He snored and twitched during the night, coughing loudly and deeply, as if he had been smoking for ages and his lungs were full of phlegm.

Bucket after bucket, we helped the janitor carry the water away and wiped the floors and walls, waiting for a plumber to come and fix the pipes. Countless hours were spent moving in and out of the camp halls aimlessly, dreaming of those warm summer days when George and I used to run wild in the neighborhoods, hoping for a water sprinkler to start and get us wet. During those days in the camp, my mood soured, and the only person I could blame for our current situation was my mother. I never fully understood: *Why are we here? Why can't we stay in Romania with my grandparents?*

When I put my tray on the cantina's long counter, I gave a faint smile and winked at Madame Maria. Long ago, I had taken Silviu's advice and prepared a few French phrases for her, which pleased her immensely. It became clear to me that behind the long faces of the people working in the camp, there were strangled souls needing human connection and to feel seen.

Just as on previous mornings, her uniform had stains on the left pocket of her blue apron, her chestnut-colored hair was arranged in a thick bun, and her face looked pale with red cheeks from the steamy kitchen. She gave me a warm cup of tea, a piece of hard-crusted bread, and a bowl of porridge.

"How are you feeling, *bambino*?" Madame Maria asked.

"Like a frozen stone," I smiled back at her.

"The rumor is that today a plumber will come to fix the pipes." She added an extra spoon of jam to my tray.

"Really? Can you imagine? Hot water and maybe even heat in the radiators? *Merci*, Madame Maria," I said. And before I stepped forward in the queue, she stretched her hand toward me with a fist closed. I also reached out my hand, and she placed a chocolate candy in my palm. I quickly took it, winked at her, and followed my mother to the table.

We put down our trays with porridge and tea and sat facing each other.

"Today, if Ms. Georgia allows me, I'll call both Ionela and Ana. I wonder if they have any news. Good or bad, anything would be better at this point," my mother said, blowing on her tea.

"What for? So she can come here and tell us that we must have patience, things will get better, or she is doing her best to get in touch with people," I answered.

"What's with you these days, Alexandru?"

"Look around you, Mama! We are living hopelessly in this damp camp, spending our days waiting and dreaming that one day someone will come and call our names, allowing us to move to another country and start all over again. Or we will probably end up like that Serbian woman who had been here for seven years and decided it wasn't worth living anymore, who knows." I took a sip of the tea, tasteless as always.

"Yes, it's hard! Nobody said it would be easy." After a dramatic pause, she continued, "It's not like I'm living better than you. I don't need you to talk to me like this." She straightened up and tapped her finger on the table, as I remembered her doing at home whenever I was in trouble.

"And how should I talk to you, Mama? You dragged us all the way here. You took us from my grandparents. If we had stayed there, we would've been just fine."

"No, we would not. There are certain things you don't understand about a single woman with a child living under the eyes of the Communist Party. Both your father and I did our best to shield you from the reality of our lives. We both dreamed you would be able to live your life in a different society, so don't take our efforts for granted." She picked up the spoon and slowly stirred the porridge in circles.

"Don't you drag my father into this. If he were still alive, he would never have let us languish in this camp." I leaned back in my chair with my heart pounding in my chest, knowing that I might have gone too far.

"I don't appreciate your tone. I didn't raise you to talk to me like that, Alexandru." She leaned toward me over the table. "And lower your voice, people are looking at us."

"Let them stare. I hear them screaming and crying all day, and I don't say anything. Why can't we go back? I want to go back! I don't want to be here anymore!" I said, burying my face in my hands.

"We cannot! You don't know what you're saying. Going back to Romania after we escaped…" She paused. "We might as well be sentenced to prison for the rest of our lives. They'll make sure there's no future left for you or me. That idea is out of the question," my mother nearly yelled.

For a moment, I was back in Zimnicea under my mother's vigilant eye. I knew that when she raised her voice and looked at me like this, I was playing with fire. As if programmed, I would lower my shoulders and look down, like Volk did after he understood he had hurt me.

But this time, fear and guilt were replaced by confidence and anger. So much so, that in protest to my mother's behavior, I got up from the table, took my tray to the kitchen, and gave it back to Madame Maria, who looked with questioning eyes from my unfinished plate to me, and left the room without saying a word. I ran quickly through the lifeless park, into the main building, up the sixteen steps to the first floor, and opened the tall doors to the *biblioteca*. There, I found Mr. Nowak kneeling on the floor, next to the piles of books as if waiting for me to arrive.

Two days earlier, when I decided to skip classes and arrange the pile of books in the *biblioteca*, Mr. Nowak took it upon himself to help me. Despite our language differences —and fashion style, for that matter—we found a way to understand each other through a world of our own, a world only divided by title, genre, and shape.

By late afternoon, however, the atmosphere improved. An old van of burgundy color parked in front of the main building, and two elderly men dressed in worn jumpsuits and rubber boots, carrying heavy tool cases, arrived to fix our pipes. Most of us gathered around the bathroom, inspecting their every move as if we had any knowledge or insight into what they were doing. At last, the pipes were changed, and hot water flowed again in both the bathrooms and the radiators.

Later that night, when everyone was asleep, I tiptoed to the bathroom, turned on the hot water, and took a well-deserved shower. I remember that one more than all the showers and warm baths I've taken since then.

* * *

The dining room, which opened into a large living room, was not a place of shadow and gloom that evening. It rarely was, of course, since Mr. Laurent never missed an opportunity to host an unexpected gathering any night of the week, a habit that both Ms. Agueda and Gloria had learned to accommodate. Even the most exquisite French recipes, which usually required complex preparations, could be ready in a miraculously short time. For there were only a few sacred customs from his heritage that Mr. Laurent had not changed, and these included his tastes for French food and wine.

With the firelight steadily burning, candles lit, music and loud chatter, a warm atmosphere imbued the dining room. The noise spread throughout the entire two floors of the house. Mr. Laurent sat at the head of the table, and the other four chairs were occupied by three younger men and a woman—artists, as they called themselves—each with a guitar. The rumor in the kitchen was that they were part of a well-known band of guitarists in Catalonia called the "Quartet Tarrago."

At Mr. Laurent's request, Gloria brought several more bottles of Jules Burdin from the cellar. Meanwhile, Ms. Agueda cleaned the plates from the seasoned salad served as an entrée and continued to present her main dish: stuffed onions baked in a cream sauce, a sauce that had been prepared for hours, originally for another dish.

"You truly are spoiled, Laurent!" said Lavel, one of the band members.

"And I love being spoiled," he exclaimed, and took yet another sip of wine from his glass. "Food and wine are my main joys in life."

"And music," said Laura, another band member.

"And music!" He winked.

"Wait until you see the dessert," Ms. Agueda said to the guests as she continued serving.

"What do we have for dessert?"

"I just took a golden honey-glazed apple tart out of the oven."

Ms. Agueda left the dining room, feeling exhilarated, for while Mr. Laurent's biggest joys were food, wine, music, and parties, her biggest joy was seeing him content. Being under his roof for the last fifteen years, she had grown a motherly affection for him, the kind that gave her purpose every morning and filled up the emptiness in her heart that was left by her lost son. Back in the kitchen, she found the sink full of unwashed dishes and glasses, bowls of food that had not yet been put to cool in the fridge. Gloria sat by the window table, her head against the window.

"What are you sitting there for?" she asked as she entered the kitchen.

"Sorry, Ms. Agueda, I was just taking a rest," she answered and lifted her pregnant body up from the chair.

"Let's clean all these dishes and put the food away. You'll have time to sit and ponder when you go to bed."

Irritated at each other, both cleaned in silence. They followed the same routine they usually did. Ms. Agueda washed the dishes, and Gloria dried them off with a dish towel and put them away in the light blue cabinets hanging on top and underneath the kitchen counter. On the other side of the counter were two other closets, also of a light blue shade, with glass windows and drawers, where special types of porcelain glasses, cutlery, and tableware were kept, together with tablecloths and other kitchen utensils. Everything was left as Mr. Laurent's mother had decorated after she moved into this house.

Therefore, contrary to the rest of the house, which had French wooden floors and doors, the tiles of the kitchen floor were green with sophisticated white details. Most of the kitchen cabinets and closets were light blue, the table, where the two maids usually sat and ate, was white, and house plants hung from every corner of the room. In a way, the room still carried his mother's presence, which was also the reason Mr. Laurent almost never set foot in there.

By the time the tart was ready to be served, the party of five had moved to the living room. The four band members started playing their guitars, and Mr. Laurent played piano in the background. Ms. Agueda contentedly took small plates of tart to the living room, only to be entirely ignored by the members of the party, as they were all engrossed in their world of music. She placed the small plates on the table and looked toward the living room without understanding much of what she was listening to. To her, it felt as if each guitar played its own song, but admittedly there was a semblance of rhythm, especially with the low keys of the piano in the background.

When she came back to the kitchen, everything was polished and cleaned, but she was disappointed to see Gloria had already left for her room without being dismissed. So, she sat alone by the kitchen table and looked out of the window until the party died down in the early hours of the morning.

37

LLOTA AND ANDOR

By the end of winter, the thin, colorful, flat-topped houses and shops of Latina sat isolated, overshadowed by long stands of barren trees. When my mother and I went strolling in the city, the day felt warm for the middle of February, and the golden sunlight beamed brilliantly throughout the streets.

With our hands on a railing near the docks, we looked out at the sea, listening to the sound of waves crashing against the harbor, growing louder and louder. The same harbor that welcomed us more than five months ago was now empty, with only a few boats mooring and swaying with the movements of the waves.

The suspense of waiting and the uncertainty were affecting our minds, much like a debilitating disease. Nothing seemed as bad as not knowing what would happen or when. We took great pleasure in Ionela's visits, which happened almost every Sunday. She told us about her week at work, her husband's high society friends, whom she found rather dull, and the museum visits she enjoyed. Every now and then, my mother managed to call Ana in Spain. These calls buoyed her spirits with promises of visits to the immigration offices in Barcelona, or even the police, all in the hopes of advancing our case.

March 4, 1978 marked a year since the earthquake in Zimnicea. Yet with everything that had happened since, it was hard to believe that so little time had passed. Not at home, not where we hoped to be, like everyone else around us, we became like ghosts with an uncertain future, stumbling around the camp.

Shortly after that date, the camp announced the arrival of a new wave of Hungarian families, and rumors suggested that more would follow in the upcoming months or years. The news created a certain tension and worry among those of us already in the camp and sparked concerns over the number of beds available and the quantity of food, which was already sparse.

Our fears were confirmed the following week when, on my suggestion, Nam and I changed our usual carving spot to the small courtyard by the entrance, where the few emerging rays of the sun would heat us better. We were sitting on the grass, leaning against the fence, facing each other. Nam was showing me how to smoothly shape the piece of wood at the right angle to create a form, when the blue gates of the camp were pulled to the side and a long bus drove in. The bus parked in front of the building, and as the door opened, a seemingly endless line of people descended the steps, one after another.

Nam and I stopped our work and sat there motionless, looking at them the same way others had looked at us when we first arrived at the camp. With red, tired eyes, they began to scan the camp's surroundings until Ms. Georgia took charge. Before she let anyone inside the building, she directed them toward the wall to have their picture taken, then instructed them to stay in line, one family or couple at a time, before entering his office to complete their registration.

Despite the overcrowded circumstances, we slowly adapted to one another within a couple of days, thanks to a common interest we all shared: the community room. The community room was so small that it barely had enough seats for all of us at that point. But we all looked forward to the hours when everyone would contribute with any skill they had. With over fifty people now in the camp, the community room buzzed with energy as if it were the backstage of a theater on opening night.

It had taken me months to adjust, but eventually I came to take great pride in my mother's sociable nature, which had previously irritated me. I smiled to myself as I barely recognized this new person, who wore corduroy mustard-colored trousers with the pant legs stuffed inside a pair of tall boots, a plaid sweater, and a thick scarf holding her red hair, as opposed to the heartbroken and restless woman that she used to be when we left Romania. Among the camp's staff and residents, my mother became a popular person, always showing her support and offering to help, even to Ms. Georgia and Mr. Giovanni in the office.

There were five of us at the table—Mr. Nowak and I were turning the pages of a black-and-white photography book, and next to us were my mother and a pregnant Hungarian girl, Llota, with her fiancé, Andor. The Hungarian couple sparked my mother's interest after hearing that they, too, had family in Alexandria, the city in Romania where my father was born. Llota was only nineteen and already four months pregnant. The couple was forced to leave the country when Andor was put on a blacklist back in Budapest.

"By Christmas, I got fired and we found out Llota was pregnant. What could we do?" Andor started their story as he was holding Llota's hands underneath the table.

"Didn't you consider leaving earlier?" my mother asked.

Llota took over. "Well, we thought about it before, but things were never as bad as they were when we left. The government got more and more strict, especially toward the working class. People could barely afford food, even if they worked all day. There were several protests that Andor participated in, so they started to watch him every day. Around Christmas, we heard rumors that they were planning to tighten security even further. We borrowed money from Andor's father. We told him it was for the baby, and Andor knew some guys who were acquainted with smugglers, so he went and spoke to them. At last, one of them offered his services. He told us the trip would be long and start on December 25, when everybody would be busy with their families."

"It was terrifying," Andor continued, his eyes moving between Llota and us. "On December 25, we went out dressed as if we were going for a walk. Llota had only her handkerchief and a notebook where she wrote her poems—do you still have it?"

"Of course I still have it."

"And a handbag, that's all," he continued. "We paid all the money we had, plus what my father gave me. The smuggler then wanted my camera, so I handed that over as well. It was my favorite thing to do, take pictures. But I guess it was also my curse, for some of the pictures I took ended my career and put me on their list."

"In the end, how did you both manage to escape, especially with Llota being pregnant?" my mother asked.

"He picked us up from a parking lot where we had agreed to meet," said Andor. "We drove for seven hours straight. I remember Llota had to pee, but we couldn't stop—it was too risky. We arrived late at night in Sopron, which is on the border with Austria. That patch of the border was treacherous, lined with watch towers and spotlights that were going round and round. We had to walk quietly and lie flat on the ground when they passed."

"That's when I peed—I peed myself one of the times," Llota said.

"Some parts of the border were mined," said Andor, "but luckily the smuggler knew how to avoid them. We heard dogs barking and even gunshots at one point, but we kept walking for hours and hours in the pitch dark until we finally reached the Austrian side of the border. We presented ourselves as refugees, and the authorities called for the Red Cross to come and pick us up."

"And the smuggler?" I asked.

"He went back. I hope he was alright. He did this often, so he must've known his way."

Llota took over again. "Then in Austria, they took us to some office, where they questioned us about our political orientation, requested our identification papers, and asked other questions. They gave us meal tickets for food and some clothing. Being pregnant gave us some kind of priority but also stopped us from being able to apply for asylum in some places. Not all places had the ability to deal with pregnant women. They asked us if we were married because they didn't recognize our engagement there. We told them we weren't yet."

"We wanted to go to the US because Llota has a distant

aunt who can help us there," said Andor, "but because she's pregnant, they didn't approve of it. They offered me Australia, but I didn't want to go without Llota, so we asked to be transferred to another camp, one where we could stay together. We heard that Latina camp here in Italy was one of the safest ones out there, so here we are."

"Where are you trying to go now?" my mother asked.

"We both decided on Canada and have already applied," said Andor. "I assume it will take a while, especially with a baby on the way. We aren't even married."

After a few moments of silence, my mother said, "Why don't you get married here?"

"Here? How? We don't have a penny in our pockets, and without our asylum approval, we can't. We eat pasta and porridge all day. Who can even think of a wedding?" Andor asked.

"We can still have a ceremony, maybe even at a church, and later on you can have it done legally," my mother said, standing up and clasping her hands together.

Llota and Andor looked at each other.

"What does it matter whether there's a signed document or not? We are all together here just once," my mother insisted. "I can speak with Ms. Georgia to see what we can do. I'm sure she will help us with it."

38

THE CAMP WEDDING

First, my mother went into town and straight to Parrocchia San Francesco d'Assisi to speak with the priest. Since neither the bride nor the groom were Italian nor members of the church and had a baby on the way, he refused to perform the ceremony. That changed one morning after my mother woke up early and followed him around town, trailing him to the market. Caught mid-conversation, the priest was taken aback by my mother's persistence. But with many eyes on him, he felt compelled to cooperate and recommended one of his friends instead, a priest from the church of St. Prius, a few kilometers outside the city, who eventually agreed to do the ceremony as long as it was on a weekday.

That Sunday, when Ionela came to visit us, she took us for a ride all the way to a place called the Gardens of Ninfa, where we could pick flowers to decorate the cantina for the gathering after the ceremony.

"What kind of flowers shall we get?" Ionela asked.

"We should try to aim for white, red, and yellow so we can create a theme," my mother answered.

Standing in the middle of the field, we looked around at the abundance of flowers: delphiniums, sweet peas, and masses of carnations of all colors—my mother's favorites. I heard Ionela inhaling deeply, taking in the sweet, earthy aroma of the garden, before she bent down to pick some.

By Wednesday, March 28, when my mother, Ionela, and the Hungarian couple got out of Ionela's car, the cantina was festively prepared. The two large windows were ornate with lights left over from Christmas, the tables were put together in the shape of a square and covered with colorful tablecloths brought from home by the kitchen staff, and flowers filled every corner. A few hours and several bottles of wine later, provided by the camp association, the atmosphere around the tables was cheerful and social.

Sitting beside Mr. Nowak I learned more about his family. His wife and sister, both former residents of this very camp, were now eagerly awaiting him in Canada.

In the middle of the festivity, a thin figure, sitting right across from me and dressed in a worn sweater with a hole right next to the neckline and its sleeves rolled up, a pair of pants, and simple shoes, got up from her chair. With her left hand she brushed strands of red hair behind her ear and turned around to face everyone. She began by congratulating the future parents on their "marriage" and shared some of the joys of her own, which led to her retelling the reason we fled the country and ended up here.

"Was it a mistake? I wonder and fear that every single night when I put my head on the pillow."

Her speech felt long and dreary to me but looking around the room I noticed everyone's attention drawn to her words, some with teary eyes, some with smiles of agreement when they recognized themselves in her story.

Her voice was of a woman who had breathed the dust of her ruined home, cried at the sight of her husband's broken body, and tasted the sweat running off her forehead and down to the factory floors. In other words, it was the voice of my mother, my best friend, and the voice of everyone else who had suffered at the hands of their country.

"*Noroc!*" she finally shouted, raising her glass in the air. "To a ragtime camp affair!" She took a sip of the wine.

A couple of days later, on a sunny April day, as my mother and I awaited the camp's blue gate to swing open, Mr. Giovanni emerged from the main building, signaling to my mother with an evident look of distress.

"Ms. Eva! Ms. Eva! Thank God, I found you! I was looking everywhere for you."

"What happened?" my mother asked, quickening her pace toward him.

"I just got off the phone with the office in Rome. The commissariat team would like to hold a few private interviews here tomorrow afternoon."

"Does Ms. Georgia need help preparing the files?"

"Yes, that too, but there's another thing I wanted to inform you about."

"What is that?"

"Among the files required, they asked for yours."

39

ARRIVEDERCI

Positioned prominently across from the office's tall doors was a grand replica of a renowned painting depicting the battle of San Romano between Florentine and Sienese forces in 1432, encased in a golden frame. My mother and I sat patiently studying it, waiting for someone to open the doors and call our names.

It finally happened. A tall brunette motioned for us to follow her inside. Without looking at us, she pointed to the chairs in front of her desk. Square glasses accentuated her elongated face, which was dominated by a notably large nose and slender red lips.

"My name is Adalgisa. Adalgisa Bonazzola." She spoke fast without lifting her eyes from her papers. "I'm a delegate from the UNHCR responsible for assisting you with your case. Before I continue to tell you the reason why I called you here, I must inform you that I'm not the one in charge of making any of these decisions. Ahead of me, several teams of people have revised your file, examined your situation, and contacted officials in Spain, and so forth."

She lifted her head to look at my mother and continued, "As you're likely aware, Spain is only just beginning to recover from its own fascist dictatorship, making this a challenging decision for them. If you ask me, I don't think it's a great idea to seek asylum there at all. But I understand you already have a family member living there?"

"Yes, my sister. And she can help me with a job as well."

"That's something at least. That's a good start." She turned to me and asked, "And you, Alexandru? Am I pronouncing it correctly? Have you adjusted to the camp here? I assume you've made a lot of friends?"

"Yes," I replied. "I have two friends, Mr. Nam and Mr. Nowak."

"How old are they?"

"I don't know—old," I said.

"Interesting choice of friends. I'll be direct because I have another meeting to attend and no time to waste. I'll have to return for the rest of the cases tomorrow. At first, Spain said that your application for asylum in their country does not fit their criteria."

My mother gasped, but Ms. Adalgisa continued, "I don't know if you're aware but there's a new wave of refugees who are due to arrive here any day now. The camp will get overcrowded again, and it turns out that other people's misfortunes can be your fortune."

"Do you need to move us somewhere else?" my mother asked.

"Let me finish, Ms. Eva. I don't have much time. It usually takes up to one hundred and eighty days just to get an answer. I don't know if it was the political pressure on the new Spanish government or your sister's insistence, but it seems as if you were lucky enough to get your case approved. You are now welcome to Spain with the condition that your sister guarantees you financially, which she already has."

A moment of silence fell over the room while both women looked at each other.

"Did you hear what I just told you?" the woman asked.

My mother sat still and quiet, staring at her as if she didn't understand her.

"You're free to leave," she said, this time louder as she stamped papers on our file.

At that moment, tears overwhelmed my mother, and she covered her face with her hands.

"I don't have time to stay and pat your back right now. I'm handing you the folder with the documents and two papers signed and stamped that you must carry with you at all times. One for you," she said, handing one to my mother, "and one for you." She handed one to me. "From here, Ms. Georgia will help you with the travel and formalities."

"I can't express my gratitude enough," my mother said, extending her hand to Ms. Adalgisa. "Thank you," she repeated one more time.

"Don't thank me—thank your sister and your friend, Ionela. They are the ones who really made this happen."

Ms. Adalgisa rose from her chair, opened the door, and promptly ushered us out of the office. In the hallway, people turned their heads, seeing my mother's flushed face. In our hands were the folder of papers and the little two-page carnet permitting us to travel.

I opened mine, and on the left side in the upper corner was stamped:

Spain, Barcelona
Transito Italia.
EuropaOCC

Further down, another stamp read:

Qestura di Latina,
April 10, 1978

On the other page were the fields:

Proroga di Validita
Prorogation di validite.

The travel permit was valid for six months.

In the days that followed, I felt like a mere shadow trailing behind my mother's skirts. She moved with a mix of urgency and agitation around the camp, double-checking our documents, packing our belongings, and making calls to Ana and Ionela. Tearful sentiments and travel advice were accompanied by warm touches and hugs from the friends who had become almost like family to us.

The last day before leaving, Mr. Giovanni called my name from the hallway, and I ran toward him. He held the door of the office open, and as I approached I could see Ms. Georgia and the camp director behind him. He bent down to my height, as he had done the first time we met.

"It occurred to us that you might like… or at some point, perhaps if you still remember us when you grow up—"

"Of course I will," I interrupted him.

He reached his right hand into his pocket and took out a photograph.

"I know you use your father's photograph as a bookmark in every book you read, so we thought you might want to add a picture from your time here to your collection, as well." He handed me the black-and-white photograph and said, "This is from Christmas. It was a memorable one, wasn't it?"

I looked at the grainy black-and-white photograph and saw the group of us sitting scattered around the community room where we had sung, danced, and talked like one big family. I hugged Mr. Giovanni, then turned around and awkwardly ran out of the building and into the shade of a tree, where I could hide the tears running down my cheeks.

That was not the last time I shed a tear that day. Before dinner, I went to the *biblioteca* to say goodbye to Mr. Nowak. When I opened the door, I found him at his usual spot, at the round table in the middle of the room, reading a book. I glanced around the room and noticed how different I felt about it now compared with six months ago, when I had first opened the same door. And it wasn't just because the books were now neatly stacked on their shelves, allowing sunlight to enter, but because it reminded me of him. With his tweed suit and the colored shirts he wore daily, it was as if he were royalty lost in a refugee camp. That day, however, he wore a white shirt with a matching white handkerchief in his breast pocket. He closed his book and motioned for me to take the chair next to him. From inside his jacket, he retrieved a small package wrapped in paper. I pulled aside the wrapping, and inside was his other handkerchief, white with red embroidery in the shape of a flower that spread around its edges.

"For me?" I asked.

"*Tak*," he answered.

"What for?"

"*Per essere qui*,"[1] he replied.

I looked around the camp all day but didn't find Nam

---

1. *Per essere qui* – For being here

carving his toys for the weekend. That evening, after dinner, I returned alone to my bed in the men's dormitory. I spent a moment looking around, from corner to corner, from bed to bed, and that's when I noticed a small wooden figurine on the corner of the bedside cabinet. The figurine had short brown hair made of yarn, a thin face with a pronounced nose, and lips drawn with a pencil. It was wrapped in a dark blue fabric that looked like my old coat. The eyes of the figurine were painted big and blue, just like my mother's, but with a tearful look and curious eyebrows.

So that's how he sees me, I thought.

That night, I found myself tossing restlessly, seeking sleep that did not come until the early morning, and we had to get going.

On April 12, 1978, my mother and I settled into the front row seats of the bus destined for Port Vell, Barcelona, Spain. The morning was fresh with a lively spring wind full of dust. We left the city behind, descending gradually past rows of white houses adorned with blue and yellow balconies, all the while taking in the endless view of the sea and clear blue sky. The sun's rays cast strong amber light over the city, with the images of closed shops, cafes, and restaurants drifting behind us.

"I wonder what my boss will be like?" my mother mused, lost in the distant view.

"What will you do? Will you sew for him?"

"No, no," she answered, laughing at me. "I'll work as a maid—one of the girls is pregnant, so I'm filling her position."

"What will I be doing?"

"That, I don't know. You'll perhaps stay with your aunt or with me. I don't know yet. Don't worry," she said, putting her arm around me, "I won't let you out of my sight no matter what."

"Will we ever make it, Mama?"

"What do you mean by that?"

"Will we ever be happy again?"

"That's a tough question to answer," she said, stroking my hair with her soft hands. "Happiness might not mean the same for us in the future as it does now. It sure means something else for me compared with when we lived in Romania. Doesn't it for you as well?"

"Like what?"

"Well, what do you most wish for?"

After a second of thought, I answered:

"To be at home."

"Exactly. Home. That is your happiness."

PART III

40

ADAGIETTO

In the late hours of an April night, a twinkling sound woke me up. At first, the melody sounded soft and playful, but the more I lay there quietly listening, the louder and clearer it became, echoing through the walls from somewhere inside the house. A piano playing from downstairs?

The chords danced mesmerizingly along the keys, starting slow and tender, with deeper and melancholic notes in between, until it suddenly turned grave and dark. I held my breath, not wanting to miss a single note, remaining motionless in my bed. It felt as if I were looking at the sea on a gloomy day, with small waves moving in and out along the shore. The waves increased their rhythm until they became rough and violent, the sky turned dark, and a storm ensued. Occasionally, the sun tried breaking through with soft notes, but the storm prevailed. Two minutes later, the music stopped. For no reason or perhaps for many hidden reasons, that melody brought tears to my eyes and remained imprinted in my mind for many years onward.

I turned my head to the right and looked at my mother. She was sound asleep in her bed. Judging by her deep breathing, the melody from downstairs seemed not to have bothered her. I sat up on the side of my bed and looked around the room. In the corner, next to my mother's bed, was the door to a French balcony. Tiny beams of moonlight shone through the glass door, enough for me to observe the furniture and the floor of polished green majolica tiles. There was a cabinet by one wall, a round table with a beautifully ornate tablecloth, two chairs around it, and to my surprise, a tall sink with a round mirror on top of it. Our suitcases lay wide open, our things thrown across the floor from when we arrived late the previous night.

I went to the balcony door, but there was nothing to see other than branches of a tree on the verge of flowering, concealing the view of the next house's courtyard. My stomach rumbled with hunger, or perhaps uncertainty. I thought of waking my mother so she could go and ask for some food from the kitchen, but the image of the woman who had opened the door for us the previous night came to my mind. Her rigid tone scared me more than the teachers at school. I didn't think she would be pleased to be bothered from her sleep again. I went back to bed and at last fell asleep.

Later, when I woke up, I found myself alone in the room. My mother's bed was neatly made and looked as if it had never been used. The suitcase was not on the floor anymore, and there was no sign of her in the room. The clothes I had worn were carefully folded on the chair. Had I been dreaming? Was my waking in the middle of the night just a trick of my imagination? What about the song that kept playing in my head over and over again? I forced myself to remember the events of the previous days—the scent of diesel from the days of traveling on the bus, which had made me drowsy, the interrogations at the borders, and the constant fear that we would have to return to the camp. It had been late at night when we finally stopped in Barcelona.

When the door of the bus opened, my mother and I were some of the first passengers to disembark. My legs felt numb as if I had forgotten how to walk, and I was painfully aware of my own odor, a sticky and sweaty scent. The noise of people in the streets and cars honking was a contrast to our days of travel. Just when we had picked up our suitcase, we heard someone yell my mother's name. From all the way down the street, my aunt, wearing a colorful T-shirt, waved at us with a hand holding a cigarette. She ran toward us and didn't stop yelling until she jumped into my mother's arms. When the crying stopped, I was finally introduced.

We walked the length of Las Ramblas as quickly as we could, my mother with the suitcase in her hand, Ana guiding us from in front, and I following them from behind. Men from all sides attempted to accost my mother and Ana, shouting at them. Women in revealing clothing stood at the street's edge. People were sleeping on the sidewalks. The whiffs of urine and sewer were everywhere.

Once we arrived at Plaça de Catalunya, Ana signaled to a yellow car and told us to get in. During the whole ride, my mother and Ana were talking in Romanian. The driver, not understanding their words, threw angry glances toward them, irritated. From the city center, the car took us uphill until we turned right, into a neighborhood of very small streets. The streets were so narrow that the car frequently had to maneuver or stop to allow pedestrians to pass on the side. At last, we stopped in front of a white house with a burgundy door and white grated glass windows. While Ana paid the taxi, we got out of the car and looked up, stunned at the hideous shape of the ornamental features above the main door. From its facade, the house seemed narrow but had several floors. The large front door was almost too big for its size.

Ana rang the doorbell repeatedly. A woman, dressed in an oversized nightgown and nightcap, opened the door, visibly irritated at having been disturbed from her sleep. She raised her tone at my aunt, but Ana didn't hold back, and soon the discussion became so heated that my mother and I wondered if the woman would even let us in. Eventually, she capitulated and showed the two of us up to the second floor, letting us into the only room there, where I had just woken up.

I got out of the bed, washed my face with cold water from the little round sink in the room, and got dressed. I left the room and continued down the few stairs to the floor below. Underneath, there was another hallway, similar to ours but longer and with two rooms. Moving on, I descended to the first floor. In front of me stood a French door I had noticed the day before, only today the curtains covering the glass windows on each half were pulled aside. Peeking through, I placed my hand on the golden metal door handle, which turned with a squeak, and I entered.

It seemed I was in the same hallway we had passed through upon our late arrival the other day. However, now I noticed a staircase on the left, leading up, which I had not seen before. French wooden floors stretched out beneath me, partially covered by a modest Italian rug. The air was laden with scents of wood, tobacco, and vanilla. I walked to the end of the hallway and turned right, down another smaller passage that led into a dining room. As I passed slowly, I took in the paintings on the walls, the tassel lamps, and the delicate vases, each depicting events from history.

In the middle of the dining room was a long table with rounded corners, surrounded by glass cabinets displaying various ornaments that looked as if they had been brought back from visits to foreign places. The dining room connected to an even larger room where seemingly thousands of books filled the shelves lining the walls and framed an unlit fireplace. Two heavy armchairs in burgundy leather, the color of wine, and a low round table faced the fireplace. A couch in the same leather and design sat against another wall.

Once inside the room, I exhaled a sigh of relief, for I knew at that moment I wasn't crazy. This was not a dream, and last night's melody was not just in my imagination. It had been real, as real as the startling voice that I now heard behind me.

"What are you doing here?" I thought the voice asked, but it was in a language I could barely understand.

Before the sudden interruption, I had only managed a quick glimpse of the grand piano sitting triumphantly by the right corner of the living room. I turned around to see a young girl, not more than a few years older than me, with her dark hair kept in a bun, tan skin, black eyes, and plump lips. Her round belly was clearly visible, even though her oversized uniform tried to cover it.

Caught in the act, all I could manage was "Aaa…" She seemed amused at the situation, took me by my right hand, and led me back through the rooms.

Once past the door I shouldn't have opened in the first place, I followed her down the steps to the level below. We entered a hallway with ceiling-height tile glass windows covering one wall. Plants and trees sat in pots and hung from the ceiling, giving the illusion of being in a greenhouse. From the previous day, I knew this hallway led to the kitchen and the door to the backyard, so I wondered whether I was going to be fed some breakfast or kicked out.

Luckily, the girl took me straight to the kitchen, where I found my mother cutting onions. Ms. Agueda, the lady who had opened the door for us, was supervising her from behind, using a tone I didn't like.

"There's my son," my mother said in Italian. "Thank you, Gloria," she added, pointing to one of the chairs. "Sit down, Alex!"

"Mama, I'm hungry," I whispered.

"Of course, of course," my mother replied, "I forgot about breakfast."

Ms. Agueda, as if she understood our language, went to the fridge and took out several plates of meats, cheeses, butter, and tomatoes. She then grabbed a baguette from the basket on top of the fridge and cut it on a wooden board in front of me. Breadcrumbs spread all over the small table, leaving a wonderful fresh and yeasty scent. Within a minute, Ms. Agueda had the table arranged for me and then continued her conversation with Gloria, gesturing toward the floors above.

41

LES DUES DONNES

Strange beds have been an issue for me ever since I last slept in my own back in Zimnicea, but this one irritated me the most. It was not positioned against a wall, and during my troubled slumbers at night, my pillow constantly fell to the floor, waking me up. Once awake, it was hard to fall back asleep. My mind drifted restlessly with memories of my childhood in Zimnicea and Izvoarele, when charcuterie, special types of cheeses, Lyonnaise salad, and smoked salmon were delicacies I never knew existed. I thought about the many times in the camp we had gone to bed cold and hungry, with not much hope for what the next day would bring.

Seeing my mother sleeping soundly was a relief, given her hard daily work assisting Ms. Agueda in the kitchen and helping Gloria around the house. In the evenings, we sat on her bed and talked in a hushed tone about her day, Ms. Agueda's sniping, and Gloria's visible eagerness to leave the house and her resentment toward Ms. Agueda. Oddly, to this day, she hadn't met Mr. Laurent—he never seemed to come down to the kitchen. Nor had Ms. Agueda offered to introduce her, since Gloria, pregnant as she was, was still considered reliable. My mother was on trial, for now.

Endless boredom and loneliness were the staple companions of my days. My only human contact was during the day's meals when I would go downstairs to the kitchen. The backyard was suggested to me as a place of recreation and to get some air, even though it looked like a forgotten part of the house, used just for its gated exit to the street behind. The stairs that flowed down from the house to the yard looked as if they were once part of a grand entrance to a ballroom but were now dirty and unkempt. Rusted metal objects were thrown haphazardly around the yard, sitting together with plants and trees that had dried and died long ago, much like my spirit.

To pass the time, I spent countless hours looking at our neighbor's garden from our room's window, wondering why their dog didn't chase their black cat, as usually happened back in Romania. I tried writing letters to people from the camp and my grandparents, only to crumple up the papers and throw them away. What could I possibly say about our new life when I couldn't understand much of it myself?

On one of those days, my thoughts were interrupted by a gentle knock at the door. When I opened it, I was met by Gloria holding a pocketbook in her hand. She was almost out of breath from the two flights of stairs, but once she was able to breathe more slowly, she started speaking so fast, as if I could understand everything she said. My confused look must've irritated her, for she stopped and simply handed me the book.

"*Gracias*," I answered and smiled politely.

After I closed the door, I threw myself on the bed and checked the book. Its corners were ruffled, and flicking through it I noticed pages stained with food, yet it had a beautiful blue cover with a yellow drawing on it. The title was *El Principito*. First, I looked at the drawings, then I started to read slowly, word by word, out loud.

It turned out that for a Romanian with a good knowledge of Italian, Spanish was not that hard to understand.

By four that Thursday afternoon, another surprising event occurred.

"Alex, guess what!" said my mother, storming into the room.

"What?"

"Ana is here. I told her to come and take you with her so you can get out of this room for a while."

"She is?" I asked, not matching her enthusiasm.

"Yes, yes, get dressed quickly. She's downstairs waiting for you," she said, looking through the closet for something presentable.

"Mama, do I have to?"

"Why? What's wrong? You prefer sitting here by yourself all day?"

"In a way… yes."

"Ana is here. If I tell her you're not coming, she'll think it's because of her. Just go for a walk, maybe an ice cream, and be back."

I got dressed as quickly as I could, fearing how uncomfortable I would feel in the presence of my aunt. I had met her just the one time, when she came to pick us up from the bus station, and it was enough to make me realize that she was way louder than my mother, and her energetic manner was entirely too much for me. Still, I followed my mother down the stairs, through the hallway, and out into the backyard. My aunt was waiting for us by the gate, smoking a cigarette. Her outfit looked so foreign to me: a casual long pleated skirt, a dark pink shirt, and sneakers.

"What took you so long?" she asked my mother, as soon as we approached the gate.

"Oh, stop it now! I can't fly, and this house has a lot of stairs," my mother answered back.

"How's it going in there?"

"It's… you know, working with Ms. Agueda…"

"She's famous for her bitterness."

"So, then you understand. I have to go. See you in a couple of hours?" my mother asked me and turned her attention to her sister. "Are you going for ice cream?"

"Yes, maybe we will. Don't you worry." Ana put an arm around me, as if I were a little boy.

The sky was light blue that day, and the streets were bustling with people going to and from work, frequently stopping and talking to friends and neighbors, while bicycles and cars drove by. For the first minutes while going down Carrer de Verdi, neither I nor my aunt said a single word, until:

"Listen, Alex, one of my girls at the bar decided to leave me all of a sudden, so I have to open by myself. That's how it is when you take care of ungrateful girls—they'll leave you when you need them the most."

I was confused because, in my head, I was already wondering what kind of flavors I should pick for my ice cream.

"I own a bar. Didn't your mother tell you?" Before I had a chance to reply, she stopped and stooped down to me. "I must be there before five to prepare for the opening, and if you help me until the other girl's shift starts, we can go for ice cream afterward."

"What can I help with? I don't understand." I tried to keep up with her as she had started walking again.

"To set up the bar." After a brief pause, while we stepped to the side to make space for a car driving by, she continued. "Alex, I have a feeling you'll love the place, and it would do you good to get out of that room. Why don't you write down the streets we pass by, so next time you can go by yourself?" She then went through her bag to find a pen and gave it to me. "I don't have a piece of paper, but write the names of the streets on the palm of your hand. We used to do that in school."

"I can't go there by myself. I've never been on these streets before."

"Alex, you have to learn to figure things out for yourself." She stopped walking again and turned to me, taking my chin in her palm, examining my face. "You remind me of a young boy, the son of Roger, who used to hang around the bar a few years ago. The girls used to call him *Bombonet*. He was your age or maybe younger. How old are you now?"

"Eleven," I said. "Almost twelve."

"Well, *Bombonet*, then you're a grown man! You can't hide behind your mother's skirts anymore. You're the only man left in her life now. You won't make it far if you don't know how to work."

Those were words I never anticipated hearing, but they woke up a range of emotions in me. I stared blankly at my aunt's curved nose and saw her intuitive brown eyes looking back at me, while I found myself fighting the urge to erupt in tears. But there was little time for that now, for she immediately handed me the pen and started dictating the streets. As she walked, she pointed out a few shops and bars I might keep in my memory, but I barely had time to write one down before we moved on to the next street.

"Now, repeat back to me what you've got so far," she said.

"I should walk down Carrer de Verdi all the way to the grocery store by the corner. Turn left into Carrer de la Providencia. Continue walking, then take the first to the right, down Carrer de Verntallat—easy to remember for the wine bar on the corner. Follow this road all the way down to the Iglesia, the church 'Saint Joan,' in the middle of a lively square full of bars, benches, and music."

"No stopping there!" she interrupted.

"Continue downward toward Carrer de Torrijos, until you get to the fruit and vegetable market. Walk a few hundred meters on that street, passing Bar Pietro, and then turn right onto Carrer de Bailen at the intersection. The bar is a kilometer away from there, on the corner of Bailen and Carrer de Valencia."

I was so confused by all the names and confident that I would never walk these streets by myself that I hardly gave any thought to what the bar might look like, until we stopped in front of it.

"There it is! Here we are," my aunt said.

From the outside, the only thing visible was a double

door covered by thick wooden shutters, closed with a big lock. My aunt opened the lock, lifted the shutters, and revealed the two glass doors behind them, artistically decorated with drawings of wine glasses, tapas, and musical notes. She carried a tall round table and two tall chairs from behind the doors and placed them outside. She flicked a switch on the wall inside, and a flickering red and yellow light, visible even in the day, illuminated a hand-painted sign above the door, saying, "Les Dues Donnes."

I read the name out loud in syllables.

42

THE RED AND YELLOW NEON LIGHTS

When I first set foot inside the bar, I was amazed by the size of the room. Who would've thought that behind two narrow doors there could hide such a large establishment?

Memories of its long history were imprinted in the marks on the worn wooden floors and white walls and on the rustic chairs scratched by numerous shoe heels. A heavy scent of tobacco mixed with alcohol greeted you as you entered. An old upright piano, in a rich brown color, stood against one wall, next to a cabinet filled with glasses.

From the entrance, I could see the bar desk, and behind it alcohol bottles in bright colors, like rows of lollipops, lined the recessed glass shelves. Above the bar and shelves, green molding in a gothic style framed a clock in the middle.

Ana went into a backroom, from where she brought a broom, a bucket with a mop, and several pieces of cloth. She told me to clean the floor and wipe the white marble tables that were now placed against a wall. After sweeping and mopping, I began lifting the tables back to their places around the room, and my aunt placed a candle and a siphon bottle on each.

"This is table four," she relayed to me, and at each subsequent table she mentioned its number for later. By my own counting, she had twelve white tables and forty chairs, plus three tall ones around the bar.

At five, she opened the doors. She put an LP on a player kept on the right side of the bar counter. Walking between the marbled tables, I imagined how it would feel if I actually owned the place. I was excited at the thought of the first customer's arrival—what they would order, and how many would come. I was impatient to be part of a lively scenario of grown-ups, as I had only seen in movies.

Luckily, I didn't have to wait long. Within half an hour, one by one, customers started to arrive. Some of them seemed so familiar with the bar as if it was their second home.

The red and yellow neon lights cast a warm glow through the glass doors and made the bottles on the shelves above the bar shine with light. On the tables, the lit candles gave a warm and mysterious feel. Soon, one could hardly make out the song playing over the murmur of conversations blending with the clink of glasses and the occasional laughter that punctuated the air.

My cheeks blushed every time my aunt stopped me at the bar to introduce me to one of her friends as "*Bombonet*" —"the nephew whom she is helping out," leaving me exhilarated at all the attention. Turns out she was right. I was going to love this place.

Around an hour later, two girls walked in together and went directly to the backroom, and my aunt followed. A few minutes later, the three of them came back out, looking flustered and mad. The girls had changed their clothes, now wearing white tops with a deep décolletage, lined with blue ruffles—the sight made me blush. I was introduced to Eulalia and Alba, who nodded at me politely before they made their way around the room.

Just when I thought the day couldn't get more interesting, an old man entered. He walked slowly, shifting his thin, petite body from one foot to the other. He wore a black suit with stripes and a black hat, which he placed on top of the piano. From his briefcase, he took out several sheets of music and arranged them on the music stand. Eulalia and Alba came to hug him, and my aunt brought him a glass of beer, a *caña*. He was Roger, the piano player, but before I had a chance to hear him play, my aunt started guiding me toward the door.

"It's time to go home, *Bombonet*."

"But it's not that late, can't I stay a little longer?" I pleaded, looking at the clock above the bar.

"No, it's late enough, and from now on it will get busy," she answered. "Your mother is probably already ready to kill me for keeping you in this bar for so long. I'll put you in a cab to take you home."

"Alone?"

"I'm afraid so. I have a bar to attend to."

Outside the bar, my aunt paused to talk with a group of men and women, smoking and chatting. Then, going to the side of the street, she whistled loudly a couple of times and held her hand up until a car stopped at the corner. She opened the rear door for me, gave the driver the address, and handed him a few pesetas. As the car started moving, I waved goodbye to my aunt, looking back through the window at the neon sign shining in the street.

When I opened the door to the house, I heard loud chatter coming from the kitchen. There, I found Gloria polishing a blue cabinet with a cloth, her eyes wandering from Ms. Agueda to my mother, who stood bent over the kitchen counter preparing the dinner.

Studying Ms. Agueda from the doorstep to the kitchen, I imagined I could feel the cold bitterness radiating from her wrinkled face. Her frowning eyebrows made her look all too serious, and her white hair was messily arranged as if she didn't have time to brush it in the morning.

"Dinner's not ready yet," Ms. Agueda said to my mother after she noticed me at the door.

My mother turned, came to me, and whispered, "You're back! You've been gone for three hours, if not more. How was it?"

"It was… interesting!" I answered.

"Why don't you go to your room and read the book Gloria gave you? Come down for dinner in an hour or so. It's not ready yet."

I went up the stairs to my room, thinking of what the day had unexpectedly turned into. Checking my palms for the names of the streets that hadn't fully rubbed off, I wrote down everything I could remember of the route we took.

43

A FAMILIAR TASTE

The following morning, feeling stuffed from finishing an *esmorzar de forquilla*, I began to help my mother with the dishes, while Gloria cleaned the table. Ms. Agueda walked into the kitchen with a plate in her hands, full of honey dripping from the comb she had cut from the beehive outside the cellar.

"Well?" she prompted, putting the plate on the table. "Go ahead, taste it! Shall we have some baguette to spread it on?"

Golden memories of my home country rushed back to me as the familiar sweetness of honey from the first spoon entered my mouth. Within an instant, I felt an urge to run through the flower-filled meadows of Izvoarele, to feel the warm sun on my skin, and breathe the fresh air of the forests.

Instead, for the time being, I was going with Gloria to the market for groceries. She picked up her shopping cart from outside, which was nothing but a long sack strapped to a two-wheeled dolly with a handlebar on top, and out the gate we went.

The narrow pathway outside led to the main street, passing the courtyards and gates of our neighbors. It was the middle of April, a day so perfectly warm and breezy that it had drawn Ms. Prudéncia from across the street to enjoy her glass of lemonade, reclining in her garden chair. She held a shiny foil reflector under her chin with her hands, and a pair of large sunglasses covered most of her face. She lifted her head to see who was walking by, and as we passed, Gloria waved at her without stopping.

In some parts of Gràcia, the yellow-brown houses blended in with the blooming pink and purple flowers spilling from branches over courtyard walls. Following behind Gloria, I walked down Carrer de Verdi, turned left on Carrer de Robí, then a quick right, until we arrived on Carrer del Torrent. The street was long and narrow, with houses of the same shape and size next to each other, painted in light shades of peach, blue, and green. Flowers and plants flowed from the first-floor balconies to almost touch the neighbors sitting on chairs by their front doors, chatting with each other.

"Have you ever met Mr. Laurent?" I asked Gloria.

"Yes, of course," she replied. "He's a strange man. One day he locks himself alone on the first floor, the next day he brings several people in for a party. But he's a great man. He just lets us be, never bothers us."

"He never comes down to the kitchen?"

"No, almost never. He's always busy with his own world and trusts that Ms. Agueda keeps control of everything." After a brief pause, she continued, "There used to be another girl, Guadalupe, but she couldn't stand working with her. I would've left too, if it wasn't for me getting pregnant and needing the money. I don't even know if Mr. Laurent is aware she left." She shrugged her shoulders.

When we turned left onto Carrer de Tordera, we saw a group of women gathered in front of a shop. The crowd extended all the way to the middle of the street, making it hard for trucks and cars to pass by.

"Here!" Gloria said. She stopped, and her eyes ran over the crowd in front of the butcher shop.

Cansaladeria Andreu had several blackboards hung on the facade, with offerings of the day. On a board to the left of the entrance was written:

Chorizo casero de Alcazar de San Juan—todo lomo de zerda criada en buen corral 17.99 pesos/100 gramos.

Above, another board had a text I hardly understood:

La miel que rejuveneze fabricada por la abeja real alarga la vida y mantiene la piel tie sa; los baturros nunca mienten 140 pts el kilazo.

Two refrigerated display cases were open onto the street, each containing an abundance of meats, sausages, cheese, olives, and other delicacies. An old man with three slick pieces of hair combed over from one side to the other served behind the left desk, and a tall middle-aged woman served the impatient clientele from the other.

Without any thought for the queue ahead of her, Gloria pushed ahead with her pregnant belly in front, nodding and smiling from left to right at the women. Most of them kindly made space for us to pass. At the counter, Gloria took her time to chat and bargain about the price with the man, whom I learned was the owner, Andreu. The playful banter and negotiation of prices took a long time before Andreu finished weighing the goods on his ancient grocery scale. I didn't dare turn around to face the crowd and let out a sigh of relief when, at last, I could put all the paper-wrapped purchases into the cart.

"Is he always this slow?" I asked after we parted with the crowd by the butcher shop.

"Slow? No, *niño*! This is how things are done here in the neighborhood. You stay and talk to them, especially if you're daily customers like we are."

"What about the rest of the women who were waiting there before you?"

"What's with them? They also stay and talk when their turn comes. Why shouldn't I?"

I remained silent, thinking of the times my mother would wait in the queue at the *alimentară* for hours and hours for a kilo of flour and sugar, no matter the weather, only to be served quickly and with disdain.

Dragging the wheeled shopping sack after me, we made our way to a grocery store on the other side of the neighborhood. As we turned right into a street full of houses under construction, the air felt saturated with dust and the scent of cement. Graffiti and flags were predominant on walls, and I stopped to read one of the texts:

Queremos el piso nuevo que el ayuntamiento nos prometió, no podemos esperar más.[1]

Several men slept on the side of the street, using bags of cement as pillows. Next to them, another group of men were working.

---

1. We want the new homes the City Council promised us, we can't wait any longer.

"Let's go, Alex." Gloria took me by the shoulder.

A few shops later, I found myself struggling to pull the heavy dolly up the stairs at the back of the house, with Gloria breathing heavily behind me. Up in the kitchen, I was unloading the cart and telling my mother all I had seen, when Ms. Agueda heard me and offered to take me with her next time she went for groceries. I smiled and nodded politely, swallowed a lump, and regretted letting my enthusiasm shine through.

On April 23, Catalonia celebrated Diada de Sant Jordi. On this day, men and women exchanged roses and books. It was a day dedicated to two important matters in life: love and literature. But for Ms. Agueda, this day was even more significant, and she had been talking about it for the last few days. Her plan was to meet with two of her friends and walk down to Las Ramblas, where people would gather dressed in medieval costumes. There would be shows, traditional dances, and songs. Later, the crowd would move to Plaça Sant Jaume, where the president of Catalonia was expected to make a speech.

Anticipating and wanting to avoid the crowds of people celebrating in the streets, Mr. Laurent had escaped to the beachside, and Gloria went to spend her day with her soon-to-be husband and his family. My mother and I were finally alone in the house.

"Take that yellow cloth, dip it in that bucket, and help me wipe these cabinets," my mother said. "Don't just stay and look at me."

"Always make sure you don't come empty-handed from the tables!" My aunt's voice came back to me when I heard my mother's orders.

I rolled up my sleeves, soaked the cloth in the water, and

wrung it with all my power. I took a chair, crawled up on it, and started wiping the cabinets from top to bottom.

The sound of a door abruptly closing made us stop and look at each other, startled. Had Gloria or Ms. Agueda returned so soon? They left less than an hour ago.

"Eva? Alex?" A voice sounded from the hallway. My mother and I wiped our hands on a dry cloth and went to meet our intruder: my aunt, Ana.

"I brought Coca de Llavaneres and half a bottle of Anis del Mono." She held the treats up, one in each hand.

"Liquor? Only you could bring such a thing." My mother laughed. "I'll take the cake."

"What? Have you stopped drinking now?"

"Ana, shhh." She made a sign to her sister. "Don't say these things in front of Alex. And no, I wouldn't have stopped if I had some."

Within minutes, the kitchen table was arranged with a white tablecloth embroidered with yellow flowers. My mother found plates and glasses for the three of us and put the cake in the middle. Despite the liquor's alluring scent, I didn't dare ask my mother for a taste after what happened in my grandfather's basement with Ionuț, and instead satisfied myself with a glass of orange soda and a slice of cake.

I sat on my chair between them, hoping to be part of their "grown-up" talk, but they became so wrapped up in their conversation, reminiscing on stories from their past and hopes for the future, that they hardly noticed my presence. Looking at them, it felt as if the years that had gone by did nothing to damage their relationship. It was rather as if two old friends were reuniting after a long time apart.

With no greater opportunity than the present, I slowly

got up from the chair and went out of the kitchen. When I opened the French doors upstairs, the scent of furniture polish mixed with a men's cologne dominated the doorway, as if Mr. Laurent was present in front of me. I did a great deal of browsing around the rooms, looking around without focusing on anything in particular, because the only thing my eyes were searching for was the grand piano.

I could sense its imperious presence close by as I made my way toward the living room, where it was sitting in plain sight, facing the considerable number of books on the shelves. Next to the piano, a small corner table held several ruffled music sheets placed casually, and a used theater ticket to a show called *Replika al Liure* from April 20 lay on top.

I ran my fingers over the piano's body, touching its elegant, curved shape, as if trying to feel its pulse. The wood, polished to a reflective sheen, revealed dark chocolate hues that mirrored the wooden bookcases in front of it. Battling a mix of urgency and inevitability, I sat down on the burgundy leather chair in front of the instrument and was surprisingly met with a feeling of interior calm. I read aloud the text inscribed above the keyboard in golden handwritten calligraphy:

"Gustav Ignaz Stingl."

At first, I brushed the fingers of my right hand over the keys, one at a time, feeling their tones vibrate in my ear. Then, as I added my left hand, my fingers tensed, pressing several keys at a time, rapidly as if I couldn't control them anymore. The sound was unrhythmical and loud, bothering my ears but animating my imagination, which was already picturing me on a stage, in front of thousands of people witnessing my concert.

"Alexandru, what are you doing? Do you want to get me fired?" my mother snapped at me as she entered the room.

"I'm not doing anything, I just touched it for a second."

"Come down to the kitchen." She waved for me to follow her. "I hadn't even seen you sneaking out on us. What if Ms. Agueda had come home early and caught you touching Mr. Laurent's piano?"

"*În pisicii măsii*," I said under my breath.

"What did you say?" My mother turned around.

"Nothing."

44

BOMBONET

Sitting comfortably in my chair by the door of our balcony, I flipped through the pages of a children's book by Samaniego, lent to me by Gloria. My attention shifted from the book when, from the corner of my eye, I noticed a figure moving across the neighbor's lot. I had seen him many times before: a boy around my age with unusually long curly hair, wearing a school uniform that seemed too small for him. He closed the door to the house behind him and slowly walked along the path next to the flower beds, which looked as if they hadn't been maintained for years. With his hands in his pockets, he surveyed the expansive lawn in front of him, where grass grew tall and unruly. After a couple of minutes, an older woman, whom I suspected was the maid, came out and brought him a plate of food. Some days he would eat quickly, standing up, but this time he chose to sit down by the dirty garden table, underneath an old, thick tree. There were days when a girl, perhaps his sister, would join him. Unlike him, she seemed energetic and joyful, her colorful laugh often filling the yard.

Watching them play, I felt a pang of loneliness, reflecting on how my childhood was slipping away, leaving me with nothing but memories of years past.

To escape the confinement of my room and with an ulterior motive, I asked my mother if I could take a walk around the streets of the neighborhood, promising to return within an hour or two.

"It's already late, and it will soon be dark outside. Why not wait until tomorrow, and we can go together?" my mother suggested.

"I'm just bored in my room. I watch the kids running and playing across from our backyard, while I'm stuck inside that attic room all day. I promise I won't be long."

"Why don't you go and introduce yourself to them?"

"To the kids? I don't want to play with them. I don't even speak their language. I just want to get out of that room."

"Fine. Go! But if it gets dark and you're not back..." she said.

I kissed her cheek and waved goodbye, ignoring the tired look in her eyes, a testament to the weeks she had spent constantly on her feet. Turning the corner to Carrer de Verdi, I saw a sidecar motorcycle parked by the entrance to our door, a sign that Mr. Laurent was home. Across the street, an old man wearing an oversized jumpsuit in a washed-out blue color, with a striped T-shirt underneath, leaned by the door to his shop, watching me. When I returned his gaze, he turned and went inside.

Above the door, a wide sign proclaimed:

Atelier Mateo: Restauración, barnizados, reparación de sabates, qualsevol altra cosa.

From inside, unknown yet appealing music played so loudly from a record player that it echoed throughout the whole street. The windows were so dirty that it was hard to see inside without first wiping them with my hand. By the look of the wooden foot-shaped form sitting on a table and a tangle of soles around it, I assumed he was a cobbler, but with all the chaos inside it was hard to say exactly what his profession was. Eventually, he turned around and caught me staring. Startled, I stumbled backward into the street, where a scooter honked at me as it sped past.

I ran down the street, my heart pounding in my chest as I reconsidered the recklessness of walking to my aunt's bar all by myself. After a few hundred meters, I stopped and bent over with my hands on my knees, trying to catch my breath.

But just as I was about to abandon my plan, I saw the familiar sight of a wine bar, where the owner was carrying chairs outside, preparing for opening. Above it, the street sign on the wall read "Carrer de Verntallat." I looked at the crumpled paper with instructions that I carried in my pocket and realized I was close to the square with the Church of Saint Joan.

From there, I knew I could easily find my aunt's bar.

The sun was setting, painting the sky in shades of bourbon and ash. Even though obscured by a mist of tobacco smoke from the people standing outside, the sign "Les Dues Donnes" above the door could still be made out from afar.

To get inside, I squeezed between four men smoking by the tall table at the entrance. It must've been later than I thought, for the atmosphere was in full swing, and Roger was already playing. Alba, dressed in a white top with blue ruffles and tight pants, leaned against the bar desk, fiddling with a customer's green tie. They seemed intimate, her right knee playfully brushing against his legs.

My Aunt Ana, with her short hair arranged in a small bun, was behind the bar, expertly swirling bottles left and right, preparing drinks for Eulalia to take to the tables.

"*Bombonet*, what are you doing here?" she shouted when she saw me.

"I thought I'd come to visit you and ask if you need any help," I answered, somewhat disappointed by her unwelcoming look.

"I can't have a child here at this hour, Alex," she said. "There's smoke and people drinking. You can come and help me during the early hours of opening, but not now."

"He could help me! I have so much to do, and Alba is wasting time with her usual customer," Eulalia said from the other side of the bar desk.

"She's not wasting time, you know that!" my aunt answered.

With a dismissive look in her eyes, Eulalia picked up a tray of drinks and went to deliver them around the room. Ignoring my aunt's remarks, I followed Eulalia, admiring her tall and slender figure, reminiscent of a lanky Florentine figurine. Her long, straight black hair flowed down her back, and her red lips starkly contrasted with her pale complexion. When I first met her a few days ago, my initial reaction was one of nervousness. She rarely smiled, and she spoke in an authoritative manner, which I found intimidating. However, as we worked together, clearing tables of empty glasses and plates with crumbs and leftovers, I found myself increasingly captivated by her presence.

The atmosphere of the bar rose when Roger gave a loud shout, snapped his fingers, and yelled, "*Uno, dos, tres, cuatro!*"

The keys of the piano started moving under the sturdy

urgency of Roger's fingers, with unexpected rhythmic changes. Just as suddenly as it began, the song ended when Roger held the final chord with the help of the right pedal, allowing his voice to fill the large room until everyone stopped talking and turned to look at him.

"*Bombonet*, does your mother know you're not home?" My aunt came up behind me as I leaned on the bar, watching Roger play.

"She knows I'm out of the house. She gave me permission."

"She gave you permission to do what? To come here? I don't think so!"

"I told her I'm taking a walk around the streets for an hour or two," I replied.

"An hour or two? She must be worried sick about you, thinking something might have happened," she yelled at me, her eyes ablaze with concern. "I'm sending you home, now!"

Furiously, she left her place in front of the alcohol bottles behind the counter, took the empty tray from my hands, and led me toward the street. As we made our way out, I took one last look around the room, hoping to catch a glimpse of Eulalia, but to no avail. My aunt hailed a cab for me, and just as I was being pushed into the back of the car, someone softly touched my hand. I turned to see Eulalia, who had followed me out, to tell me, "Thank you for the help, *Bombonet*." She smiled and winked at me playfully before running back inside.

My aunt closed the car door, paid the driver, and went back inside without a backward glance. As the cab drove off, I feared what my mother would say about my late return, but my thoughts were consumed by Eulalia. That night, I lay in bed with my right cheek red and burning from my mother's hand, but my mind was filled with thoughts of nothing but Eulalia. The nickname *Bombonet* had a different appeal, especially when it came from her.

45

MEETING MR. LAURENT

During those first weeks in the new city, the sun never abandoned us, shining like a golden ball from a clear blue sky. The view from the balcony window became more and more obscured by the pink magnolia tree that grew thickly in front of it, making it hard for me to see the neighbor's boy, who had taken up a new pastime these last days: smoking.

On a Friday evening, I was sitting on my bed reading and occasionally thinking of Eulalia, when noise coming from somewhere on the main floor distracted me. The talk of the kitchen had been that Mr. Laurent would celebrate a well-achieved triumph in the art society of Barcelona with a group of friends over dinner. Nonetheless, the more I listened to the laughter and talking, the more I became aware of the sound of screams coming from another part of the house: the kitchen.

I closed the book, placing the black-and-white photograph from my Christmas in the camp between the last two pages I had read, and ran downstairs. Steam and a heavy scent of boiled meat filled the hallway to the kitchen. There, I saw Gloria sitting on a chair, legs apart, hands on her pregnant belly, with water all over the tile floor beneath her. Her black hair, usually tied tight in a ponytail, was now in complete disarray. Her face was sweaty, and her eyes were wet and puffy from crying. My mother sat on her knees next to her, wiping her face with a moist cloth and helping her breathe. As soon as she saw me entering, she told me to take a mop from the corner of the room and clean the floor.

"I called Doctor Aleu several times. No answer," said Ms. Agueda as she rushed into the kitchen. "Ms. Eva, the marrow and sauce are ruined now."

"She's in a lot of pain!" my mother answered.

Ms. Agueda went to the cooktop, turned off the gas under the boiling pan, and began chopping the greens. Occasionally, she would turn around to glance at Gloria, a worried expression on her face.

"Ms. Eva, please let your son know this is not a good time for a fourth person to be in the kitchen! We have enough to worry about right now," she said to my mother in a low tone, as I finished cleaning the floor.

"What are we going to do about Gloria?" my mother asked. "She needs a doctor urgently! Are there any others close by?"

Gloria started on yet another round of screams, holding her belly with one hand and my mother's left arm with the other. Together, they tried to slow her breathing, one deep breath at a time.

"My doctor is Doctor Aleu—I don't know anybody else," said Gloria between breaths.

"Oh!" Ms. Agueda gasped. "I think I know someone! She's a nurse, not a doctor, but I assume she has experience with births as well."

"Can we call her then? Where does she live?" my mother asked, looking up toward Ms. Agueda.

"She lives ten minutes' walk from here, but I don't have her number. I can give you directions, and you can take her there."

"What's happening here? Ms. Gloria, are you alright?"

A male voice made everyone's eyes turn toward the door. The unanticipated arrival of Mr. Laurent in the kitchen took everyone by surprise. With his shirt collar halfway unbuttoned and his cheeks flushed with color, it looked like the gathering upstairs was well underway. He walked straight toward Gloria's chair, bent down on his knees next to my mother, and took Gloria's other hand.

"I think it's time, Mr. Laurent. I'm giving birth!" Gloria said in a painful tone.

"We must take you to the hospital, then," he suggested, getting back up.

"Ms. Agueda knows someone close by who might be able to help her," my mother said.

"I'm sorry, who are you?" he asked.

"She's the new maid, Ms. Eva. She's here to replace Ms. Gloria," Ms. Agueda answered before my mother had a chance to open her mouth. "And he," she said, pointing toward me leaning by the wall of the kitchen, "is her son, Alexandru—Alex."

"I see!" Mr. Laurent said, looking confused at Ms. Agueda, then nodding to me and my mother. "Well, then, Ms. Agueda, why don't you and I help Ms. Gloria to the person you've mentioned?"

"Me? But I must start all over again with dinner. The sauce is split, and your guests are waiting," said Ms. Agueda.

"Ms. Eva can stay here with her son and prepare something for the guests."

"But she hasn't learned my recipes yet," Ms. Agueda insisted.

"Then she can cook whatever she desires," he said, gesturing to Ms. Agueda to get her going.

While Mr. Laurent helped Gloria from the chair, Ms. Agueda took off her apron and threw it in the corner of the counter, then followed them. Alone in the kitchen, my mother and I looked at each other in complete awe of what we had just witnessed.

"What do I cook?" my mother asked, mostly to herself.

"Something you know, from home?"

I cleared the pots of Ms. Agueda's unfinished *Os à Moelle* and cleaned the kitchen counter while my mother took ingredients out of the fridge and placed them on the counter: mushrooms, onion, chicken breast, sour cream, and butter. The result was not the sophisticated French cuisine the guests were used to, but my mother's dish was still pleasantly received by the guests, who were polishing the sauce from their plates with the remaining pieces of bread when I entered to clear the table.

Not long after we had cleaned the kitchen, as we were setting the little table for us to eat, Mr. Laurent returned.

"Mr. Laurent, we were just about to have dinner. Your guests have already eaten," my mother answered. "How is Gloria?"

"Gloria will be fine. At this moment, she's delivering her son. Ms. Agueda will stay with her for now."

"That's great news. Poor Gloria. I don't know what we would've done if Ms. Agueda hadn't known someone who could help."

"True, then I would have driven her to the hospital," he said, putting his hand inside his pockets and looking down at his shoes without saying anything else.

"Would you like some dinner, sir?"

"Yes, that would be nice, it smells very tempting."

"Should I bring the plate upstairs so you can be with your guests?"

"I was hoping I could eat here with the two of you. I'm a bit tired of loud company."

"Then please have a seat," my mother said, gesturing toward the empty chair at the table.

Carefully, he made his way around the kitchen, admiring the light blue cabinets and the china bought by his late mother, the flowers hanging by the window just like in old times, the silver trophy cup on top of the fridge from a long-forgotten award, and his mother's flower-decorated enamel bowl filled with fruits and vegetables sitting on the counter. It was as if he was seeing them for the first time. He pulled out the chair between my mother and me and sat down.

"Alex, you know where the cellar is?"

"Yes, I do," I said, having secretly browsed his wine collection the day I found out where the door behind the stairs led to.

"Bring me a Sauvignon Blanc, maybe a Château Filhot, please."

Mr. Laurent's voice had the deep tone of someone who had smoked many cigarettes in his time. He spoke Spanish with a strong French accent, making it hard for us to understand at first. I ran quickly down the stairs to the courtyard and through the door to the cellar behind. After finding the right bottle, I grabbed it and hurried back, eager to be a part of the dinner.

Before I entered the kitchen, I hesitated for a few seconds, looking at the scene inside. At the small table, under the now dimmed kitchen lights, Mr. Laurent sat with his right hand on his hip, his body turned in my mother's direction, giving her his full attention. He had an intriguing face, with strong features, a crooked and overgrown V-shaped mustache that covered his lips, and full, thick curly hair that spread widely, covering most of his ears. When he smiled, a few golden teeth were visible on one side. His eyes were focused on my mother's lips and gestures, doing his best to understand her. She, on the other hand, struggled to explain herself, using a mix of the Italian she had learned in the camp and what Spanish she had picked up from the kitchen.

I came in just as my mother had started the story about when she decided to leave our country. Following his advice, I put the bottle of wine in a bucket of ice as my mother served dinner. Mr. Laurent said very little, allowing my mother and me the chance to speak uninterrupted, only asking a few questions here and there.

At last, he thanked us for the evening and excused himself to attend to the guests, left in the sacred company of wine and music. Just as he was about to leave the room, my mother called after him:

"Mr. Laurent! Could I use the house phone to call my parents in Romania?" she asked, gesturing with her hand, imitating a phone placed by her ear.

"You can use it anytime you want—you don't need to ask my permission," he answered and wished us a good night.

When I was small, we were often told stories of an angel patrolling the night, checking on the people in each house. The story was that he could read people's innermost thoughts, and if they were good he blessed them with happy dreams, but if they were bad… he would not allow them any dreams at all. And if by chance these fairytales were real, when he would stop above the white house with burgundy frames on Carrer de Verdi, he would see three people lying with their heads on their pillows, unable to sleep.

One was thinking of the last time he visited a bar and saw the girl he liked. One was tired and content from her employer's praise and attention. The third one was tossing and turning, thinking of the encounter with his new maid.

The only soul that would be without dreams that night was the one not entirely pleased that the situation had been handled well enough in her absence: Ms. Agueda.

46

JE SUIS FOUTU

Mr. Laurent woke at half past eight to the sound of two truck drivers arguing in the street while unloading their goods. With half-opened eyes, he pulled off the covers and climbed out of bed. He picked up his green robe from the chair where he had thrown it the previous night, then put on his slippers and went out of the bedroom. As was his custom, he loudly shut the door to let Ms. Agueda know that he was now awake.

The place where he usually took his breakfast was nothing but a small room that connected his bedroom to his office. Several decorations and ornaments sat on shelves hanging on walls dominated by wooden panels, as in the rest of the house. On a wall between the windows hung *La Régalade*,[1] a painting by Édouard Manet. In the middle of the room was a round glass table and two armchairs, strategically placed in front of the windows, where the sun shone the most.

1. *La Régalade* – *Boy with Pitcher*

The *El Nacional* and *France Soir* newspapers had already been laid out on the table for him. He sat down in one of the chairs, took one of the papers, and glanced over the headlines on the front page without paying much attention. He let it slide from his fingers and stared into the sunlight, lost in thought.

Recalling his encounter with the new maid last night and everything she had said over dinner, he tried to remember her face and what drew him to her, but all he could remember was the lively look in her blue eyes, her smile, and her full lips. In a way, her experiences made him feel inferior, thinking that he had more to learn from her than the other way around, as it usually was with the other women he had in his life.

"That's what this is all about!" he said out loud to himself. "Her story is just different—it's the story that intrigues me."

He didn't even know how long he had been sitting there contemplating when Ms. Agueda knocked at the door, startling him.

"Good morning, Mr. Laurent. How did you sleep?" she asked. Backing into the room with her round backside first, then the rest following, she carried a silver tray with breakfast and coffee.

Watching Ms. Agueda enter, he remembered yet another situation that he had to deal with that day and felt deeply uncomfortable.

"Good morning. I slept well, thank you," he said, picking up the paper again.

With the tray placed on the table, Ms. Agueda poured coffee from the pot, added a small spoon of cream, and handed him the cup. On a different plate, she had two croissants, jam, butter, and a slice of crisp apple tart that she had made that morning. Now, the room smelled of freshly brewed coffee and apple tart, and so delightful was the atmosphere that Mr. Laurent almost felt lonely not having anyone to share it with.

"How is Ms. Gloria feeling?" Mr. Laurent asked. "Tell me about her newborn."

"She's feeling fine. She gave birth this morning at three forty-five, and struggled all night, the poor woman. The boy was so small, with dark hair just like hers, and round, puffy cheeks—those I think he got from his father, who, by the way, also managed to arrive at last. Today they will be a new family, even if they're not married yet."

"What time did you get back then?"

"At around four-thirty," she answered from the bedroom, while pulling the curtains to the side and opening the windows.

"Why didn't you sleep in then? I'm sure Ms. Eva could have brought breakfast for me."

"Of course she could," answered Ms. Agueda with a forced smile on her face, "but I wasn't tired. How was last night? Did you and your friends have a good time?"

"It went perfectly fine. Ms. Eva cooked and managed very well. I was impressed," Mr. Laurent said, following her into the bedroom.

At this, Ms. Agueda didn't have anything else to add and, not wanting to hear more praise about Ms. Eva, she started to make the bed.

"I must ask, how come Ms. Eva's been living in my house for a few weeks and I was not introduced to her?"

"She hasn't been here that long, and you haven't been home much, sir. I thought I would find the proper time to do so," she answered.

"Still, I think there should have been many right

moments to introduce me to a new person who lives under my roof, and especially a mother with a teenage son."

"Sorry, Mr. Laurent. Truth be told, I was unsure whether she would be a good substitute for Gloria. She seems to have her head in the clouds sometimes. Very difficult to deal with—her Spanish has only now improved."

"Last night, she managed very well—friendly enough with my friends, and they loved her food."

He went to the window and looked outside.

"Tell me, Ms. Agueda, what's the boy doing while she's working? Does he stay in the kitchen?"

"He mostly stays in his room or outside in the courtyard. Sometimes, he visits his aunt, who has a bar. It was through her that I was recommended Ms. Eva."

"What kind of bar is that?"

"I heard from a neighbor across the street." She paused, looked around, and continued in a lower tone. "It has a reputation. It's called something with *dones*, but I never go to those kinds of places. Imagine someone like him hanging around drunks and girls. But I guess it's normal in their culture, there in Romania."

"Les Dues Donnes?"

"Could be."

"How much are you paying her per month?"

"Fifteen thousand pesetas."

"That's less than what Ms. Gloria gets."

"Yes, but Gloria's an experienced cook. She's been here for more than two years."

"You must give her at least what you gave to Ms. Gloria," he interrupted her. "Keep in mind she also has a child to maintain."

His request left Ms. Agueda rather annoyed, and she sensed that Mr. Laurent was not done talking yet.

"Is the boy not going to enroll in school at least?"

"I have no idea what they will do. It's their business."

"Between us, I would like you to set aside a small sum of three thousand pesetas each month for his education, whatever or whenever his mother decides it will be."

"But, Mr. Laurent, that's unnecessary! You barely know..."

"I don't want to hear it," Mr. Laurent stopped her. "For as long as the kid lives under my roof, he deserves the chance of an education. I trust you to make sure they feel welcome and part of the household."

Ending the conversation, Mr. Laurent walked out of the room without closing the door, leaving Ms. Agueda in shock, holding a pillow in her hands, watching her master leave. After she finished the bedroom, she returned to the kitchen without saying a single word.

Oh, what is wrong with you, Laurent! Why did you have to get involved in that boy's future? These ideas have got to stop, this was a reckless initiative, he thought to himself, shaking his head in dismay.

He leaned back in his chair and surveyed the room, watching the particles of dust floating in the air, now visible against the sunlight. Ahead of him was a wooden cabinet with four wide shelves, packed with folders and documents, books about art, and drawings from last month's gallery preparations. He had no further use for them, but he couldn't bring himself to go through them. Piled in a corner was his hiking gear, boots, and a leather backpack that he rarely used.

His eyes stopped and reflected on the black-and-white photograph of his late parents, framed in rough pine. The photograph showed his parents on one of their vacations, his father with a thick mustache, the kind that he aspired to grow, smoking a cigarette, wearing short safari pants and his hunting hat. Next to him was Laurent's mother, Amélie, in a long summer dress, leaning against his father's shoulder with a big smile.

They used to be so happy, those two, he thought to himself. "Love is but a treasure that not everyone will find," his father used to say.

On the table next to him sat a pack of opened envelopes containing letters from his sister in France, that he did not have the will to answer.

Shaking his head, he snapped out of the moment and started planning the day ahead. A quick trip to the barber. Lunch at 7 Portes with Louis from Galería Joan Prats. Maybe he could sign with a new client. A new client, more work. Losing himself in work, this was the plan! Keeping himself busy with other matters, important matters, not some silly crush. Within a week, he would laugh at himself for spending a sleepless night romanticizing and thinking about, of all women, one of his maids.

This determination seemed to give Mr. Laurent some satisfaction, and he was enjoying it until a soft knock sounded at his door and Ms. Eva entered, displaying a soft smile toward him.

"Mr. Laurent, Ms. Agueda told me to come pick up your breakfast tray. I hope you don't mind."

Mr. Laurent's heart started to beat so fast that it felt like it was about to jump out of his chest. Sitting in his chair, he found himself covering his pajamas with his robe, feeling ashamed to be seen unwashed and unshaved in front of her, his curly hair unbrushed and unruly.

"Yes, of course, Ms. Eva. I'm done with breakfast."

"You haven't touched your croissants," she mentioned.

"I'm not that hungry today. You may take the tray." He gestured.

Since it was the first time Ms. Eva had visited the first floor, she took her time to admire every antique piece, vase, and decor that caught her eye, with uninvited excitement.

As much as Mr. Laurent felt drawn by her company, at that moment, he was cursing his mother's taste, collecting as many things as she could, and placing them on shelves.

Sensing that Mr. Laurent was not much for talking that morning, she left, leaving him sitting in his chair, looking more worried than ever.

"*Je suis foutu*," he said under his breath.

47

PLAÇA REIAL

"What do you mean they came to the house? Have they taken something?"

"Mama, let me talk! I want to talk to her as well." I pulled the sleeve of my mother's uniform.

"*Aham, da,* and they took all your chickens? What about the firewood?" she asked.

"You're using all our minutes and not saving even one for me," I insisted, pacing back and forth around her.

"Alex, stop it! I can't hear anything with you nagging me. Wait for your turn."

The phone sat on a round table in the entrance hallway, right next to the stairs to the first floor. Ms. Agueda was working in the room next to us, thoroughly dusting one of the antique vases, occasionally glancing in our direction.

"I wish I could send you money, but I can't exchange for lei here, and if I send you pesetas, they'll probably confiscate them," my mother said.

"Mama, please!"

"Fine, take the phone," she yelled at me. "Mother, I'll go

now. Your impatient grandson won't let me talk. I'll try to see when I can call you again."

"*Mămaie?*" I finally had the phone.

"Alex! Alex, how are you doing?" Her voice was tired and hoarse, as if she had just woken up. My mother leaned on the wall next to me, with her arms crossed, looking down at the parquet floor.

"*Mămaie*, we're good, but we miss you. Is *Tătaie* with you?"

"No, he left for the garden this morning. Valentina hurt her leg the other day when one of the dogs barked at them. He has only Țugui today."

"Is Mr. Constantin coming to look at her leg?"

"He doesn't live in Izvoarele anymore. He had to move to Alexandria."

"Mr. Constantin? But he's been there all his life! How could he move? What about his house and the grounds?"

"He left with only a few things on his back. It wasn't really his choice. Guess what?"

"What?"

"His daughter!" she said, laughing. "In the end, she married Grigore, Kabucs' boy. Remember Constantin swore to the whole village that it would never happen, but it did. They also had to leave the village."

"Why did they have to move? Why couldn't they stay in Izvoarele?"

"Ehh, politics, Alexandru. Politics." She sighed. "What are you doing? Are you in school?"

"No, not yet. We're staying in a big house. I'm mostly in my room, but sometimes I go out. Mama works all day, and at night she snores." I smiled at my mother.

"She got that from her father," my grandmother said in

a voice that sounded like a mix of laughter and crying. "I hope you're helping her. She needs you."

Ms. Agueda passed by us, clearing her throat loudly.

"We're always thinking about you. Remember to eat! You were so skinny when you left," my grandmother continued.

"We have to go, *Mămaie*, but I'll write to you. Take care of yourself and *Tătaie*."

"I pray for you both every night. May God be with you two." She ended the call.

As soon as I put the receiver down, I hugged my mother tightly, wetting her uniform shirt with my tears. My mother's blue uniform and white apron reeked of fried onions and cooked meat. She patted my head, keeping her chin close to my ear.

We must've been caught up in our own world, for when we let go of each other, we noticed Mr. Laurent standing at the bottom of the staircase, looking at us. He was dressed as if he couldn't be bothered that day, holding a brown leather suitcase in one hand, and a briefcase and a hat in the other.

"Mr. Laurent, are you going somewhere?" my mother asked.

Mr. Laurent didn't seem to hear her.

"Mr. Laurent?" My mother took a few steps toward him.

"Yes. Was everything alright with the phone call?" he asked.

"Yes, everything was fine. It's hard to understand what's going on there from a phone call, but we're grateful for you letting us speak to them."

"Mr. Laurent, where are you going? I didn't hear you!" Ms. Agueda's voice sounded behind us.

"I'll be gone for a few days. I'm going to see my sister and then to Paris."

"I didn't know you were planning to travel."

"I wasn't planning. I just thought of it last night. I'll see you when I'm back."

"When will you return?" Ms. Agueda insisted.

"I'll call a day ahead," he answered. "I have to go—my car is waiting outside."

He put his hat on, gave a slight bow toward us, picked up his suitcase where he had placed it on the floor, turned around, and went out the door.

In the days that followed, a gloomy silence descended over the house. Even though Mr. Laurent was rarely seen, his absence was felt throughout the entire house. The sound of doors closing and shoes walking over the wooden floor, late-night melodies on the piano, and the occasional gatherings with his friends were now replaced with the sounds of brooms sweeping, the squealing sound of cloth polishing the furniture, and the mop washing the floors. With Mr. Laurent away, Ms. Agueda's tight grip relaxed, allowing my mother and herself some time off.

By the end of May, I could really feel the warmth of summer settling over the city. I was leaning on the frame of the balcony door when my mother entered the room out of breath, holding several banknotes in her hand.

"Guess who got her first salary?"

With the bills in her hands, she danced and twirled around the room, as if she had won the lottery. Three times, we counted the money laid out on her bed. We then split it into three piles: one for us, one to send to my grandparents, and one to be kept *la saltea*, for rainy days. The next day, my mother and I took our first trip together into the city center.

It cost us fifteen pesetas each for a ticket from the station in Gràcia to Plaça de Catalunya, where we spent the first half hour gazing up at the tall buildings surrounding the plaza. From Plaça de Catalunya, we went down Las Ramblas. My mother stopped to look at or enter almost every shop on the way, bargaining with vendors and checking fabrics between her fingers with an expert's touch. For six hundred pesetas, she bought a new pleated skirt, a white shirt, a T-shirt, and for me, a pair of pants and black leather shoes.

By one o'clock, the tables of the *terrazzas* had filled with people having drinks. We followed an obscure street to the left and arrived at Plaça Reial, a town square flanked by yellow stately buildings, with wide colonnades underneath. Restaurants with red-and-white clothed tables fenced by palm trees and ornate wrought iron streetlamps made for a picturesque setting.

We picked one of the tables underneath the colonnades and waited patiently for our order of vermouth for my mother and seltzer for me. With our stomachs rumbling, we watched the waiter place the cutlery and the two plates on the table in front of us.

"Five years I've been working here, and this is the first time someone has asked me to add cheese to *tortilla de patatas*," the waiter said with a thick accent we could hardly understand.

My mother simply smiled back at him without saying anything.

A man and a woman sat down on a bench near us. The man opened his guitar case, took the instrument out, and began strumming a few notes, adjusting the pegs. Within a few minutes, the woman started to sing along with the guitar, her voice echoing in the square as everyone turned to look at them.

On the other side of the square, an old lady stood in front of a box camera on wheels. She held a sheet of fabric over her head and looked through the viewfinder. With one hand she adjusted the focus, and with the other she pressed the release button: *click*.

I turned to my right and watched my mother smile to herself. The rays of the sun brought color back to her cheeks, making her freckles visible again. That morning, she had brushed her hair to the side and powdered her nose, as she used to do when my father was alive. Her dark circles had slowly disappeared, and her body had begun to gain a well-nourished shape.

At a certain point, her eyes focused on a couple to the right of us, who had just finished their meal and a bottle of red wine. Their chairs were pushed close together, and the man had his arm around her shoulders. They shared passionate kisses that made me blush, as if they were the only people in the square.

"Why are you staring at me like that?" my mother asked, turning back toward me.

"No reason," I answered, although inside I wondered if she was melancholic or envious of the couple. I could only imagine how much our lives would change if she were to ever fall in love again, to be married to someone else but my father. I shook my head to get the thought out of my mind.

48

NEVERMORE

The sound of running water from the marbled bathroom in Mr. Laurent's suite at the Le Meurice woke him up. Papers from a notebook, a passport, empty whiskey glasses, and a book were spread on the bedside table. With his head spinning fast, he squinted and noticed the blue floral wallpaper on the wall. Naked, he left the double bed and went straight to his clothes, which were thrown over various chairs in the room.

He searched in his pants pockets until he found his tobacco pouch, matches, and pipe. Filling the bowl halfway with a loose pinch of tobacco, he pressed it down gently with the tamper. He added another pinch of tobacco, then tamped it down again, leaving a little space at the top of the bowl. A match was struck, allowing a few seconds for the sulfur to burn off. Skillfully, he applied the match to the bowl of tobacco in a circular motion, inhaling gently from the pipe at the same time.

He opened one of the doors that led to the terrace and took a big drag from his pipe, the tobacco calming his senses. The view from the terrace looked over the uneven tile roofs of the apartments ahead. Flashes of memory from last night's event at the restaurant came back to him. He recalled a heated conversation with the owner of the Menier de Noisiel factory, who was boasting loudly to everyone at the table.

"All you need in life is ignorance and confidence, and then success is yours," Mr. Laurent had said. He watched the dumbfounded look on his opponent's face with slight satisfaction. "Mark Twain said it—I'm simply quoting him."

Judging by the way Menier furrowed his eyebrows and clenched his jaw, he was not entirely pleased with Laurent's sarcastic comment. He straightened himself, revealing a tall, robust physique underneath his luxurious tailcoat.

In all truthfulness, Laurent's reason for attending this event was not simply for the presentation of the new chef's exquisite tasting menu; it was mainly to confirm the rumor that was going around on the pitiless lips of Paris high society. Whispers insinuated that Monsieur Gary Menier's mistress had left him due to his substantial financial problems, which were putting even the future of his factory in jeopardy. Being a private art collector with an inherited collection, he was desperate to sell some of his works to cover his debt.

"I beg to differ," Menier had answered, taking another sip from his glass of red wine. "What about hard work and perseverance? What about dedication and sleepless nights?"

"I think we define success in very different ways, Monsieur Menier." His gaze shifted to the woman sitting next to Menier.

That morning, Laurent recalled the rest of the long and uncomfortable conversation of the previous night. Everything came back to him now.

At least, for the time being, I'm not thinking of the maid anymore. He laughed to himself. *At least that, I managed to fix.*

"What are you doing outside, all naked?" A light, girlish voice sounded from behind him.

He turned around to look at Sophie Menier standing in the door. She wore a short, light pink slip with lace around the décolletage. Her face was bare of makeup, allowing her wet hair to cascade casually over her back and shoulders.

"*Ma chérie*," he said, going to her for a kiss.

The couple spent the whole morning and afternoon in bed, followed by an early aperitif and a bottle of Louis Roederer champagne before a walk in Jardin du Tuileries and dinner at La Tour d'Argent.

"A woman could get used to this," she said to him on their way back to the hotel.

"To what, exactly?"

"To dinners and walks with you," she said, taking hold of his hand. "But I'm not stupid enough to not realize the reason you're with me."

"What do you mean?" he asked, stopping and turning to face her.

"I know what you want, Laurent. You have a reputation, as I'm sure you're aware. You started a fight with my father so he would notice you—last night at the party."

"And exactly why would I need him to notice me?"

"Because even though things look as usual on the surface, I know of the financial troubles my father got himself into. He's on the verge of losing his company."

"What does that have to do with me, then, *ma chérie*?"

"That's what I'm trying to figure out. Is it the paintings?"

"It's already too late for those. At this moment, he's in talks with Alex Smith, from Glasgow," Laurent replied.

"So it's true, you're interested in his paintings," she interrupted him.

"That's true, yes. Although it's not his paintings—just the one. *Nevermore* by Paul Gauguin. But you do understand that his seeing you with me erases all my chances, right?" he said, continuing walking.

The two of them walked the streets of Paris in silence, hand in hand. The following morning, shortly after breakfast, Laurent was sitting on the couch of the hotel suite reading the newspaper, with Sophie leaning on his shoulder. He put down the newspaper and took a deep breath, caressing her hair softly.

"What are you thinking?" she asked.

"That it's time. Time for me to go home," he answered.

She got up and turned to him.

"So, that's it?"

"Well, other than spending time with you, which I enjoy very much, my deal is pretty much off. I can't stay in this hotel forever."

"You could stay at my place."

"*Ma chérie*," he said, touching her face lightly, "I must go home. I have matters to take care of. Especially now, I must find another option, something that would be even better than *Nevermore* for my buyer."

"And what if the deal were on? Would you stay then?"

"I don't see how that can happen."

"I could talk with my father and persuade him to meet with you and hear your offer. Hopefully, you'll be more careful with your words." She smiled at him.

"If that's the case, it'll have to be fast, for I'm sure the painting is promised and sold already."

"I'll do it today," she answered. "I'll go over to his office and talk to him. But then, would you still leave?"

"Sophie, I have to be honest with you, the answer is yes. I must return home." After a moment of silence, he continued, "Why don't you come with me?"

"To Spain?"

"Yes, you could stay at my house. I can take you out and show you the city—it'll be fun. You could stay as long as you please, until you get bored of me."

"That's a big step, Monsieur Laurent. Are you sure about it?"

"It's only big if we make it big. For starters, let's just enjoy the moment."

As he had hoped, that evening Laurent was extended an invitation for dinner at the Menier house, where the whole family would be present. While waiting for dinner to be served, Sophie and her mother kept Laurent entertained, taking him on a tour of the two-story mansion. The large house, located well outside of Paris, used to belong to Menier's father, and had kept its century-old decor along with a predominant scent of mold and burning candles. Straight after dinner, Menier invited Laurent to follow him into his office, closing the two wooden doors behind him. The painting he had his mind on was already promised, but not to the right buyer as Laurent suggested.

According to rumors, Menier's grandfather had bought the painting from the artist Delius in 1910, and the family's interest lay in keeping the painting within the exclusive circles of private collectors, such as the one Laurent worked for, rather than museums. When Menier heard the name of Laurent's client, a well-known Swiss-Dutch citizen, his offer suddenly became more tempting. Of course, Laurent carefully neglected to mention that his client's ultimate plan for the painting was as a centerpiece in the opening of his upcoming museum in Madrid, within a year.

"I'll have to think about it, Mr. Laurent," Menier said, taking a sip of his scotch. "As you can understand, I've already agreed to sell it to Mr. Smith."

"There's just one problem. I'm leaving tomorrow morning for Spain, with Sophie. I don't know if she told you," Laurent said. "Should you accept my offer, which I believe is one of great merit, I'm afraid it'll have to be tonight."

"And what exactly are your intentions with my Sophie, Mr. Laurent? She's practically close to being half your age, if you don't mind me saying it."

"No, I don't mind," Laurent answered, smiling. "I'm well aware, but my intentions are nothing but good. My being older, as you pointed out, should reassure you that she'll be treated in the most respectable way."

Shortly after the conversation came to an end, Laurent thanked the hostess, Ms. Menier, who seemed thrilled to have received him as her guest. Laurent politely bid his goodbyes and went on his way to the hotel. Early the next morning, Menier made three important phone calls: one to Laurent, one to the shipping office, and one to Mr. Smith, who was not pleased at the latest news and swore to never do business with the French again.

By late afternoon the following day, Laurent arrived back in Barcelona, with not one but four suitcases in tow. On his arm was a tall, slender woman with chestnut hair and a pale complexion, reminiscent of a bright petalled flower blooming in May.

49

ALEX'S IDEA

"Too sweet!" Ana's husband, Gael, said after taking a bite of the lemon layer cake my mother baked that morning. "Not for me," he continued, waving his hand.

He moved the plate with the unfinished piece of cake to the side of the table in the enclosed balcony and turned to look over the street.

"You barely even tried it!" Ana tried to feed him another bite with a small fork. "It's quite refreshing on a hot day like this."

"I really would prefer if we just stuck to the usual *crema catalana*." He pushed her hand away.

"Oh, damn you with your *crema catalana*! God forbid you try something different!" Ana turned away to face my mother and me.

Gael seemed indifferent to my aunt's comments and instead looked hypnotized at the world moving below on the busy street of Carrer de Roger de Llúria. Seen from the street, their misty, green-colored balcony, located right on the corner of the third floor of the building, provided a striking paradox to the plethora of buildings in the neighborhood.

It was one of the examples of the Modernisme movement in the city, making it hard for people passing by not to stop in their path and admire it. Yet, what they couldn't see, through the colorful windows of the balcony, was the sadness of the sixty-seven-year-old wheelchair-bound man, who, since an unfortunate accident, had been feeling like life was wasting away before his eyes.

Pretending to listen to my aunt reiterating the altercation she had with the neighbor from the fifth floor after she saw their dog relieve itself against the building entrance, I watched Gael from the corner of my eye.

A bushy mustache sat twitching above the line of his upper lip. A few thick, curly black hairs escaped from his eyebrows, and from his ears sprouted similar hairs—black, curly, and comically arranged. But what truly distracted me was the extreme length of the hair coming out of his nose, like a black-and-white bush.

Not long after dessert, we said our goodbyes and went on foot all the way toward Gràcia, gossiping about Ana's spacious apartment. Back home, my mother was quickly ushered into the kitchen by Ms. Agueda, hastening to prepare lunch. It turned out that shortly after we left, Mr. Laurent, forgetting to call ahead, had arrived home with a guest who was to settle in the house for an indefinite amount of time. According to Ms. Agueda's description, the guest, a lovely young lady with delicate facial features and an elegant, classic style, was involved in a relationship with the master of our house. Her name was Sophie, and she was from Paris, Ms. Agueda stated in an enthusiastic manner.

With a tignon bandanna tight around her head, hiding

her unbrushed hair, Ms. Agueda hobbled in and out of the living room, setting the table while my mother finished the lunch in the kitchen. The menu held nothing extravagant for that June day: cod fish, parmesan risotto, and of course a bottle of Chablis.

Throughout the course of the lunch being served, Ms. Agueda returned to the table more often than was truly necessary and didn't hold back in asking questions about Ms. Laurent's trip and how the two of them met.

A couple of days later, I woke up feeling slightly dizzy and heavy in my head, a consequence of the previous evening, when, as I passed through the empty kitchen, a half-empty bottle of white wine between the dirty plates had caught my eye. Thinking that no one would notice, I downed it all in a few big gulps. I left the empty bottle on the table and went straight to bed.

That morning, my mother's bed was tightly made, the cover stretched to every corner, so smooth it appeared as though she had ironed the bed itself. Despite the open window, the air felt warm and humid, my body was moist from sweat, and my mouth felt dry. I got up, washed my face, and cleared my mouth with the cold water from the sink. I grabbed my clothes from the chair and went out of the room, my stomach rumbling and craving something salty and rich.

I stopped for a second in front of the French doors on the main floor and listened to the sound of a melody coming from the piano inside. Carefully, I opened the door and walked in. I continued to the living room but remained standing just outside the door, close enough to watch Mr. Laurent's fingers master the keys, seamlessly gliding between notes, making it look natural and fluid.

He stopped playing to take a drag off his pipe, but then picked it up again.

"Did you like it?" The voice emanated from inside the room as soon as the music stopped.

Embarrassed, I remained staring at the wall without saying a word.

"Alex, I heard you coming all the way from the entrance." Mr. Laurent smiled and turned to look at me.

"I'm sorry to interrupt you, sir. I was just listening to you play. It's fascinating."

"Why, thank you," he answered. "'La plus que lente'—that's what it's called, the melody," he said in his thick French accent. "Have you ever heard of Debussy? Claude Debussy?"

"No, but it's beautiful. It reminds me of summer back home."

"We used to listen to Debussy as kids, my sister and I, on my grandmother's gramophone."

When I told him we didn't have a gramophone, only a radio on which we mostly listened to the news, he looked astonished.

"I grew up with music. My parents made me sing in all sorts of choirs and participate in plays, but it wasn't until I first touched the piano that I felt in my place." He effortlessly played a few chords. "If I remember correctly, I was just about your age when I first got acquainted with it."

"I wish one day I could learn to play like you."

"You should start learning then." After a small pause, he asked, "But what about school—don't you think that's more important, in your case?"

"I don't think I speak Spanish or Catalan well enough to understand the classes."

"That's an issue, agreed." He placed his hands on his knees. "How about this? I'll hire a tutor to teach you Spanish this summer, and maybe in September you can enroll in school?"

"That's very generous of you, but I don't think my mother could afford to repay you."

"I'll pay for it, and maybe, who knows, one day you'll return the favor. How about that? It's better than sitting around the house, sipping from my wine bottles." He looked me straight in the eyes.

"Oh, I was not… it was not my intention," I answered, my cheeks and ears burning.

"Don't worry about it. I know what bottles I have in the cellar, and I saw you last night in the kitchen. Just promise me you won't make it a habit."

Sophie entered the room with a delicate stride, settling onto the burgundy couch at the room's center. She wore a white peignoir with a V-style cleavage that left her shoulders bare—innocent but revealing enough to make a young boy wonder. As the two of them started talking to each other in French, I slowly withdrew from the room, trying to give them privacy. Some words kept coming up—*moda* and *robe*—and I suddenly thought I understood what she needed. With an impulse and eagerness to repay Mr. Laurent's generosity, I blurted out, "My mother can make you the dress you desire!"

I held my breath for a moment as I looked at them.

50

THE DRESS

July 15 marked the seventy-fifth anniversary of the Cooperativa d'Alta Costura, an event Mr. Laurent and his plus one, as the invitation stated, couldn't miss. It was expected to be the year's most prestigious fashion show, featuring the biggest brands in high fashion and demanding a guest list of the finest caliber.

Having spent her entire career as a seamstress in Romania, sewing standard models of pants, dresses, and skirts that were suitable to wear in our little town, my mother never imagined creating a dress for an actual fashion show. At first, she was annoyed with me for having suggested it and outright rejected the idea. But when Mr. Laurent came down to the kitchen in person and asked her, she felt compelled to accept.

"What about a sewing machine?" she asked him.

"As a matter of fact, my mother had one. She used to sew, there in the hallway." He pointed. "Right, Ms. Agueda?"

"I remember it like it was yesterday. I still have two of

the dresses she made for me. What a seamstress she was. Can't imagine anyone better." She sighed.

"Whatever did we do with the machine, then?" asked Laurent.

"It must be here somewhere," she answered, continuing to chop onions.

"Ms. Eva will need it. Can you help her look for it?" he insisted.

"When I have time," Ms. Agueda answered.

To my mother, he continued, "Sophie has so many ideas, the whole living room is a library of cutouts and magazines. I'll be there to translate and help if you need." He smiled kindly at my mother and, with a slight nod of goodbye, turned and left the kitchen.

As it turned out, the sewing machine had been right under our noses the entire time. It was still in the long hallway, sitting in a corner, next to one of the tall windows, its table covered in pots and plants. Having removed them all, I helped my mother lift the machine and move it toward the center of the room. She dusted it off with a cloth and pulled the extension plate to the side, revealing the machine underneath. With an experienced hand, she lifted the old Singer until it locked into place. Pulling up a chair, she turned the hand wheel while gently pressing the pedal underneath to check its movement. With a yellow thread found in a small drawer, she threaded the needle and ran a few stitches over a corner of her uniform.

"With a bit of oil, I think it'll be as good as new. It's almost like the one I had back home, isn't it?" she asked.

"Yeah, it's the same brand, but this table extends further. Have you noticed?" I replied, studying it.

The following day, with her heart pounding, she went upstairs to discuss the design with Sophie and Mr. Laurent.

For over an hour, they delved into discussions about fabrics, colors, and designs, going over pages of the newest magazines. In the end, Sophie fell in love with a pale rose pink that she saw on one of the models, certain it would complement her complexion, but selecting the perfect fabric remained a conundrum, and the only detail she decided on was that there would be lace at the front.

During the following two weeks, my mother thought of nothing else but her project. At night, she often sat in bed sketching designs until late.

With a page ripped from one of Sophie's magazines in her hand, she frequented store after store in search of the perfect fabric. She would hold the page next to the material while imagining what the dress would look like. Cotton, linen, chiffon, not even satin and silk quite matched the vision in her head. She hadn't even considered velvet until her fingers brushed against what the shop assistant called "summer-velvet." It was light, soft, and smooth, like marshmallows.

By the time my mother had shown the fabric to Sophie, there were only two weeks left until the event. Sophie unwrapped the pile of fabric my mother had bought and draped it over her shoulder, admiring the contrast to her pale skin in the mirror.

When it was time to start sewing, I would find my mother in the hallway, her back arched over the machine. Occasionally, she stopped to wipe the perspiration from her face. Meanwhile, she did her best to ignore Ms. Agueda's comments, now that she was left with extra work around the house.

Even in the most trying circumstances, when Sophie would come with Mr. Laurent for fittings and "a few small changes," my mother remained calm, accommodating each new whim. Initially, the dress was meant to be long, with a slit on the left side, to discreetly show a bit of the leg. The latest change, however, altered the shape and length of the dress by eliminating the open slit and adding ruffles around the now asymmetric hem.

After a week and a half, the hallway began to look like a tailor shop, with fabrics and pieces of thread strewn across the colorful tiles.

The day before the event, I took advantage of my mother's excitement over having finished the dress and saw my chance to ask for permission to escape the house, assuring her that I would be careful and that I knew my way home. I went all the way to Casa de les Punxes and paced along Avenue Diagonal, the long street with shops and restaurants. But as much as I tried to push it out of my head, my only desire was to go back to my aunt's bar, and so I did.

As fate would have it, I entered the crowded room, but Eulalia and Alba were nowhere to be seen. I found my aunt at her usual spot behind the bar. Like everybody else, she was anxiously waiting for a special guest to arrive and perform tonight.

"*Bombonet!* Go in the back and see what is taking those two so long," she said to me.

In the back room, I found both Alba and Eulalia taking turns in front of the round mirror on the wall, applying makeup and adjusting their uniforms. The room felt humid and carried a damp scent. Along the far wall sat boxes and crates full of alcohol. Several fridges hummed noisily. On the right, a spiral staircase led upstairs.

"I can't wait to see him!" Alba said, applying even more lipstick. "I heard he's only twenty-four but looks older."

"His manager wants him to look like that, so people will take his music seriously," said Eulalia.

"Ladies, ladies, everyone is here, and Tony just arrived with his crew," my aunt said, walking in. "Everyone out. *Bombonet!*" she shouted, pointing at me. "You as well. Come outside! Don't stand there snooping—help me with the drinks."

The two girls dashed around the bar to take the last-minute orders, my aunt prepared them hastily, and I delivered them. Gradually, the lights of the bar dimmed, and the activity slowed down until the room went nearly dark. Four guys gathered around the piano, one of them taking Mr. Roger's usual seat.

A short, stocky man was holding a trombone. Next to him, another band member blew a few notes on a saxophone. Sitting on a chair, another one held a tall double bass. Once the room became quiet and the public focused on the band, a guy dressed in a white Italian suit and a hat walked out of the backroom. He seemed to be the one the girls were so obsessed with—Tony! He was tall and good-looking with a boyish demeanor that made him seem vulnerable yet dangerous. A girl would want to be protected, held in his arms, yet serenaded and courted by him. He bowed and accepted the applause with his own charming grace.

Once he started singing, his voice led the band and audience, which he handled with an easy assurance, giving time for each band member to show their own skills on the instruments. After the first couple of songs, he loosened his tie, revealing the sweat running down his neck, and started walking around the room, in between tables and chairs, singing to each guest willing to give a few extra pesetas. With the doors and windows open, his voice traveled through Valencia Street, sparking the curiosity of several people outside, who queued to get a glimpse of the show.

When the band finished the set, they bowed gracefully to the excited audience. The lights came on, but the applause continued along with insistent stamping and demands of "*Más, más.*" Tony stood by the bar, smiling and looking flustered at the audience's response, leaned close to Alba, and asked if she would like to hear him play an extra song. She answered with a smile so wide it lit up her whole face. "*Sí, por favor!*"

I left before the encore was over. It was a warm evening, and the sun was setting later than I expected, so I walked home, replaying bits of Tony's show in my head, wondering what it would feel like to have so many fans wherever you went.

When I arrived home and went upstairs to our room, I found my mother standing alone, staring at herself in the mirror. To my surprise, she was wearing the dress she had made for Sophie, running her fingers over the soft fabric hugging her body. The dress had thin lace straps and delicate embroidery around the plunging V-shape neckline and chest. Below the chest, the dress flared out into a wave of velvet and lace ruffles, giving the illusion of the skirt hovering like a cloud around her, light and structured all at once.

"What happened, Mama?" I asked softly as I walked into the room. She was silent and lost in her thoughts, staring at herself. "You look like a princess from the movies."

At the sound of this, she turned toward me and smiled. "Who's going to see me anyway?" she said, holding back tears.

"Father saw you," I reminded her.

"Your father is not with us anymore, Alex."

"Then, who do you want to see you?"

"Oh, no one. It's just a silly thing. I got carried away."

"Mama, what happened? Why are you wearing Sophie's dress?"

"Because she gave it to me. Some big-name designer gifted her a dress at the last minute. Someone called Pertegaz—Manuel Pertegaz." After a brief pause, she continued, "Her new dress was beautiful too—beige and long, like she wanted it first, with a round neckline and open back. It fit her like a glove."

"I'm sorry, Mama. You worked really hard on this dress. I was actually happy to see you behind that noisy machine again. It reminded me of home." I sat down on her bed.

"I like mopping floors too," she said, chuckling. "Now get out so I can change!"

I left, softly closing the door behind me, and sat outside on the courtyard steps. An hour later when I returned to the room, I saw she had placed the dress on a hanger and left it hanging from the closet door, as if it was now part of the room's decor.

Life moved on, and so did my mother's blues, and after a month, the dress would find its place, hidden in the back of the closet.

51

AN UNEXPECTED OFFER

The next day, when the sun's crown faded behind the robust towers of the cathedral, the two of them, Laurent and Sophie, were driven to the fashion event they had prepared so much for. In the backseat of the black sedan that had picked them up, they sat on each side, looking out their respective window, each lost in their own world. Only their hands reached for each other across the middle seat.

It seemed as if the agitation of two hours prior, when the house was in complete disarray, was now long forgotten, a distant memory. Yet, back at the house, the hairdresser, who had carefully arranged Sophie's long curls to cover part of the backless dress, was still putting away his tools, his hands shaking, longing to get out of there. Eva, who had mended a small hole in the delicate fabric made by the puncture of a heel, was now in the kitchen drinking tea to calm her nerves. Ms. Agueda, who had been told that "she was always in the way" and "could never get anything right," was polishing the silverware in the living room out of frustration.

During the ride, Laurent, who had spent the last hours trying to compliment Sophie and reassure Ms. Agueda that he was still proud of her, remained quiet and listened to Sophie's admiration of the city's architecture. His mind drifted somewhere else entirely, or rather, to someone else—someone who might be feeling hurt by Sophie's last-minute change of mind.

Following the red carpet into the hotel, Laurent and Sophie spent the first hour mingling with people they hardly knew, until it was announced that the fashion show was about to start.

After the main event, a dinner was held on the hotel's rooftop, serving a seven-course menu with liberal amounts of wine and champagne, with Mar Bonet and Pi de la Serra playing in the background. Afterward, Laurent withdrew to the railings and looked down at the city's blinking lights. Berenguer, another art dealer linked to Galería San Joan, approached him.

"I must not forget," said Laurent, taking a sip of champagne from his glass, "I ought to congratulate you, Mr. Berenguer."

"Well, I've accomplished many triumphant things in my life—exactly which one are you referring to?"

"Modest, as always." Laurent laughed. "I couldn't believe it when I heard that you installed a sculpture by Eduardo Chillida in Park Ciutadella. I had to go and see it with my own eyes. Such an eccentric work of art, and it is now on display to everyone."

"Ah, yes, the *Lugar de Encuentros III*,"[1] he answered,

---

1. *Lugar de Encuentros III – Meeting Place III*

looking over the city. "Magnificent piece."

"I really wanted something that would create a conversation among the community, something that when people stopped to look at it, they would wonder, *What the hell is the meaning of that?*" he said as they both started to laugh at the thought.

"Have you procured anything for the upcoming exhibit?" Laurent asked.

"Nothing in particular, not yet. And you?"

"I've secured a promise for one of Miró's latest pieces—he's always a crowd-puller."

"How did you manage that?"

"Well, it was a collaborative effort. I know the owner very well. I've worked with him before, and I persuaded him to loan the piece for the exhibit, in exchange for a contact from City Hall, which, to be entirely honest, I have yet to secure."

Berenguer shifted his attention to the guests on the rooftop terrace.

"I see you brought company this time." He took a sip of his champagne. They both turned to look at the pool area, where Sophie was laughing with three other guests. After a moment, he continued, "I look at you and think you must be one of the luckiest men I've ever known."

"I suppose at the moment, everything seems to be going rather well for me." Laurent looked in Sophie's direction.

"Laurent, you won't believe what Alain asked!" Sophie said, walking over.

"What is that?"

"He wants me as press representative for Pierre Cardin. He says I'm exactly what they're looking for."

"I can see that," Laurent said.

"But there's a small detail." She gulped a sip of

champagne from her glass. "It's at their headquarters in Paris."

"In Paris?"

"You love Paris! What keeps you here anyway?"

"Let's talk about this a little later, Sophie," Laurent said softly, motioning toward Berenguer, who was watching the interaction with interest.

A little after midnight, the party was winding down, but that was just as well. While Sophie celebrated the new opportunity with way too many glasses of champagne, Laurent remained quiet and reflective, caught in his own thoughts. On the drive back, Sophie fell asleep on his shoulder. After the car pulled up to the entrance of the house, Laurent took her in his arms and carried her all the way to the first floor. He helped her change into her nightgown, put her in bed, and pulled the linen cover over her.

Unable to sleep, he went downstairs to the living room, poured himself a glass of scotch, lit a cigar, and stood in darkness and silence.

For two days straight, Ms. Agueda and Eva took turns polishing the floor and dusting the ornaments on the main floor and in the entrance, eager to overhear some of the couple's heated conversations. By the time the floor was polished to a sheen, Sophie's bags were already downstairs. The following morning, Sophie waited for the car to pick her up, with her head low to hide her tired eyes. She wore a pair of pleated trousers that hugged her thin hips and flared at the ankle, a short-sleeved T-shirt, flats, and a necklace of tiny pearls, a gift from Laurent.

After the car pulled up in front of the house, the driver began loading her suitcases while Laurent followed quietly behind Sophie. Just before she left, she turned to him one more time, caressed him, and kissed him on his right cheek. Then she straightened herself up and left without saying a word.

Inside, Laurent remained by the door with his arms at his sides, as if hoping for someone to open it and jump into his arms again. When it didn't happen, he went upstairs and secluded himself on his floor.

52

AUGUST IN THE CITY

The humid August air blanketed the city, making it insufferable for those of us who could not take refuge by the sea. All the flowers were in full bloom, and the usual green trees lining the streets had started to wilt slightly under the scorching sun. The air felt stuffy and heavy during the day, while at night the unpleasant odor of sewers rose and entered through the open windows. It soon became unbearable to sleep or even stay in our room on the second floor without being bathed in sweat. I longed to escape the monotony of August, to run in the fresh forest air, and to jump in the chill meadow ponds back in Romania.

After Laurent's breakup with Sophie, we barely met face-to-face. He packed his bags and went first to the seaside and then to his sister in Bonnieux, France. Whenever he was at home for a few days at a time, he spent them dining out and entertaining friends. Having to cook at that time of the year, even with all the windows open, made everyone in the kitchen irritable. Laurent's frequent absences often made my mother feel insecure about her position. Was there really any need for a second maid at all? But in time she forgot about her fears, and one day Ms. Agueda came back from the city and said that her friend, the Spanish tutor, was now available. My mother wholeheartedly supported the idea.

Her name was Ester Ferrer, a married woman in her late fifties, a retired schoolteacher and mother of five now-grown-up children. She valued discipline, education, and most of all, dedication. To me, she bore a vague similarity to Ms. Agueda, due to her formal clothing and age. However, her manner was completely different—she was nothing but kind, gentle, and patient.

From the first class, I became attached to her. Her manner of teaching and love for books reminded me so much of my grandmother. Even if I would still drop by the bar for an hour or so, I never skipped my homework and always respected everything she asked of me. When I told her the memories of my childhood in Romania or experiences in the camp, she would smile and caress my cheek as if I were her little boy, while correcting my grammar and pronunciation in the gentlest way. I hoped there was a way to continue studying with her, for the idea of starting at a new school terrified me.

August brought changes for my Aunt Ana, as well. At her husband's insistence, she agreed to leave the bar for a few weeks and stay with his family at the seaside. If for some a long vacation by the beach would be a well-received experience, for my aunt, who couldn't imagine a day in her life away from her work, it was an annoyance that she felt obliged to endure.

Before her departure, she and my mother prepared a package for my grandparents, containing all sorts of goods, together with a substantial number of pesetas sewn inside a dress made for my grandmother. They spoke with Costel Carp on the phone, who, dealing with visitors coming in and out of the port, promised to exchange the money into lei and deliver the package to my grandparents' home, taking a minimal cut for the trouble.

My aunt's absence from the bar was a joyous opportunity for both Eulalia and Alba, now left in charge. However, the few times I dropped by, I often found the two of them arguing about the alcohol they hadn't ordered in time, the food that wasn't prepared, and the disorganized bar. That month, I took advantage of the fewer customers and the absence of my aunt's diligent eye to ask Roger to help me fulfill the fantasy that had been nurturing in me during those last months: to learn how to play the piano.

"Playing piano is like learning a whole different alphabet," he said to me, pressing the keys one at a time, from left to right. He lent me a pocketbook with the scale and told me to read it, even though it was in Catalan. It was satisfying to finally learn the name of each note: do, re, mi… and even more satisfying to attribute my own number to each one.

As August came to an end, I dreaded the thought that soon, my aunt would return and put an end to our lessons. The day came sooner than expected. After a class, just as I was sneaking a sip of wine from behind the bar, she walked in!

53

THE GIFT

When I was six years old, Matilda's parents got in touch with my mother and invited me to her birthday party. George and other kids were invited as well, but since manners required guests not to come empty-handed, not everyone could go. Twenty minutes after my mother dropped me off at their place, all of us kids and the grown-ups were told to gather around the table in the living room and sing for her.

Matilda, directed by her father, was placed at the head of the table. That day, her hair was full of small clips of all colors, shaped like butterflies. With all eyes in the room on her, she stared at her feet, only looking up when her father nudged her slightly on the back. When her mother walked in holding a plate with a white birthday cake and placed it in the middle of the table, we began to sing.

Matilda's happiness at being the center of attention was grand, but it couldn't begin to compare to the excitement the rest of us felt, seeing her birthday cake with different fruits on top, a rare treat that only the richest could afford.

As soon as she blew out the candles, we all cheered and clapped, our eyes never leaving the cake. It was my first birthday party with a cake so big that they could cut each of us a slice. Afterward, my belly felt completely stuffed from two glasses of orange soda and a slice of cake. I even dared to ask for another, thinking, *Who knows when I will have a chance like this again?* When it was time to go home, my mother arrived to pick me up, and then there was another surprise. Matilda's mother walked out of the kitchen with a second cake, this time a charlotte cake encircled in a layer of ladyfingers, a rose-colored cream in the middle, and filled with pieces of fruit. To my disappointment, I was too full to eat another bite, and my mother was eager to leave.

For several days, I made a point of telling my parents that if they truly loved me as they claimed, I would have a cake just like Matilda's for my birthday. I carried the frustration of not being able to eat that second cake for several weeks.

On September 12, 1978, the four of us—my mother, Ana, Ms. Agueda, and I—gathered around the little kitchen table in Mr. Laurent's house. They took turns to sing to me, both in Romanian and Spanish:

Happy Birthday to you,
With health,
God may give you all that you wish,
Beautiful days,
And happiness,
Happy Birthday, may you live long.

As the singing thankfully came to an end, I closed my eyes to make a wish, then blew out the single candle in the middle of the birthday cake. When I opened my eyes again, on my right was my mother and Ana, laughing between themselves, and on my left Ms. Agueda was smiling. So joyful was she to be part of the celebration that she even gave me a hug. My mother pulled a thick envelope with three letters out of her uniform pocket, two from her friends back in the camp and one for me, from Mr. Novak.

Ms. Agueda was the first one to notice Mr. Laurent standing in the door, his arms crossed in front of him, looking at us. By instinct, she stiffened and got up from her chair. He wore a striped T-shirt and brown pants, and his hair was significantly longer and more unruly than when I last saw him.

"I heard the noise from upstairs and wondered who was torturing cats in the kitchen. What are you all celebrating here? I see cake and a bottle of liquor," he asked, making his way to the table.

"It's my birthday!" I answered. "It was a song for my birthday—the cats you heard must have been my mother and my aunt."

"I assumed so. How old are you now, Alex?"

"Twelve, twelve years old," I said. "Cake, Mr. Laurent?"

"Please. Let me bring a bottle of champagne."

By the time Mr. Laurent returned from the cellar with the champagne, my mother had already cut five big slices from the cake, and he opened the bottle with a pop. Ms. Agueda eyed Mr. Laurent's unusual familiarity with suspicion as he took the chair next to my mother. They sat so closely at the small table that their arms touched with every bite of cake they took.

"Sewing. It was the only thing I was good at," my mother confessed, cleaning the plate with her fork. She placed the empty plate on the table and took a sip of champagne from her glass.

"I'm sure that's not true," Mr. Laurent said. "What about school?"

"Frankly, I don't remember much of my time in school, nor how I spent my days in Romania. Sewing clothes and staying for hours in queues, that's all that comes to my mind."

"What for?" Ms. Agueda asked.

"For everything—eggs, flour, meat, oil, butter, even toilet paper. It's a Romanian tradition, you could say," she went on. "I can still feel the infernal cold creeping into my bones during those winter mornings. We would spend hours and hours queueing, from four in the morning until seven or eight, for a chance to buy something."

"I'm so glad I left when I could," Ana said.

"In our country, each family has a certain ratio," my mother continued. "It's not like here. We could buy around three hundred grams of bread and half a kilo of cheese, about ten eggs, one kilo of sugar, and flour. It was enough, I can't complain. And with Cornel working in the butcher shop, he could bring some meat home, sometimes even extra butter and milk. Keep in mind, this boy here," she said, pointing toward me, "refused to touch butter or drink milk, when others didn't even have the chance."

"Was that food for a whole week?" Mr. Laurent asked.

"Yes, even longer. It's funny but sometimes I miss those long hours spent in queues. We all talked to each other, strangers or neighbors, we were all the same. As long as we kept the complaints to ourselves."

"I could never do it," my aunt interrupted. "I can't see myself standing in queues for a kilo of flour. I was so lucky to find my Gael—he treated me like a queen from the moment he saw me."

Ana talked about my grandparents—who, she had been

sure, planned to marry her off to a villager's son—how traditional Grandfather had been and how difficult life was during her teenage years.

"They raised me the best they could, and for a long time I felt terrible about not saying goodbye to them before I left the country. But after years of working hard on my own, I realized that I owed them nothing, after all." She talked without interruption, jumping freely from one topic to another, leaving the rest of us confused and exhausted.

Looking around the table, I could see everyone's eyes lowered to their glasses, avoiding her gaze. I wondered whether anyone would even notice if I left the table, but thankfully Mr. Laurent finally broke the flow of her stories.

"Ms. Eva, if you don't mind me asking—what happened with your husband? Your father," he said, shifting his gaze from my mother to me. Silence entered the room, and seeing that my mother was making no attempt to answer, I did.

"He died."

"That's terrible," Mr. Laurent said, resting his hand on my mother's shoulder. After a moment, during which nobody spoke, he continued, "I'm sorry to ask yet another question—how did it happen?"

"It was an earthquake. We were at a gathering at City Hall in our old town. He had to go back to pick up something he forgot at home. When the earthquake hit the city, all the buildings on the right side of the…"

The sound of my mother bursting into tears interrupted my story, leaving a poignant silence in its wake. Her face was red and flushed as she blew her nose into a handkerchief she kept in her uniform pocket. With a brief apology, she excused herself from the kitchen. My Aunt Ana followed her, while Ms. Agueda began cleaning the plates in uncomfortable silence.

"I'm so sorry, I had no idea," Mr. Laurent said. He took a quick look around and said, "I see that I've ruined your birthday with my inappropriate questions."

"It's alright, you didn't ruin my birthday at all. This is, in fact, one of the birthdays I'll keep safe in my memory."

"Let me make it up to you. I have quite an idea. Come!" He got up from the table, bidding Ms. Agueda goodbye.

"I have a feeling you might be interested in music?" he asked, turning back toward me as we walked up the stairs.

"Very much."

We went up the stairs to the first floor and entered his office. He placed a chair in front of the library shelves behind his desk, climbed onto it, and reached for the top shelf. He picked up something heavy and rectangular, placing it on the many papers, magazines, and newspapers stacked on his wooden desk. It was a Zenith integrated record player from the early seventies, dusty but in immaculate condition. Mr. Laurent blew air over the lid and wiped off the dust on top with his hand. He lifted the transparent lid and scanned over his records on the shelves with his hands until he found the one he was looking for.

On the cover, there was a painted portrait of a man dressed in old-fashioned clothes, his gaze profound and introspective. Next to it, the text read "Beethoven, Moonlight Sonata." With a slight tip of his thumb, Mr. Laurent removed the record from its cover, holding it gently by its sides. He placed the record on the spindle, then moved the pickup on top of the record and released it. He moved a selector down to where it said "auto" and pressed a button.

When nothing happened, Mr. Laurent looked around, then remembered.

"Aaah! I forgot to plug it in," he said, connecting the wire to the outlet. The record started spinning, and rich harmonies of piano started playing.

"It's all yours! Now you can listen to music in your room!"

On impulse, I almost hugged him but instead withdrew and thanked him kindly.

54

A NEW CHANGE

For hours on end, I listened to the LP, curled up in a chair, with the record player on the little table next to me.

By then, I had read Mr. Nowak's letter twice and was happy to hear he was now on his way to reunite with his family. Thinking back, even though the time spent in the camp had a range of challenges and hardships, we had left a family of friends behind.

Several days after my birthday, I was returning from Cansaladeria Andreu with a cart stuffed with lamb legs and ribs, squeezing through the people going to and from work, moving to the side whenever a truck or car drove by in the narrow streets at the usual snail's pace. Above the overwhelming noise from the street, my ears caught a peculiar sound that I had previously only heard in movies. It seemed to come from the little shop on the corner of our street. I stopped in front, hesitant about my next move, but placed one foot on the high doorstep and entered. I greeted the man who was standing by a table with his back turned toward me, working on a golden picture frame. He turned around, and just as he had the first time he saw me, he eyed me from head to toe and turned to his work again.

There seemed to be an abundance of objects in an organized chaos. Masks hung prominently on the wall, as if they once were part of a costume or decoration. The shelves and tables were cluttered not only with tools but also with painting supplies, and several handmade toys and dolls. Posters and images adorned the walls that were lined with broken chairs set to be repaired. Leather shoes and two half-full bottles of liquor were piled underneath a table.

"What music are you playing?" I asked, seeing that he had not taken his eyes off his work.

At my question, he turned around and looked from the stereo to me, then went to pick up an album cover and showed it to me.

"Louis Armstrong!" he said, pronouncing the name with a strong Spanish accent. "Louis Armstrong!" he repeated.

"Can I buy it?" I asked, looking at the cover featuring the singer's wide smile.

"No. You can buy this one." He pulled another record from underneath a pair of shoes. The cover featured a charming, boyish-looking young man who was photographed playing the trumpet. He looked clean-cut and wore a pair of black trousers, a white T-shirt, and a hat. Underneath the picture, in capital letters, was his name, Chet Baker, and on the back, a list of songs and the album title: "Chet Baker Sings."

"How much?"

"One hundred pesetas."

"One hundred? That's a lot."

"It is what it is. It wasn't easy to come by."

I checked the change I had left in my pocket—some

small bills and a few coins. It was enough for the LP but not enough to come home with the change expected, unless I told Ms. Agueda that the lambs were seven hundred grams instead of five hundred, and the same with the rest of the groceries.

I paid him and left in a hurry. Ms. Agueda was not in the kitchen when I arrived, so I quickly emptied the dolly, putting each purchase in its place as I had been taught, and ran back to my room, taking the stairs two steps at a time. I gently removed the record Mr. Laurent gave me and slid it back in its cover. Just like he showed me, I took out the new LP, placed it on the player, moved the arm on top, and pressed the button.

Baker's voice was so seductive and mysterious, just as I imagined the men in my aunt's bar when they whispered in the girls' ears. I read on the cover of my new record that it was called jazz. It consumed me entirely, and I willingly surrendered to it as I sat breathless on my chair with the album cover clutched to my chest.

Inside the album cover were several blurry black-and-white photographs of Chet Baker in the studio playing trumpet, sitting on the edge of a balcony window holding his trumpet, or smoking. After a few days of looking at the pictures of him, I became infatuated with his style, his hair, and his voice. I insisted my mother take me shopping for new clothes and even a long overdue trip to a barbershop. I wanted to look like him.

I cuffed my black trousers to showcase the patent leather shoes and the new socks my mother bought for me, and tucked my white T-shirt inside the trousers.

The classes with Ms. Ester advanced day by day, with much more interesting topics such as mathematics and physics—all knowledge that I would need if I was to enroll in public school for the second term of Educación General Básica.[1]

The realization that Ms. Ester's payment was not deducted from my mother's salary, as she had assumed, did not sit well with her, and she bombarded Ms. Agueda with questions. That went on until one day, Ms. Agueda revealed that the payment came from a sum that Mr. Laurent set aside monthly, so I would have a chance at an education. When she heard this, my mother's face flushed. She threw her apron on the counter and left the kitchen in a fury of mixed emotions. As she walked up to Laurent's floor, she didn't know whether to feel enraged, grateful, or ashamed. Standing in front of his door, she thought again, turned around, and instead went upstairs to our room.

I was doing my homework by the little table when she burst in, talking rapidly.

"Does he pity us because we're immigrants? Does he think I can't provide for you?" She was pacing back and forth, with one hand on her hip and the other holding her head. "First he gives you a record player, then he pays for your tuition."

"Maybe that's just how people are here, Mama. We do live in a different country after all. We can't expect the same customs as at home, can we?"

"Maybe. I don't know what to think." She sat down on the side of her bed. "I'm scared that somehow it might get me in trouble. I don't want to lose the only job I have."

"Mama, he just wants to help us. What's so bad about that? Don't we deserve a bit of luck, after all we've been through?"

"I guess." She considered this for a moment, then stood

---

1. Educación General Básica – Basic General Education

up and went to the small mirror on the wall. She glanced at the image in the mirror, put a few small hair clips in, fixing her unruly hair, and went for the door.

As I watched her, I wondered if it was possible that she didn't see what was really happening? Before leaving, she turned. "By the way, what's this music you've been listening to lately? A week ago, you were listening to piano music, sitting there, all melodramatic?" she asked, mocking me with an exaggerated gesture.

"Mama! Leave me alone!"

"Now it's new music I hear. With the loud trumpet?" She laughed.

"It's Chet Baker—it's called jazz, Mama! How can you not know about it?" I asked, as if I had known about it for years.

"It sounds funny. I like it." She went out the door.

"Can I have some privacy once in a while?" I yelled after her.

"Privacy would be nice for me, as well," she yelled back while going down the stairs.

One day, after walking Ms. Ester to the gate after our lessons, I came back to find the sewing machine table, which I had been using for my studies, occupied by a big pile of fabrics and magazines. My mother lifted the machine from underneath, planning to sew herself a new skirt she fancied from a magazine. On the machine's extension board, she placed a heart-shaped needle pad, several jars filled with all kinds of buttons, and a cookie box containing threads in several colors.

"Imagine if we could use different kinds of buttons for one skirt, instead of having to find three matching ones," she remarked as she threaded the needle and began to sew. With her head bowed and eyes focused on the needle's course over the fabric, she pressed down on the pedal with her right foot.

How I loathe the sound of that machine, I thought to myself as I swept up my notebooks.

A loud bang was heard from the first-floor door being closed, followed by soft footsteps on the stairs until they reached the hallway. Mr. Laurent came in, looking disoriented, his hair tousled as if he had just woken up from a nap.

"Did I wake you, Mr. Laurent?" my mother asked, pausing the machine.

"Yes, you did!" he said, his voice still hoarse.

My mother and I looked at each other.

"But now that you've woken me up, maybe you could make a pair of trousers for me as well?"

"I don't know if it's such a good idea."

"I promise I won't change my mind at the last minute and buy from somewhere else," he answered. "I'll be your most devoted customer."

I left the two of them discussing styles and materials. Of course, the thought had crossed my mind before, but now I was feeling increasingly sure of how Mr. Laurent felt, and I wasn't sure I liked it very much.

55

MR. LAURENT IN DENIAL

When Eva came to look for him, Laurent was sitting in his usual burgundy armchair in the living room, legs crossed, holding a book in one hand and his reading glasses in the other. At a slow pace, he passionately intoned Éluard's words, whispering them to himself.

La courbe de tes yeux fait le tour de mon cœur,
Un rond de danse et de douceur,
Aurore penchée au-dessus de ma nuit.[1]

Standing on the doorstep, she found herself looking at him with a certain sense of reluctant admiration. At last, she cleared her throat to make her presence noticed, rubbing her hands together as if she was about to give a speech in front of a large crowd, then asked him to come downstairs

1. *The curve of your eyes goes around my heart, / A circle of dance and sweetness, / Dawn is bending over my night.* – "La courbe de tes yeux" by Paul Éluard

for measurements. Laurent closed the book, placed it on the side table, and laid his reading glasses on top. With a wave of his hand, he gestured to her to lead the way. From the living room, they passed the entrance and kept going down the steps to the hallway next to the kitchen. Along the way, Laurent took in every single detail of Eva's figure. With her hair in a bun, her neck above the collar of the uniform was bare. Her shoulders were small as she wasn't very tall or broad, but her hips were a little wide. Through the uniform, it was hard to make out the shape of her backside, but he was well aware of the fullness of her chest.

It was a short walk down the stairs, but Eva talked continually on the way. She told him about Ms. Ester, Alex's tutor, how much his Spanish had improved, and how even hers had gotten better. She shared her fears that Alex was not socializing with anyone, having instead acquired strange interests for a boy his age—listening to trumpet music and going to Ana's place to play piano.

"Trumpet music? You mean jazz?" Mr. Laurent asked.

"I suppose so, I haven't a clue," she answered, searching for a magazine among the pile next to her sewing machine.

"I don't know him that well, but I believe jazz suits him. Yes, thinking about it, I can see him in a jazz band."

"Oh no, Mr. Laurent, I didn't come all the way here to work so he can listen to music and play piano—don't scare me like that." She laughed at the idea.

"Well, he's still young and has a lot of time to decide, but for the time being jazz and piano are both great interests to have. Not everyone understands jazz." He seemed lost in his thoughts and continued, "Jazz is so much more..."

Without understanding much of Mr. Laurent's reverie, she showed him a page torn from a magazine and pointed to a pair of light beige men's pants, labeled "straight trousers with herringbone."

"I did this model a few years back for my husband—that's why it caught my eye. Of course, that time I used polyester, but I found a great fabric for you." She pointed to the meters of wool spread out on the sewing table. "Touch it! It's soft and it'll be good in the cold," she said to him in a motherly tone.

"You don't have to make these ones if it brings back memories." Laurent felt the fabric with the tip of his fingers.

"To be honest, it's the only model of men's trousers that I know how to sew. It has a straight cut, which I've noticed in some of your other pants. Two pleats on the waist, that's easy to do," she said to herself. "And how long do you want them?" She pulled a tape measure from her uniform pocket.

"Well, I'm 1.76 meters tall. I prefer the pants to finish just above the shoe. Not so long that they touch the shoes, not so short that they show much of the socks."

"You don't want them rolled up, like my Alex?"

"Yes, I saw him the other day. No, I'm too old for that fashion. I would like the bottom of the trousers to be unhemmed. I prefer a more classic look."

While Eva started to measure him, Laurent was suddenly conscious of the tension and blood flowing through his veins. With each touch of her hands on his legs, he felt as if he had just woken up from a long and deep sleep. Seeing her at his feet, with her notebook and pencil in hand, amounted to a type of unforeseen torture.

"How much longer for the measurements?" Laurent asked.

"I think I got them all. Now I need to create the pattern, then I'll take the fabric and…"

"Good, good," he interrupted. "Just call for me when

they are ready." And he awkwardly headed for the stairs, without another word.

Rapidly walking up the stairs, he thought that he would lock himself in his office until he could leave for dinner. "I should dine out tonight," he said to himself as he closed the door to the room, then stood breathing heavily on the other side.

"Are you alright, Mr. Laurent?" Ms. Agueda asked, causing him to jump.

"Ms. Agueda, I didn't see you over there."

Ms. Agueda was standing on a chair, dusting the high shelves of his office.

"I thought you noticed me when you entered—I'm not that small," she said, getting down from her chair with a grunt.

"Say, Ms. Agueda, I meant to tell you, I won't be dining at home tonight, so don't bother preparing anything for me."

"Very well, we won't prepare anything then."

She continued dusting the lower shelves and asked, "Are you changing your wardrobe, Mr. Laurent?"

"*Mon dieu,* no! I'm simply getting a pair of pants made. Why would I change my wardrobe?"

"Because I saw Ms. Eva working on your trousers, and I wondered why you didn't go to your usual tailor."

"Why should I go to him, all the way in El Born, when we have a perfectly good seamstress in the house?"

"Why eat out when you can have a perfectly well-cooked meal at home?" she returned. "It's for the right company, I would assume. Of course, I don't know much—I don't eat out, nor do I have my clothes made by a tailor. I just buy them from Mercado de Santa Catarina."

"True," he answered.

"Do you consider me good company as well?" Ms. Agueda asked.

"Yes, of course. You're like family, not just company."

"Then how come, in all the years I've worked here since your mother died, I can count the times you've been down in the kitchen on one hand?"

"I see you around the house every day. You know all my doings and wrongdoings. Should I come help you cook, or what do you expect, Ms. Agueda? Or is there a problem that I've asked Ms. Eva, who, if you will remember, works for me, to sew me a pair of pants?"

"Stubborn like his father," she said to herself. Then louder, "So, you're trying to tell me that there's no ulterior motive to your need to look after her boy or seek her company at every opportunity?"

Laurent sat down on his office chair, resting his head in his hands. Ms. Agueda took the empty chair in front of the desk and put her duster and cloth on top of some of his papers.

"I hate to see you torturing yourself like this, Mr. Laurent."

"I don't know what to do," he gestured helplessly. "I tried, I really did! When my mind started to toy with the image of her, I instantly left for Paris where I met Sophie. I thought I had fallen in love, and I would forget everything. But that didn't work out! I left my home almost for the whole of August, just to get away, but I barely closed an eye those nights, thinking of her, worrying about her life, was she safe in the new city? Now, I just can't ignore this feeling inside of me anymore. Also, I really need a new pair of trousers."

They both laughed.

"I'm even considering firing her, selling the house, moving to the Canaries, and never coming back."

"What about me? What would happen to me if you decide to fire her and move?"

"I would take you with me. You know I can't live without your cooking."

"But Ms. Eva is no young girl. She's a woman who's been through a lot, and she comes with a child—a boy who is old enough to see what I see at this point. What will happen to them if you fire her?"

"What other choice do I have, Ms. Agueda?" he said, waving his hands in protest.

"There is another, but that's up to you," she said as she got up from the chair. "Think of how much your father fought to be with your mother when your grandparents didn't allow him to marry her at first. And I don't think I ever saw a couple happier and more in love than them."

"That's the thing. I can't imagine any of my relationships getting close to what they had."

He put on his glasses and opened a random folder on his desk, signaling to Ms. Agueda that he was going to work. He wanted to be alone with his books, the papers on his desk, and the freedom of his thoughts.

"I'm sure at the right time, you'll know what to do." Ms. Agueda smiled at him, a motherly and heart-opening smile, picked up her duster and cloth, and quietly left.

56

THE ENCOUNTER AT THE BAR

It was bright and sunny outside, and our balcony door was open to let the surprisingly warm October breeze drift into our room. The insistent chirping from the birds outside grew louder and louder, making it hard for me to go back to sleep. My mother sat on the side of her bed, dressed in her nightgown, brushing her hair with a sizzling sound.

What our room lacked in decorations, she compensated for with a vase of white carnations, her favorites, which was always present on our table. Next to it was a long, unfinished letter to her sister Alexandra and my grandparents, which my mother had started a few days ago. A pen still lay next to it in case she forgot to mention something. Having received confirmation over the phone from Costel that the package she and Ana had sent had arrived safely at my grandparents, and that it had come most providentially, she had woken up in high spirits.

Later that day, we sat down at one of the four tables lined up outside a pintxos bar on Travessera de Gràcia. It was the only table directly in the sun. The bar itself and the few tables outside were separated by a pedestrian walkway, the perfect spot to people-watch, an essential aspect for our own private game.

From across the table, I watched my mother take a compact mirror from her handbag, checking that her red lipstick was still intact. Then, with a snap, she closed the mirror and put it back in her purse, instead getting out her sunglasses in their case. I always teased her about them being too big, making her look like a fly.

To think that this time last year, we had just arrived in the refugee camp with no idea how our lives would unfold. My grandmother was right—life is full of surprises. A waiter came out carrying several small plates on his tray and arranged them on our table—*platillos de gilda, jamón serrano, y pintxos de boquerones en vinagre.*

"*Gracias,*" said my mother, looking up toward him.

"*Grácies, senyora,*" he answered in Catalan.

I unbuttoned my sweater and moved closer to the table. My mother fished up the toothpick with olives that had marinated in her glass of vermouth and emptied the drink with a gulp. Having lowered a slice of jamón into my mouth, I suddenly became aware of my mother's peculiar demeanor. She ate slowly, looking out to the street, as if I wasn't even there, and if her mouth had not been full of *boquerón*, an involuntary smile might have crept onto her lips. I wondered if it had something to do with Mr. Laurent's latest incursions into the kitchen, which would confirm my worries and dark thoughts. I lost my appetite completely.

As the only man in her life, maybe it was time to have a conversation and explain to her what she was getting herself into. But how would I begin? What if it ended in a fight and she wouldn't allow me to go to Les Dues Donnes later? I sat there, squinting at the sun burning my face, struggling with the two choices. I could tell her what I thought of Mr. Laurent or lighten up her mood by starting our usual game, where one of us would pick the first letter of a color from someone's clothing, and the other had to name a famous person from our country whose name started with that letter.

I made my choice.

"Mama, to your right," I said, gesturing discreetly toward a young man wearing a speckled brown jacket with a turquoise shirt underneath. "Look at the color of his shirt—*turquesa*. Tell me someone famous whose name starts with T."

"With T? That's a hard one, let me think. Aah!" she said, after she finished chewing.

"Toma. Toma Caragiu," she said. "I don't know if you've heard but he died in the same earthquake, just like our Cornel."

After my mother paid the bill, we crossed the intersection and turned onto Carrer de Tordera, a narrow street in Gràcia, known for its artistic flair and local shops.

A familiar woman caught my attention as she was coming out of a shoe store. She was dressed in an impeccable coffee-brown dress and held her daughter by the hand.

"*Marrón*—Spanish for brown, like her dress," my mother signaled with her eyes to the woman and her daughter. My mother's attention was on the dress, but my eyes, on the other hand, were on her daughter, having recognized her from our neighbor's lawn. Judging by the look on her face, I had a feeling I wasn't a stranger to her either. She must have seen me leaving the house or in the balcony door where I spent most of my time listening to music. Either way, I felt as though we knew each other.

"*Marrón, marrón,*" I repeated, trying to focus after we had passed them. If it wasn't for the girl distracting me, I could have answered the riddle in a heartbeat. I knew my mother's favorite poet by heart, but I took my time to look behind us before I recited the poem.

In vain you gather rivers in the sun
In your thoughts,
And the yearning fields
And the dark sea;
The ancient pyramids
Climb their tall peaks to the sky—
Don't seek happiness in the distance,
My beloved![1]

"Mihai Eminescu," she answered. "I used to know his poems by heart."

Of course, we were both fully aware that inventing this game "to challenge our memory" was just another way of remembering the homeland we had slowly begun to forget. Underneath it all, hiding in the depths of our minds was a feeling of guilt for how our lives had turned out. Guilt for building a better life for ourselves. Guilt for enjoying pleasures we never knew existed: French food, jazz, piano, and occasionally dining out.

Later, when I went to the bar, my aunt was behind the counter, talking with two customers. As always, her voice carried so loudly that it almost overpowered the music. From the door, I watched her then wipe the counter with a

1. "Blue Flower" by Mihai Eminescu

fast, meticulous motion, as if she was in a hurry. I imagined how life must've been when she came here twenty years ago, leaving her family and country for Barcelona.

In my mind, I saw tears running down her cheeks, ruining her black mascara and streaming lines down her face. She would then wipe them away with the same meticulous motion I saw her use on the counter, take a deep breath, and wash her face with cold water, as our grandparents taught us to do every morning. Year after year, fewer and fewer tears would flow, until there would be days when she would forget her past and fully embrace being Ana Borges.

"Can I play the piano for a while?" I asked her.

"You don't help much around here anymore. Lately, you only come to play," she said.

"I looked around—there are no empty glasses," I answered, turning my back to her and sitting down at the piano.

The scent of old wood from the piano reminded me of leafing through the pages of an antique book. Looking down at the black-and-white keys in front of me, some of them washed up and dirty from the years of use, I wondered what my father or George would think if they heard me play. I opened the book Roger lent me over a month ago at the usual page and started playing a few chords with my right hand, as he had instructed me, and gradually added voicing here and there with my left. The melody became playful until I reached the group of mi, fa, sol, and continued progressions going one note down at a time. Now it started to sound familiar. It was the first song Roger had taught me and the only one I knew how to play —"Autumn Leaves." No matter how many times I practiced it, it still felt mechanical and simple compared with when Roger played it.

With my full concentration on playing, I was completely oblivious to the customers behind me, although I eventually noticed them getting louder and impatient. I finally stopped when I felt a hand on my shoulder.

"Someone should get their mojo playing for an entirely different audience," a familiar voice spoke from behind me.

When I turned around and looked up, my heart stopped in my chest. A curly-haired figure with a crooked mustache, dark brown eyes, and a pipe hanging from the corner of his mouth: Mr. Laurent.

"Mr. Laurent, what are you doing here?"

"What am I doing here? The question is, what are you doing here?" he replied, smiling.

"This is my aunt's bar. I come here to help her sometimes and to practice piano."

"I see. You were doing quite well, but I believe you deserve a better audience than a bunch of drunken fools loitering around." He took a pull on his pipe. "Has your mother ever heard you play?"

"No, never."

"Then, maybe the next question is, is your mother aware you're here in this bar?"

"Well, she knows I'm at my aunt's, but she's never seen the bar. She told me she would come one of these days," I said, unsure if my mother had actually said so or if I was just convincing myself.

He abruptly turned away from me and went to the bar, where Ana was chatting with one of the guests. After a few minutes, he came back.

"Alex, I spoke with your aunt. I'll take you home," he said in a calm yet patronizing tone.

"Why? I can get home by myself."

"Alex, I'm offering you a ride—it's safer than walking these streets alone."

He gestured with one hand for me to walk ahead of him, then followed slightly behind, passing through the people who were entering the bar. Once outside, I walked with him to where a motorcycle with a sidecar was parked. He unclipped the helmet from the handlebar, took another from the sidecar, and gave it to me. Even though he told me to get behind him, I pretended I didn't hear it and instead sat down in the sidecar. Kicking a pedal, the engine ignited with a powerful vroom that echoed through the streets. The vibrations made my stomach shudder as we rode from the bar in Eixample all the way to Gràcia.

Parked in front of the house, I got out of the sidecar and returned the helmet to Mr. Laurent, but he remained sitting on his bike, helmet in hand and following me with his eyes.

"Alex, I'll be honest. I find myself in a bit of a pickle. Should I tell your mother about you hanging out in that bar, or will you?"

I stopped abruptly when I heard the question and turned to him. "Thank you for your concern, but I don't think it's your responsibility. I'll tell her," I answered.

"It may not be, but living under my roof for the past months and knowing how much your mother has sacrificed for you, I think I'm entitled to tell you that that bar is no place for a twelve-year-old to hang out. I can't speak for your aunt, but I have a feeling your mother won't be entirely pleased when she hears, either."

"I might be twelve, but I'm not a kid anymore!" I said, louder than I intended to. "If you tell my mother about this, she'll forbid me to go. There goes the one place I've felt happy since I arrived in this country."

"Aren't there other places for you to go? If it's piano practice you're after, I'm happy to give you a few lessons."

When I heard this, I stopped right in front of the main door with the burgundy frame around it, which had scared me the night we first set foot in Barcelona, and looked at him. Inside, I felt in turmoil. My conscience was telling me to stop talking, but the thought of my mother and Mr. Laurent together raised an uncontrollable rage inside me, a rage I couldn't control anymore.

"Of course, that was your plan all along." Mr. Laurent looked as bewildered as if I had stabbed him with a knife. Yet, I continued, "You pay for my tuition, you ask my mother to sew your new pants, and now you offer to teach me piano. All this is to get to my mother! As if she would be impressed by all your generous efforts. Just so we're clear, neither I nor my mother are looking for someone to take care of us! That role is long gone, and it can never, ever be replaced!"

Hearing myself say these words out loud, my face turned red, and my heart began throbbing. Before Mr. Laurent had a chance to answer, I turned and ran into the house. In our room, I threw myself on the bed and began crying ferociously until I fell asleep.

57

AN UNEXPECTED PROPOSAL

On a late night in November, under the intimate mellow lights at the club Jazzsi, a crowd of jazz enthusiasts amassed in the small room, which by the shape and scent of it looked like it had recently been a cellar. There was barely enough space for the waitress to bring the drinks to the round tables in front of the stage, and the scent of women's perfume and tobacco filled the thick air.

Laurent was sitting at one of the tables close to the stage, with an empty bottle of red in front of him. Three empty glasses flanked the bottle—his and his two friends'. As the band began their number, he could feel each instrument loudly penetrating his ears, making him squint and turn, in a need to get away. He tried to get up from his chair, but a spell of dizziness hit him, and he felt the eyes of everyone on him as he slumped back down in his seat. After a round of applause and a solo from each member of the band, his head felt a bit clearer, and his ears became more accustomed to the volume.

He looked to his right, where his two friends sat on their chairs, also lethargic as if they had fallen asleep, lifted his right hand, and waved to the waitress for another bottle of wine. The night was young after all.

As the first notes of a cover of Miles Davis' "Generique" filled the air, Laurent closed his eyes and leaned back in his chair, letting the deep tones of the trumpet resonate through him, like a revelation.

After the show and on the spur of the moment, Laurent went backstage and decided to invite the band members and a few of the other guests to continue the party at his place.

It was an agitated Ms. Agueda who opened the door to this sudden and unplanned event. A long queue of people pushed their way inside, one after the other, with muddy shoes and the smell of alcohol on their breath. Instrument cases scuffed her freshly polished floors as the guests spread around the rooms. Last came Laurent, who, before entering, took a deep drag of his pipe and blew the smoke out.

"Mr. Laurent, what happened to you?" Ms. Agueda asked, examining him with her motherly worry.

"What do you mean?" he said, entering the house.

"Your hair! It's completely disheveled, and your white shirt," she said as she tried to button it. "Open like that!" she berated him. "Where's your blazer?"

"I really don't know," he answered, pulling away from her. "Say, do you think we could have some snacks for the guests, *chère* Agueda?"

"I guess I could prepare something quickly. I need to check with Ms. Eva in the kitchen."

"Oh, and don't forget the wine! Bring many bottles—we're going to need them," he said on his way to the living room, where most guests were gathered.

"But of course! Continue with this lifestyle, Mr. Laurent, and you might accomplish in one month what your father couldn't in his lifetime—to empty the cellar."

"What a feat that would be!"

Three men and a woman stood in the hallway, resting their glasses on the round telephone table. In the dining room, a group sat playing cards and smoking, while others slowly circulated the rooms. Through the clouds of tobacco, Ms. Agueda passed around smoked salmon canapés, socca, and charcuterie from a tray prepared by Eva. Angrily, she placed coasters under glasses, wiped tobacco ash from the furniture, and collected empty glasses, wondering if fifty-five was too early to consider retirement.

The doorbell rang again, and she rushed to answer it. A young woman with red buckled shoes, matching the bright red feather on the collar of her jacket, entered the house.

"Yes, sure, come in," said Ms. Agueda as she took the woman's jacket. *What does one more matter after all?* she thought to herself. *Between the tobacco ash all over the floor, the rings from glasses on the furniture, and the muddy carpets, one more guest won't make a scrap of difference.*

In the living room, Laurent leaned on the shelves next to the grand piano with a glass of wine in his hand. His eyes ventured from the young boy in front of him, who couldn't believe his luck being invited to such a party, to the blonde girl sitting at the table in the dining room, smiling at him from time to time. The boy, Marc, had just graduated and moved from Madrid to Barcelona, where he lucked upon an internship at Galleria Sant Joan. While Marc carried the conversation by asking pompous questions and answering them himself, Laurent's mind began to drift.

"And just like wine, each artwork has its own terroir—the artist's background, the cultural influences of the time, and the emotional landscape that shaped its creation," ventured Marc. "So in a way, understanding art is like understanding a good wine."

Laurent, hearing a pause in his tirade, felt obliged to answer for once.

"Yes, it stimulates the mind," he said absently.

"Are you feeling alright, Laurent?"

"Yes, yes, I just need some air," Laurent answered, leaving his glass of wine on the corner of a table and excusing himself from the room.

Initially, he walked to the front door, but, holding the doorknob, he sighed and turned around. Walking down the steps to the hallway, the laughter and music from upstairs combined with the clatter of pots and pans from the kitchen created an unsynchronized melody of their own. Deciding on being forthright, he planned on adopting a serious tone when telling her how he felt. What he didn't foresee was that his body had its own quirky ways of expressing itself, making him unexpectedly hiccup as he reached the kitchen.

"Mr. Laurent, are you well?" Eva asked, looking at him with worriedly. He was holding his mouth closed with one hand, hiccupping.

Getting no response, Ms. Eva insisted, "Would you like some water? Or maybe I should try to scare you?" She laughed.

The kitchen counter was filled with dirty dishes, cutting boards, and a new round of *gougères* baking in the oven. Eva left the two trays she was preparing and wiped her hands on her apron. She filled a glass with water from the tap and handed it to Laurent.

"How's the party going upstairs? It seems like a merry crowd, and I can hear music playing." She continued to assemble food on one of the trays.

"You could come upstairs, as well," he replied quickly in between hiccups, sipping from his glass of water.

"How I'd love to! But look at all this!" she said, gesturing around the room. "Imagine me dancing around in my dirty apron." She laughed. "You keep us busy these days, Mr. Laurent."

The laughter and the footsteps gradually mellowed to nothing, and the only noise coming from upstairs was the smooth sound of the trumpet and a piano playing blues. Laurent watched Eva and closed his eyes for a moment, only for the image of her to reappear. He opened his eyes and smiled to himself. There were no doubts. There never had been. From the moment he saw her there in the kitchen, the image of her had never left him. Now, it was clear to him what he needed to do.

58

JANUARY 1990

On the morning of January 19, like so often, I found myself sitting on a chair in front of the open balcony doors, my legs crossed and balancing a book on my thighs. The sky was still the nostalgic, soft blue of summer, yet a dry cold had started creeping through the walls of the house. Once in a while, I took my eyes off the book and looked out at our neighbor's lawn. Javier, who lived there, was now a good friend of mine. In the garden, nothing much had changed. The grass remained unkempt and grew tall and green, hiding a few wildflowers here and there, like in a painting. Their garden furniture still sat unused underneath the old tree. If there was something missing from that painting, it would be Javier sneaking food out through the kitchen door, as I had watched him do over and over for so many years. That, and Imea, his sister, playing in the tall grass.

Cuckoo! The bird from the clock on the wall sounded eight times, signaling it was time for me to get ready for work. I placed the old black-and-white photograph of my father and me between the last-read pages of the book and studied it for a moment. Its corners were now damaged, and the contrast had faded, but the day the photograph was taken was still etched in my mind with extraordinary clarity, as if it were yesterday.

It was the morning of my first day of school, shortly before I turned seven years old. The photograph was taken in front of our old block in Zimnicea, with the steps up to the building in the background. My father kneeled down to put an arm on my shoulder, and I, dressed in my school uniform, stood still with eyes wide open, fearing the flash would catch me with them closed.

I tried to remember my father's features, and the more I thought about it, the more I realized that I was nothing like him. During my teenage years, my mother always said, "You will grow as tall as your father," yet I'm of rather normal height, certainly not tall and slender like him.

"His nose, he has from his father," my mother would say to other people here in Barcelona. But he had a prominent nose, being tall and skinny with a bony face. I have a small nose and round cheeks full of red freckles that darkened in the sun.

"Your father was a hardworking man—he did everything for us." Yet I'm now twenty-two years old and work in my mother's tailoring shop. I skipped attending public school and got my *bachillerato certificado* only thanks to the years of Ms. Ferrer's homeschooling.

Unlike my father, I've developed a fondness for alcohol that took hold from an early age, and to my mother's disappointment my aspirations don't involve a high position in society as she had always dreamed for me. Instead, I dream of playing music—"trumpet music," as she would call it—now being a member of a still-unpopular jazz band here in Barcelona.

Would my father be proud of me? Is this what he imagined I would become? If he saw me right now, what would he say?

I closed the book and placed it on the small table next to the chair. I went for a shave and a shower, wondering how my mother and Laurent were doing back in Romania. They had promised to call daily, but in the two weeks they'd been there, they only called once, when they first arrived. How was my grandmother coping, living alone since the death of my grandfather? Had it been three years already? How was Romania after all these years?

Even though it happened a month ago, I cannot stop thinking about the cataclysm that changed the fate of millions of Romanians, including us. On the morning of December 23, I had woken up to the sound of Ms. Agueda's heavy breathing when she entered my room. She handed me a newspaper, then sat down on my chair, trying to catch her breath.

"You should come downstairs. Your mother and Mr. Laurent are watching it live on the news," she said and left again.

I rubbed my eyes and looked at the first page of the copy of *El Nacional* she had left behind.

Over the years, the faces of people dear to me had begun to slowly fade from my memory, but his face had remained imprinted at the back of my mind, watching over me like the pictures that used to hang on every wall in Romania. Now, the image of a confused Ceaușescu claimed the front page of the newspaper, holding his hands up, trying to calm an angry crowd in front of him who were holding banners and waving Romanian flags in the air.

When I opened the newspaper to page four, a photograph showed streets with bodies on the ground and military trucks patrolling the city. Another one showed thousands and thousands of people packed tightly together in front of the balcony from where Ceaușescu had made his speech. A close-up of a man sent chills through my body. He was dressed in a brown coat that was ripped open. A Russian-style fur hat sat at the back of his head, almost falling off. He held his hands up in front of his unshaven face, seemingly screaming or shouting. His eyes were black and bloodshot, and they shone with signs of sadness and desperation.

The title of the article read "Romania in Revolution!" and under it was a quote from the Romanian newspaper *Scînteia*:

"Mircea Dinescu: We must have patience! We waited for twenty-five years, we can wait a few more minutes. The people have won!"

I immediately grabbed my bathrobe and ran downstairs to the living room, where my mother and Laurent were watching the TV. My mother sat with her head so close to the screen as if she was trying to transport herself back to Romania, right then and there. The news said that Nicolae Ceaușescu and Tovarășa Elena Ceaușescu had been on the run but were captured early in the morning. They were held at the military base in Târgoviște.

We barely slept during the days that followed and spent most of our time in front of the TV waiting for news. Like a ghost, my mother paced restlessly around the house, talking to herself, while Laurent, now her husband, did his best to calm her. Through the black-and-white screen, Bucharest looked like an aged city, with its population in pain and anger, striving to throw off the burden of the past and frustration of the present.

I felt both grateful to have left when we did and uneasy for not being there, alongside the thousands of others making history. Watching the events unfold from afar, I felt like I was just part of a river instead of the whole ocean, letting down the people we had left behind.

On December 25, we watched Nicolae Ceaușescu and Tovarășa Elena Ceaușescu shot by dozens of bullets on live TV. Ms. Agueda, Gloria, Laurent, my mother and I all sat in front of the TV, the volume turned up as loud as the radio in my grandparents' kitchen. When the shots rang out, my mother yelled as if she could feel the bullet hit her own heart. *Bang! Bang!* We hugged each other, tears rolling down our cheeks.

I didn't know why I was crying, but it felt as if the pain of losing my father and my best friend George, my grandfather, and the separation from my country all had gathered in one emotion.

After all those years under dictatorship, the people of Romania had finally triumphed—or so it was believed.

Now, I stood in front of the open closet doors with a towel wrapped around my waist. I flicked through my small collection of suits and shirts, pulling one hanger at a time until I stopped at the right one—a morning ritual that I was convinced would determine the fate of the day.

Dressed in a pale gray suit and Mr. Nowak's handkerchief, with its red-and-white details peeking squarely from my breast pocket, I skipped down the stairs two steps at a time and walked to the kitchen.

At that hour of the morning, I knew that Ms. Agueda would be at the market, leaving only Gloria in the kitchen. When I entered, indeed, I found Gloria humming a song while arranging a breakfast board with tartines, two types of jam, and butter for her younger son, Emiliano. He was short, with curly black hair like his mother, full of energy, which was a given for a boy of six years.

Before I got a chance to say something, I heard the ringing of the phone by the entrance. I turned around and ran toward it. As soon as I put the receiver to my ear and said "*Hola?*" I heard someone crying.

"Alex?"

"Mama? Why are you crying? What's happening?"

"Oh, Alex! Izvoarele is deserted, everything is so gray. All that's left are shadows. You must come home."

ACKNOWLEDGMENTS

The story of Alex and Eva would probably not have seen the light of day the way it did if it weren't for a team of editors (thank you, Matthew), illustrators (Oksana and Monica), and my husband, Brian. Brian was my rock through this whole process, and without him I wouldn't have been able to accomplish my dream.